REBECCA REMAINS

JESSICA AIKEN-HALL

MOONLIT MADNESS
PRESS

ISBN-13: 978-0-9993656-9-4(paper)

Library of Congress Control Number: 2021900720

Moonlit Madness Press

Cover Design © Indigo Hearts Design

Editor: Proofreading by the Page

*Warning- Contains sensitive subject matter including, but not limited to rape, domestic violence, and murder.

jessicaaikenhall.com

For everyone tossed away by their family simply because of who they are. You are worthy of love.

The wind blew the branches against the bedroom window, causing a screech so loud I jumped out of bed. My heart thumped against my chest as I made my way over there to check things out. There was no breeze. I swallowed the lump that formed in the back of my throat and climbed back into bed. Keith was fast asleep, like all the other times it didn't appear that he heard what I did.

This wasn't the first time a noise had pulled me out of slumber, but it was the loudest. I pulled the pillow over my head and closed my eyes. The beating of my heart lulled me back to sleep as my breathing returned to normal.

"Get out while you still can." The voice danced off the walls in the empty room.

I looked around for her, but I was the only one there. "Hello?" She didn't answer. I opened the door and walked to the living room. It wasn't me with Keith in our wedding photo. A gorgeous redhead with a face full of freckles stood in my place. My heart sank to the pit of my stomach as tears rushed down my face.

"Who are you?" Still no answer. I was nowhere to be seen in any

of the photos. Every picture, she stood in my place. A beautiful smile on her face was pressed behind the glass. "Who are you?" I fell to the floor as I waited for her answer. My head rested on my knees as my tears soaked my nightgown.

"Get out while you still can. Get out before you're just a forgotten memory."

When I opened my eyes, she wasn't there. The room was still empty. I picked the photo up off the coffee table to get a better look at the mysterious woman, but it was me this time. I wasn't smiling, but it was me. The once happy photo was tainted with misery.

"Who are you?" My voice took me out of the dream and woke Keith up.

"What are you talking about Tessa?" He squinted his eyes as he turned on his phone. "It's two o'clock in the morning."

"Sorry. I had a bad dream." I pressed my body into him to try to push the images from the nightmare out of my mind.

"Another one?" He pulled me close and fell back to sleep.

How could I make my dreams match my life? Keith was everything I ever wished for in a husband. He took care of me, and I knew he'd do the same when we made our perfect little family. He had a great job and he was thoughtful. What could these dreams be trying to tell me? And who was that woman who kept appearing when I closed my eyes?

In Keith's arms, I let the warmth of his skin keep me safe from the unknowns that lingered in the air of the night. Last month marked our first anniversary. The months passed by so quickly. It was hard to believe we were standing on the beach almost a year ago when we eloped.

After just a couple months of dating I knew he was the one. I knew I wanted to spend the rest of my life with him, and he knew it, too. He asked me to marry him on our two-month anniversary. A big, traditional wedding was planned, but Keith said he couldn't wait any longer. Three months after the engagement, we found a Justice of the Peace and took a day trip to the New Hampshire seacoast. It was so spur of the moment, it was romantic. Not a single person knew what we were up to. We stopped along the way and I found the most beautiful, sheer white dress that blew in the sea breeze as we exchanged vows.

My sister, Emily, still wouldn't talk to me. She was supposed to be my maid of honor, and still hadn't gotten over being left out. She had the audacity to tell me she thought Keith was trying to control me, but she didn't know him like I did. Maybe that was what these dreams were about. I did miss Emily, maybe I just needed to give her a call and try to smooth things over.

When morning finally came, Keith was already in the shower. I slipped on my lavender bathrobe and slippers and went to start his breakfast. The smell of coffee hit my nose as I entered the kitchen. I opened the refrigerator and took out the eggs and wheat bread. After slipping two slices of bread in the toaster, I cracked two eggs into the frying pan and listened to them sizzle.

"Good morning sleepyhead. I didn't think you were ever going to get up." Keith wrapped his arms around my waist and kissed my neck.

"Sorry, I guess I didn't hear the alarm go off. I didn't get much sleep last night; I had another bad dream."

"Again?" He sat at the table and opened the newspaper. "What was this one about?" He raised his eyebrow as he looked over the paper at me.

"Oh, nothing really. Just the same old stuff." I hadn't been able to tell him about the details. Something inside me told me to keep it to myself. I placed his breakfast in front of him and sat at the table as he began to eat. "Can I ask you a strange question?" I pulled my robe tight against me.

"Go ahead." Keith took a bite of toast and focused his attention to the sports page.

"Do you know anyone with long red hair? And freckles?"

His coffee spilled on the table, dripping onto the floor and his lap. "Jesus fucken Christ." He stood up and brushed the coffee off his lap before leaving the kitchen.

I rushed to grab a towel to clean up the mess before he returned and refilled his mug. "I'm sorry. I didn't mean to upset you." I dropped my head as he sat back down.

"Why are you sorry? Did you spill my coffee?" His sigh hung in the air as he picked up his mug and took a drink.

"No."

"Right. I didn't, either. Must be the uneven floorboards in this place."

"Yeah, that must be it." I picked at the pink polish on my nails.

"What was your question again?"

"It's nothing really." When my eyes met his I felt better. He always had a way of making things better with just a smile.

"No, what did you ask me?"

"I just wanted to know if you know anyone with long red hair and freckles?"

"No." The safety of his smile faded. "Where did that come from?"

"I'm sorry. I know it was a stupid question. It was just something from my dream."

Keith stood up, pushed in his chair and walked over to me.

He bent down and kissed the top of my head. "Why don't you just drop it? You know dreams don't mean anything."

"Yeah. I'm sorry. I shouldn't have brought it up."

"Have a good day. I'll call you at lunch."

After Keith left, the desire to call Emily overcame me. I was ready to do anything to make the dreams stop. With the phone in my hand, my palm began to sweat. I just wanted to get back to normal. I hoped enough time had passed and she felt the same. "Emily?"

"Yeah? Who's this?" The voice on the other end of the phone sounded like a stranger.

"Em, it's Tess." I cleared my throat as I waited for her to answer.

"I'm surprised you're still alive." The sting in her words made me instantly regret my decision.

"What are you talking about?" A sigh lingered between us. "I just wanted to call and tell you I was sorry. And I miss you. I miss us."

"I miss you, too. The you before your husband brainwashed you."

"Em, I don't understand why you hate Keith so much. He's a really great guy once you get to know him."

"Tess, have you ever Googled his name?"

"No, why would I?" I wrapped the string of my bathrobe around my finger.

"Oh my god, you don't know." Emily's voice softened. "Tessa, can you meet me at the Swiftwater Café?"

"Don't know what? What's going on? What are you trying to prove?"

"Nothing." She paused, the silence in the air made my stomach flip. "I just miss you, and I want to see you."

"I'd like that. I've missed you so much."

"Okay, see you in an hour."

What was she talking about? I knew she hated Keith and she had tried to get me to leave him before we eloped. The desire to know what she was talking about made me want to log onto Google, but there was no time if I was going to get to Swiftwater on time. It would have to wait. A quick shower was all I had time for. I didn't want to be late to meet Emily after a year apart. I was glad she wanted to see me. I didn't know what to expect when I called her, and I'm still not sure what will come of this meeting.

When I pulled into the parking lot I noticed Emily sitting in her car. Still the same blue Subaru Outback she had the last time I saw her. She never did like change. Emily got out of her car, her enormous pink tote bag on her shoulder as she waited for me to approach her. "Hey Em." I dropped my head as I walked closer to her. "I missed you."

"Get over here and give me a hug." With her arms open I fell into her. "I missed you, too, Tessa." She took a step back. "You look great. Are you still going to yoga a hundred times a week?" Her sarcastic tone hadn't changed.

"No. I actually haven't been to yoga in ages." I straightened my jacket and took Emily's hand. "You look great, too."

"Yeah, I'm sure I'm a beauty queen." She brushed her ash blonde hair with her hand. "Let's get some coffee."

I followed her into the café, she tossed her tote bag into our usual booth and took off her jacket. After unzipping my coat, I tossed it on the bench and pulled my wallet out of my purse. "My treat."

"I'll have my usual. I bet you don't remember what it is anymore." Emily placed her hands on her hips.

"Of course, I remember. Mocha latte with skim milk and three sweeteners. Do you remember mine?" I raised my eyebrow as I waited.

"Vanilla iced coffee, less ice, half cream and half sugar."

"I'm impressed."

"We used to come here all the time. I'd be a complete asshole if I didn't remember what my baby sister likes."

"I've really missed this." I smiled and walked over to place our order.

"Me, too. It's just not the same here without you."

Her words stung a little more than they should have. This was *our* place. I wouldn't have dreamed of bringing anyone else with me. With our drinks in hand I headed back to our booth. Emily had her iPad on the table.

"Tess, come sit over here. I have to show you something." Emily patted the seat next to her.

I closed my eyes and took a long breath before handing her the cup. "Em, I don't want to talk about Keith today."

"Tess, I can't live with myself if I don't at least show this to you. Do what you want with the information, but if anything were to happen to you, I'd never be able to forgive myself."

Curiosity got the best of me and I squeezed into the seat next to Emily. "What are you talking about?"

"Has Keith ever mentioned Rebecca?" She pushed the iPad across the table. A photo of the red head from my dream was smiling back at me.

The moisture left my mouth, not allowing me to speak. I took a sip of my iced coffee to try to wrap my mind around what I was looking at. "Who is she?"

"Tess, Keith was married before. I guess technically he still is. This is his wife."

I picked up the iPad to get a better look at Rebecca. She was beautiful. Her long, flowing red hair framed her perfect, freckled face. "I don't understand."

"Click on the picture." Emily reached over and tapped the link to open the article. "She's missing. Well she was, now she's presumed dead."

I scrolled through the article, trying to make sense of it all. I couldn't. No matter how hard I tried, I couldn't understand why Keith hadn't told me about Rebecca. I handed the iPad back to Emily. "I can't read this. Do you know what happened to her?"

"I've been following this story since I Googled Keith last year. I've read every article I could find. There really isn't anything that says what happened, but people think Keith did it. They think he killed her."

"Why would people think that?" I held my drink in my hands as I examined the cup, not able to look at Emily.

"Tess, they had a history."

"What do you mean?"

"There had been multiple reports of domestic violence. The cops had been called to their house so many times. People speculated that he finally killed her."

I shook my head. "Why didn't he tell me about her?"

"Why would he? I mean honestly, I get why he didn't, but that's what makes it worse. If he were innocent, wouldn't he have said something?"

"I don't know. Maybe he just needed to move on. Maybe it's nothing. Keith's a great guy. You should give him a chance. If you get to know him, you'll see he's nothing like what those articles are painting him to be."

Emily shook her head. "I had a feeling you wouldn't

believe me. He really has you brainwashed. I thought you were smarter than this."

"Em, that's not fair."

"Remember how Gram always told us to trust our guts?" She placed her hand on her stomach. "I have never had a good feeling about Keith. I thought in the beginning I was jealous that he was taking you from me, but I know now it was more than that. Please just listen to me. At least open your mind to the fact that he might not be who you think he is."

"I remember." The memory brought a smile to my face. "I miss Gram so much."

"Tess, I'm not usually wrong about people. I love you and I want you to be safe." Emily put her hand on top of mine and looked into my eyes. "I don't know what I would do if something happened to you."

"I'll be fine. I know Keith would never hurt me. He's never laid a hand on me."

"I'm happy to hear that." She gave my hand a squeeze before taking a drink of her latte. "Just be careful, okay?"

"Okay. I will." I got up to sit on my side of the table. I felt my purse vibrating when I sat next to it. I pulled my phone out and saw Keith's name light up my screen. "Oh, here he is now." I gave Emily a smile before answering. "Hey babe."

"Where are you? How come you haven't answered my calls? I've been calling all morning." The worry in his voice confirmed that Emily didn't know what she was talking about.

"I'm sorry, I'm at Swiftwater Café with Emily. I had my phone in my purse."

"I called you fifteen times. You didn't hear it ring?"

"No, I had it on silent. I guess I forgot to turn it back on."

"What if there was an emergency? What if I needed to get ahold of you?" The concern oozed off his words.

"I know. I'm really sorry. I didn't mean to worry you. It won't happen again. I love you."

I pushed up a smile as I turned the ringer on and slipped the phone back into my bag. Emily had her hands folded in front of her and matched my smile. "He was just worried about me."

"Does that happen a lot? Does he always call to check up on you?"

"No, that's the first time." That was the truth. It was also the first time I had left the house without Keith since the last time Emily and I hung out. He didn't usually call me during the day. It was strange that the one time he called me was the one time I wasn't home. I should be grateful he loves me so much that he was so worried about me.

2

Rebecca was all I could think about. I wanted to know more about her. There was still a chance she was still alive. People do run away. I wished I had thought of that when Emily was telling me about it. Rebecca might not need any help at all. Keith might be the victim in all of this. He must have been heartbroken when she left.

A pang of jealousy rushed through me as I thought about the life Keith had before we met. He was fifteen years older than me. A lot could happen in that time. I liked that he was older, it made me feel safe. When my dad died when we were kids, I never had that safe feeling again, not until I met Keith.

Emily didn't know him the way I did. He was a little gruff when you first got to know him, but if you looked past that he was a sweet guy. He would do anything for the people he loved. If they would just get to know each other I know I could make Emily see the *real* Keith.

I had never seen a picture of Rebecca before my dream, and then this morning. He'd never mentioned her name, or even told me that he was married before. This wasn't something I'd be able to ask him. I knew it must be too painful for him to talk about. I couldn't imagine Keith disappearing on me. How did you ever get over something like that?

The more I thought about Keith and Rebecca, the more I wanted to know. I just wanted to know more about the lady in my dreams, and why I was dreaming about her. On the computer, I Googled Keith's name. Pages of results populated. I scrolled down the page and clicked on Rebecca's photo to open the article Emily tried to have me read at the café.

A local Drakesville, New Hampshire woman was reported missing ten years ago by her mother. Keith was quoted saying they had been having marital problems and she had taken off for some time alone to think. Rebecca's mom wanted the police to look into Keith when she hadn't heard back from her daughter. After reading all I could find in that article, I clicked on the next one. There were speculations that there was abuse in the relationship, but there were never any formal charges brought against Keith. Emily must have been confused. I knew Keith wasn't like that.

I closed out the search page and started doing dishes from breakfast. I didn't want Keith to come home to a messy kitchen. It was the least I could do since I wasn't working anymore. I kept the house clean, my husband fed, and soon, hopefully, I'd have a baby to raise. I closed my eyes and rubbed my belly as I imagined a baby growing inside me. It was the only thing our perfect little family was missing.

A glass fell off the counter as the hot water ran to fill the sink. *Strange.* It was pushed all the way back with the others. I took out the broom and swept up the glass, making sure I got all of the splinters off the floor. When the mess was cleaned up, I filled the soapy water with the dishes. The hot water felt good on my cold hands. Fall was in the air, and the warmth of summer was a distant memory.

The red and yellow leaves danced in the wind as I looked into our backyard. I loved our home. A modest three-bedroom ranch on a dead-end street. The closest neighbor couldn't be seen from our yard. It was almost like we lived out here by ourselves. It was just the way I liked it. The house was starting to feel empty as we waited to fill the bedrooms.

As the thoughts of motherhood bounced around my head, the ding dong of the doorbell echoed through the house. "Just a minute." I dried my hands on the dish towel and went to the door. On my tiptoes, I looked through the peephole to see who was out there. There was no one. I opened the door and didn't see a car in the driveway or in the road. *Strange.* Maybe the wind was strong enough to ring the bell.

Back at the sink I slipped my hands back in the hot water to finish up the dishes. There were so many strange things happening today. The one thing I was grateful for was that Emily was back in my life. She was my go-to person when I needed to talk about stuff, and she didn't look at me funny when I talked about *strange* things.

After our mom and dad died, it was just the two of us. Emily was four years older than me and always took care of me, even before the accident. Mom used to say that I was Emily's baby. This past year was the only time I remember us fighting. It was so lonely without her. I couldn't wait to get her and Keith together so she could see who he really was.

After the dishes were done, I decided to start dinner. It was still early enough that I could have it ready and still have time to do a little yoga before Keith came home. Until Emily mentioned it, I had forgotten how much I missed the peace it brought me. It kind of felt like I wasn't the same person I was before Keith. That wasn't a bad thing. I didn't like who I was then. Keith had only improved who I was.

With the soup simmering on the stove, I went to the basement to find my yoga mat. The basement was the one place in the house that I didn't like to go to. Keith didn't like me down their, either. He said there was so much stuff down there that I might get hurt. I flipped on the light and started down the stairs. When I reached the bottom, the light flickered. I pulled my phone out of my back pocket to have in case the light went out.

The stuff from my apartment was all in the back corner. The last time I came down here was when I moved in. I found my purple yoga mat on top of the pile of boxes and hurried back to the stairs. In my attempt to be quick, I tripped over the bunched-up carpet and fell to the floor. *This is why Keith didn't want me down here.*

When I stood up, I noticed an upturned box. I flipped it over to restore the contents and saw Rebecca's face smiling back at me. As I picked up the photos, I examined each picture. She looked happy. I couldn't believe they were unhappy, and I certainly could not believe Keith abused her. "Where are you Rebecca? You gave up a good man." I tossed the picture back into the box and stood up and continued on my way to the stairs. As I started up, the lights went out and the door slammed shut. I raced up the remaining stairs and turned the door handle. It wouldn't open.

I dropped the yoga mat and used both hands to try to pry the door open. My heart beat against my chest as I realized I was trapped. "This isn't funny. Let me out of here." Tears fell down my cheeks as I continued to pull on the handle. I pounded on the door with my fists when my attempts failed. I sat on the top stair and hid my head in my lap. Oh my god, the soup is still on the stove. What if I burn the house down? What if Keith comes home and finds me down here? The thoughts flew threw my head like a freight train.

My sobs echoed off the concrete walls. *I've got to get out of here.* The thought left my mouth and when I stood back up and turned the doorknob, the door swung open. A cold breeze filled the kitchen. When I shut the basement door behind me, I pulled my sweater tight against my body. When I turned the corner to get back to the stove, I found where the cold air was coming from. The front door was open.

What the hell is going on? "Keith, are you home early?" I cleared my throat as I walked through the house. There was no one else here. In the living room the words *Get Out* were typed across the screen of the computer. I went to turn the monitor off when the last page I had searched opened. Rebecca's picture stared back at me. As I tried to close down the window, another one popped up on the screen. An article I hadn't read yet.

A picture of Keith in handcuffs was halfway down the screen. *He was arrested?* The date under Keith's photo was two years before Rebecca went missing. He was arrested for domestic violence. Emily *was* right. My heart ached at the thought. I loved Keith. I couldn't imagine him being all of the awful things the article said.

"Who's doing this?" Fear turned to anger. "Who's here?" My voice shook as my fingers trembled to turn off the computer screen. "What are you trying to prove?"

A painting fell off the wall. "What do you want from me?" I walked over to replace the picture and noticed a hole in the wall, it had been hidden by the painting. I traced the outline of the hole. Chills ran through my body when I looked closer and saw what looked like dried blood. It was too big to be from someone's fist, but it was the perfect size to be from someone's head. "Oh my God. Rebecca, it's you, isn't it?"

I replaced the painting and went into the kitchen to turn the stove off. What was happening? I didn't understand how Keith could be *that* man. How could someone so loving be so awful? My tears hit the stove as I stood in a trance. A warm embrace helped soothe some of the uncertainties. "Rebecca, what do I do?" I wiped the moisture off my cheeks.

The front door swung open. "Tessa." His voice blasted past me as I remained at the stove. "Where are you?"

"Right here." I cleared my voice to try to shake out any hesitation that lingered. "Is everything okay?"

"Yeah." Keith cocked his head and smiled. "I just wanted to make sure you made it home alright." He walked over and wrapped his arms around me. "I love you."

"I love you, too." I closed my eyes tight as I fell into his arms. It was too much to wrap my head around. How could he be so evil and so wonderful?

"How was your day with Emily?" He placed his hands on his hips as his smile beamed.

"It was nice." I pushed the hair out of my face and focused my attention to the pot of soup in front of me. "I've missed her."

"What's new and exciting in her life?"

"I don't really know. We didn't have a lot of time to talk."

"Oh? What did you talk about then?" His smile faded as he crossed his arms.

"Nothing, really. She wanted to know if I was still into

yoga. I think I want to get back into that again. I've missed it, too."

"Hmm. So, that's it?"

"Yes, that's all we had time for."

"You should invite her over here for dinner some time. I'd love to get to know her."

"That's a great idea." I nodded as I maintained my concentration on the soup. It wasn't a great idea, but it wasn't a bad one, either. It might be good for Emily to get to know Keith. She'd be able to tell me if he's changed. People change. It happened all the time. Good people made mistakes. The pit of my stomach burned with uncertainty.

3

"Don't let him fool you, honey." Rebecca sat with her legs crossed on the couch. "He's good at pretending." As she moved the hair off her face, her blackened eye peeked out from under the makeup.

"What do I do?" I sat next to her and took her hand.

"You don't let him know you know."

"What do you mean?"

"Sweet girl, I'm not the first." Rebecca's grip tightened around my hand.

"Not the first?"

"No, but I want to be the last."

"He's killed before?"

She wiped the tears off my cheek. "No, but I was warned by the others. I didn't listen to them. I loved him, and I was sure he loved me. When he found out I knew, he changed."

"How did he find out?"

"He's sneaky. Just promise me you'll be careful."

Keith's alarm pulled me out of the dream. Still unsure what to think, I didn't dare open my eyes. Why was Rebecca able to come to me? Maybe it was just my imagination. I rolled over and laid my head on Keith's chest. As I listened to his heartbeat, I couldn't imagine him as the man Rebecca was trying to make me believe he was. But maybe she wasn't. It was possible that my wild imagination was getting the best of me. It's happened before.

Keith kissed the top of my head before he stretched. "Another day, another dollar."

"I wish I could help. I'd love to be able to contribute to the household."

"Don't be silly, a woman's place is in the home. I don't want to come home to an empty house. Besides, when the house is filled with babies, who is going to take care of them?"

"I know, but until that happens..."

"I said don't be stupid." Anger coated his words. "You know where you belong."

Taken aback by his tone, I wasn't sure what to say, so I said nothing. Don't be stupid? That was the first time he ever called me a name. Maybe all this thinking had made me too sensitive.

"Oh, baby, you know I don't mean anything. I just want to be able to take care of you. I love you, Tessa."

"I know. I love you, too." I swung my legs over the bed and into my slippers. I tied my bathrobe tight against my waist and went into the kitchen to get Keith's breakfast started. As he took his time getting ready, I sent Emily a text inviting her over for the day.

Keith sat at the table, the newspaper covering his face as I served him his fried eggs and toast. My phone dinged alerting me of a message. "Who's that?" Keith put the paper down.

"I don't know." I picked up the phone and saw Emily had responded. "Oh, just Em. She wants to meet at the café again."

"Again?" Keith raised his eyebrow.

"Yeah, I guess she's missed me, too." I typed back my reply and set my phone on the counter. "Guess I need to get dressed, too."

"You're seriously going out, again?"

"Yeah, is that okay?" I swallowed the lump in my throat.

"You're sure it's Emily you're meeting and not someone else?"

"Are you serious?" I pulled my robe to cover more of my body. "Of course, it's Em. I told you yesterday we've missed each other. We have a year to catch up on."

"No, I'm just messing around." His smile grew as he opened the paper.

In the bedroom, I couldn't shake the uneasy feeling Keith's behavior left me with. This wasn't the Keith that I knew. Maybe I was just being too sensitive. I threw on a pair of jeans and a white sweater and ran the brush through my long brown hair. I didn't want to take too much time and give Keith more of a reason to suspect anything. I was just going to see Em after all. She didn't care what I looked like.

In the kitchen I noticed my phone was on the table now, not on the counter where I left it. It wasn't worth an argument, so I didn't say anything. I took Keith's lunch out of the refrigerator and placed it in front of him and gave him a kiss. "Have a good day at work."

"You're leaving? *Now?*"

"Yeah, I don't want to be late. It takes a while to get there."

"Hmm. Okay. Make sure you're home before dinner."

"I won't be gone that long. We're just getting a coffee."

"We have coffee here."

"Yes, I know, but Swiftwater is *our* place."

"Have fun." The coldness of his words made him a stranger to me. "Here, don't forget this. I made sure the ringer was on this time."

I took my phone from him and gave him the sincerest smile I could muster. "Thanks."

It was hard to know what was happening. I'd never left the house without Keith before, so I guess there was never a chance for me to see how he would have acted. If it was Rebecca in my dreams giving me a message, I had to be sure he never figured out that I knew anything. It was all too much. I really hoped Emily could help me put things into perspective. Maybe she was right about her gut feeling about him. Gram was never wrong.

A sigh of relief flooded me when I saw Em waiting for me at Swiftwater. The tears I had been holding back came rushing out like the levee let loose.

"Oh my god, Tess, what's wrong?" Em shut the car door behind her and ran over to me.

"Nothing. I'm okay. I'm just glad to see you."

"Tess, are you sure? Those don't look like I'm happy to see you tears."

I nodded and squeezed her hand. "Let's just go get our drinks. We can talk inside."

I was relieved to see our normal booth was open. I tossed my purse in before I sat down.

"My treat today." Em winked before she walked to the counter.

I pulled my phone out and scrolled through the messages. A new one from Keith arrived just as I was about to set it down. "I love you. Have a good time with Emily today."

And just like that I wasn't sure what to think anymore. Everyone had bad days, maybe today was his. I sent a quick response back before tucking my phone back into my purse.

"Here you go, sis." Em handed me my iced coffee and slid into the bench across from me. "So, tell me, what's going on? You Googled him, didn't you?" She took a sip of her latte.

"How did you know?"

"I could see it on your face. You're afraid, aren't you?"

"Well, I'm not really sure. I've been having these dreams. I think they scare me more than the search results did."

Emily raised her eyebrow. "Dreams? Do tell."

I let out the breath I had been holding. "I think Rebecca has been visiting me. Well, more like haunting me."

"Haunting you? Have you seen her?"

"No, well, yes, but only in my dreams. The night before I saw you last, I had a dream where she was in all of our photos together, and then you showed me the stories online, and it was her. I had no idea who this woman was before, but she has been coming to me in dreams since I moved into Keith's house."

"I have so many questions."

"I knew you would." A nervous laugh escaped before I placed the straw between my lips. "I had no idea why she kept coming to me, and the more she came, the angrier the dreams became."

"Angrier? What do you mean?"

"I guess that's the wrong word. She's trying to tell me something, and up until yesterday, I wasn't listening."

"What happened yesterday?"

"Where do I start? The better question is what didn't happen yesterday."

"Okay, so, tell me what's going on."

"I went to the basement to get my yoga mat, and I got locked down there. I tripped on a box and Rebeca's pictures fell out on to the floor. The doorbell rang and there was no one at the door. The computer turned on and had an article about Keith being arrested for domestic violence. A painting fell off the wall and I found a hole in the wall, that looked like it had dried blood around it."

"Hold up. Dried blood? Oh my god, Tess, you've got to get out of there."

"Oh, but there's more. She came to me in my dream last night and told me she wasn't the first. She said the reason he hurt her was because he found out that she knew what he had done." I waited for her to respond. The color had drained from her face. "What do you think I should do?"

"Tessa, it's obvious. You've got to get out of there."

"It's not that easy."

"What's not easy about packing your shit and getting the hell out of there?"

"I'm just not sure. I…"

"You're not sure? Are you kidding me?"

"What if I'm making more out of this than it is? What if…"

"No, Tessa, you don't tell me all this and then try to explain your way into making him a saint. That's fucked up."

"I'm not. I just don't know what to think anymore. You've got to understand this isn't the man I married. I love him."

"Ugh. Gross. After all this, everything that you know, you still love him?"

"It's not that easy to just turn off my feelings. I do love

him, but I'm scared now. I don't know what to think. I need your help, not for you to be mad at me."

The heat from Emily's sigh warmed my forehead. "I'm not mad at you. I just don't want anything to happen to you." She reached across the table and took my hand. "I'm not going anywhere. But you have to promise me that you'll listen to your gut."

"I will. I promise."

"What else was in that box?"

"What box?"

"The one you said Rebecca's pictures fell out of?"

"Oh, I don't know. I didn't look. Honestly, I was a little jealous that he still had her pictures."

"Tess, that's… understandable."

"What were you going to say? That's what? Crazy?"

"No, I guess I get it. I'd be hurt, too, especially if I didn't know the whole story."

"I just don't know what to think, but if I trust Rebecca, I can't say anything anyway. I have to keep pretending that I don't know anything."

"But the box. Don't you want to know what's in it?"

"I do now, but I'm not sure I want to get locked in the basement again."

"I'll come with you."

"You want to know that bad? You're willing to risk seeing Keith?" I laughed as I thought back to our childhood when I'd always catch Em snooping in our parents' room.

"You know who I am right?" We shared a laugh as we reminisced. "I'll grab some stuff, and I'll invite myself to your place for a sleepover."

"Oh, I'm not sure that's a good idea."

"Why not? It's your house, too. Right?"

"Let me ask him first. I just don't want him to be mad."

"Yeah, and I don't want you to be dead." Emily lifted her shoulders and widened her eyes.

I sent Keith a message, asking if he'd mind. The ring pierced the air of the café, making me drop my phone on the table before answering it. "Hello." I shot Emily a smile and nodded my head. "I just wanted to check with you to see if it was okay for Emily to stay over tonight?" I twirled my hair around my finger as I waited for his response.

"Sure. I said your sister is always welcome at my, I mean, our house."

I turned my phone off and slipped it back in my purse. "Okay, let's go get your stuff."

"This is going to be fun, like old times." Emily finished her latte and scooted out of the booth. "You'll have to come with me and meet Mandy."

"Mandy? Who's she?"

"My girlfriend."

"You have a girlfriend and you haven't mentioned it?"

"Well, there was never a great time. We've only been talking for two days, and we've been consumed with your life."

"I'm sorry, I want to hear all about her."

"She works from home, so lucky for you, you get to meet her today."

"Oh, you two are already living together? Have you put a ring on her finger yet?"

"Whoa, slow down. We've only been dating for ten months. I'm not you. I like to take my time."

"True. I'm surprised you even found anyone."

"What's that supposed to mean?" Emily crossed her arms as she stood by her car.

"Just that you're so picky. I never thought anyone would live up to your standards. That's all."

"Hmm. I guess you're right. After what happened to Mom and Dad, I didn't want to end up with an asshole."

"No, I guess that's my job." I put my hands in the air before opening the door to my car. "I'll follow you."

I was so happy to know Emily hadn't been alone over the past year. I felt guilty when I thought about her spending the holidays alone, I was glad to know she hadn't. Emily and I had always been different. I was the one who seemed to need someone by my side, but she had been independent our whole lives. She was just as happy at home with a good book, but that was never enough for me. I needed a man's approval to feel good about myself. I'd always admired that about Emily.

At Emily's house, I pulled in behind her car and followed her to the front door. "Is she going to be mad that you're coming to my place?"

"No, she's not a dick. She doesn't have one, either." She laughed as she opened the door. "Honey, I'm home."

An older woman with salt and pepper hair sat in front of an iMac in a makeshift office in the living room. With her index finger, she pushed up her glasses. "Hey, Em, this must be Tessa." She stood up and extended her hand to me. "I've heard so much about you."

"Oh no. That doesn't sound good." I shot Emily a smile.

"Yeah, it wasn't the first few months." A deep cackle left her mouth. "Oh, I'm just kidding. Your sister has said nothing but great things about you."

"Geeze, Mandy, don't go spilling all the beans." Emily gave

her a kiss. "Hey, I'm going over to Tessa's place for the night. We've got some investigating to do."

"Oh, good. I get the bed to myself tonight."

"I'll miss you, too." Emily shook her head. "This is what I live with." She laughed as she went into her room.

"I see she's still a smartass." I stood in the middle of the living room, not sure where I should go. This wasn't Emily's place anymore; it was now Emily and Mandy's place.

"You can sit down you know. Being a lesbian isn't contagious."

"Oh, I get it, you're a smartass, too." I picked up a pile of magazines and sat on the recliner I used to always claim. "That must be why she loves you."

Mandy's cackle returned. "Yeah, I guess we are a lot alike. But different enough we don't want to kill each other."

"Glad to hear." I smiled as I noticed the photos covering the walls had been changed to cute couple photos of the two of them. I couldn't help but smile. Emily must really love her. She was never one for the lovey dovey stuff. "What do you do for work?"

"I'm a freelance writer. I ghost write people's books."

"Oh, that sounds cool."

"Yeah, if you like trying to get into someone else's head and coming up with eighty-thousand words in their voice. It's a blast. But I have written some best sellers. I'll just never get any credit for them, and I can't tell anyone I wrote them."

"It's losing it's appeal."

"Yeah, it's like being paid to do the jock's homework at school. But I love writing, and I hate people, so it's a win-win for me."

"I miss people. I used to love to work."

"Why don't you?"

"Keith, my husband, thinks it's best if I stay at home and take care of the house. We're trying, or we were, to start our family."

"Whoa, hold on, is this the Donna Reed show? It's not the 1950s anymore sunshine."

"Yeah, I know." My head dropped as what she called me registered. "Wait, did you call me sunshine?"

"Yeah. Sorry?"

"No, it's okay. It's just that's what my gram used to call me. Did Em tell you?"

"No, she never mentioned that. Sorry. I didn't mean to bring anything up."

"It's fine. It was nice to hear, actually. I really miss her."

"She sounds like a great lady. Em has told me a lot about her."

A smile spread across my face as I remembered the time we spent with Gram. She was an angel sent from God. If it wasn't for her, I was sure Emily and I would have been sent to foster care. She gave up her life to take care of us after the accident. I hadn't thought about that nickname in ages.

"What did you do to her out here?" Emily tossed her duffle bag on my lap. "Tess, you alright?"

"Yeah, I'm fine. I was just thinking about Gram."

"Geeze, I know Mandy's old, but she's not *that* old."

"No, smartass, I called her sunshine. I had no idea, I guess it's an old lady thing."

"It's good, I'm glad she did. I'm not some kid, I'm a grownup now."

"I know. I miss Gram, too. I think about her a lot."

"Have fun, girls. I can't wait to hear about the results of your investigation."

"You and me both." Emily bent down and gave her a kiss before we left for my house.

"You can follow me this time." Butterflies took up residency in my chest as I thought about what we were going to find, and what I was going to do about it. Was I ready to give up on Keith? I loved him, at least I loved who I thought he was. I guess there was something to the saying ignorance is bliss.

4

<hr>

There were still a few hours before Keith arrived home. That would allow us some time to start the search. Guilt washed over me as I thought about betraying my husband. He was supposed to be my forever and ever. There was still a chance that there was nothing to find. It could all be a big misunderstanding. My heart wanted that, it needed that.

"You can sleep in the guest room. You'll be our first guest."

"How special." Emily raised her eyebrow as she tossed her bag on the bed. "Why do you have a guest room and no guests?"

"I guess in cases like these?" I shrugged my shoulders. "Do you want a tour?"

"Sure."

"This is the guest room." I giggled as I turned off the light. "This is our room." I opened the door and saw I hadn't made the bed before I left that morning. I pulled the blankets up and straightened the bed as Emily stayed in the doorway.

"What's this room here?" Emily opened the door. "Oh my god, Tess, please don't tell me…"

"I'm not pregnant, at least, I don't think I am."

She wiped the sweat off her brow. "Phew. You know that would make this so much more complicated, right?"

"Yeah, I know." I hung my head as I flipped off the light in the nursery. "I just really want to be a mom."

"Oh, Tess, I know you do, but not with him. Promise me you'll stop trying."

"How? He'll know."

"No, he won't. Get on the pill or something. He'll never have to know."

"I guess you're right. I don't want to raise a baby on my own."

"Tess, there are lots of other guys out there. I know how bad you want to be a mom, but maybe there's a reason it hasn't happened yet."

"Alright, want to finish the tour?"

"I think the only place I haven't seen is the basement."

"You're not excited about this, are you?"

"You know my sleuthing skills are top notch. I have to keep them in shape. I don't understand how you've lived here this long and haven't snooped at all."

"I guess I'm not interested in getting in other people's business. What I don't know doesn't hurt me."

"Except in this case, it could."

"Yeah, you're right. Come on, let's go."

My heart began to race as my hand turned the doorknob to the basement. "Rebecca, I'm doing this for you, please don't hurt us."

"Tess, I'm sure her plan isn't to hurt you. She wants to save you. Do you really think she's using her energy to hurt you?"

"No, I guess you're right. It's just scary. I've never been

haunted before."

"I'm sure her intention is not to haunt you. She comes in peace. Isn't that right, Rebecca?"

Chills traveled through my body as my foot hit the top stair. The creak of the wood under my feet intensified the uneasy feeling swirling inside my body. The hair on the back of my neck stood up when we reached the box I had tripped over the day before. "Here it is." I pointed, not daring to touch it.

"Open it." Emily gave me a shove.

"I can't. I don't know what's in there."

"Isn't that the whole point to this? That's what we're about to find out."

With my arms folded tight against my chest, I couldn't budge. "Go ahead. You do it."

Without hesitation, Emily opened the box. The photo of Rebecca was the first thing she pulled out. "My god, she was beautiful."

"She was."

Emily pulled out an envelope addressed to Rebecca. She handed it to me. "Here, open this."

I shook my head. "You."

Emily carefully slid her finger under the flap as she reopened the envelope. She pulled out a stack of papers and gasped. "Holy shit, Tess, jackpot."

"What is it?"

"It looks like a protection order Rebecca had." Emily scanned the document. "It's dated two years before her disappearance."

"What's a protection order?"

"Essentially it's an order from the court to keep an abuser

away from their victim." Emily's eyes didn't lift from the paper. "Oh my god. This is Rebecca's story, in her handwriting."

"What?"

"Rebecca had to explain why she needed the protection order. There are questions about some of the abuse." Emily shook her head as she turned the page. "Wait, did you say there was a hole in the wall?"

"Yeah. Why?" The echo of my heartbeat was louder than my words.

"Look at this." Emily handed me the paper.

On Christmas Eve, Keith was angry with me when I didn't want to make love. I was tired after getting things ready at work, and I just wanted to go to bed. First, he called me a whore and accused me of having an affair. When I didn't disagree fast enough, he threw his beer bottle at me. It smashed when it hit the wall behind me. I had never seen him like this before, and I didn't know what to do. I stayed on the couch and cried. This made him even more angry. He came over to me, pulled me off the couch by my hair and hit my head against the wall. I didn't know it then, but when I went to shower, I noticed I was bleeding. I had to go to the hospital to get stitches. Keith wouldn't let me tell the doctor what really happened. He made me tell them that it was from a sledding accident. He wouldn't even let me repair the hole in the wall, because he used it as a threat in future fights. He told me it was to make sure I knew what he was capable of. He said he would kill me if I ever told anyone.

"Oh my god." My voice was unrecognizable when it left my mouth. "He sounds like a monster."

"You think?" Emily handed me another piece of paper from the box. "Here, check this out."

"I don't want to read anymore. I can't."

"Tess, you have to get out of here. You're not safe." She held up the paper. "This is a letter from Rebecca's doctor stating that she was mentally unfit to testify. It looks like Keith paid someone to say she couldn't be trusted."

"What if that's real? What if she was sick?"

"Tess, don't. Don't try to defend him. You said you saw the hole, and didn't you say there was dried blood?"

I closed my eyes as I remembered the find. "Yeah."

"I'm worried about you. You have to get the fuck out of here. Rebecca needs you to get out of here. You can come stay with Mandy and me."

"It's not that easy. I can't let him know I know. I have to act like everything is normal. Rebecca warned me. She said he could never know what I know."

"But why stay here? Why risk it?" Emily's sigh circled around us.

"Trust me, Em. I know how to deal with him. I can't just disappear. I need to take my time."

"How will you be able to act *normal* knowing this?"

"I know he won't hurt me. Maybe he actually loves me."

"Don't even tell me…"

"I know I need to leave, but I have to be smart. I need to keep our relationship intact while I figure it out."

"You have a month before I do something stupid."

I turned to look at my sister. "Like what?"

"You don't want to find out." She crossed her arms and tapped her foot.

"Em, it might take longer, but trust me. Okay?"

"We'll see."

"Thank you."

"Don't thank me yet. I haven't agreed to stand back."

"No, for being here for me. I'm grateful to have you back in my life."

"That's what sisters are for."

"What time is it?" Panic set in as I noticed the sun was setting through the small basement windows.

Emily looked down at her watch. "It's almost 5:00. Why?"

"We've got to get out of here. Be sure to close that box, leave it the way you found it. Keith will be here any minute." I ran my hands through my hair. "Oh, shit, I didn't make dinner."

"Hey, calm down. Let me order a pizza." Emily bent over to replace the contents of the box.

"No, Keith hates takeout. It's my job to cook."

"Like hell it is. We're having a sleepover, and your guest wants pizza."

I swallowed the lump in my throat as I thought about how upset Keith may be. "I don't know. I guess we could get one, and I'll make him something."

Emily put her hand on my arm. "No, he's a grown-ass man. If he wants something else, he can make it. You are going to spend time with your sister tonight."

I exhaled the panic and tried to stop the anxiety from building. Keith had never actually said no to takeout, I just felt like it was my duty to make sure he had a hot meal on the table before he got home. It was the least I could do since he worked all day. This new dangerous Keith was one I wasn't sure existed. Sure, there were signs, maybe even evidence, but until I *knew* for certain, I didn't want to wish for something that wasn't.

Emily placed an order for two large pizzas to be delivered. They should arrive before Keith did. Knowing food would be on the table for his arrival helped ease some of my worry. I tried to breathe away the unknown and hold tight to what I knew. Forty-eight hours ago, I was a happily married woman trying to start a family. I just needed to get back to that place until I could figure everything out.

The front door opened, jarring me out of my seat. On my feet, I met Keith at the door. "Hi, sorry, dinner isn't here yet. Em, ah, we wanted to get pizza."

Keith bent down and kissed me. "Didn't you get my message?" He handed me a bouquet of roses.

"No, sorry, we were busy. Ah, we were talking, I must have left my phone in my purse."

"Oh, that's okay, honey. I have takeout in the car. I hope you girls like Chinese."

"You did? I didn't think you liked takeout?" I pulled out a vase and arranged the flowers.

"Of course, I do, don't be silly. I wanted you two to have more time together, that's why I sent you a message. I wanted to catch you before you started cooking. Everyone needs to have a little fun once in a while."

"That's very sweet of you. Do you need some help getting anything out of the car?"

"No, that's fine. Just get back with your sister and have some fun. Oh, hi, Emily. I didn't see you over there."

Emily was at the table watching us. A forced smile was plastered on her face. "Hey, Keith. Thanks for bringing us dinner home."

"Anything to make my baby happy." The door closed behind him as he went to retrieve dinner.

"Oh my god, gross." Emily pointed into her mouth with her index finger.

"What? I think it's sweet."

"You've got to be kidding me, Tess. Do I need to go back to the basement?"

I put my finger to my mouth and widened my eyes. "Shh."

This was the Keith I knew and loved. This was what made it hard for me to believe everything that was being presented. What if Rebecca was crazy? What if she wasn't really dead? There was still a good possibility that she left on her own to start her life over. I mean, why would Keith keep that stuff if he was guilty? I wanted more than anything for everything to go back to normal. I missed having Emily in my life, but now, my life was in shambles. I didn't know what to think anymore.

The pizza delivery guy and Keith met in the driveway. Keith brought the pizzas and bags of Chinese food in, stacked on top of each other. "Let's eat." Keith laughed as he put the food on the table. "I hope you're hungry."

"Look at me, does it look like I ever miss a meal?" Emily rubbed her belly. "It's just like old times, Tess, remember when Gram would let us each pick what we wanted for special occasions?"

"Oh, yeah. I had forgotten about that. No one ever went hungry at Gram's." We shared a laugh as Keith put plates on the table.

"You never told me about that." Keith rubbed my shoulder as he sat next to me.

"It's hard to talk about Gram. I miss her so much. It was even harder to talk about her when Em and I weren't talking." I dropped my head as I thought back to the last year. I couldn't risk losing her again. I just needed time to figure out what to do.

5

The door closed behind Keith as he headed for work, leaving Emily and me alone in the house. I knew what she was itching to say, but I wasn't up for it today. I just wanted to curl back up in bed and go back in time a few months, when things were normal, at least our normal. The heat from the mug between my hands filled my entire body with warmth.

"I see why you fell in love with him." Emily's words startled me more than the tap on the shoulder that followed them.

"Wait. What did you just say?"

"I can see why you loved… I mean love him. He seems like a nice guy."

"Really?"

"Yeah. If I didn't know all of the other stuff and get that twinge in my gut." Emily shrugged her shoulders.

"So, it's not just me?"

"No, but don't let his acting fool you. You know it's all an act, right? Abusers do that shit all the time. They work so hard to make you think they're nice guys. He must be exhausted."

Emily shook her head. "You know, I almost feel sorry for him."

"How do you know it's an act? How can you tell?"

"Tess, how can you not? People aren't ever *that* nice, not unless they are hiding something."

"But, would you know that without knowing what you know? I mean, would it be that easy to tell if you didn't Google him?"

"Yeah, I'd know." Emily's hand went to her stomach. "This thing is never wrong."

I placed my hand on my stomach. "I wonder why mine is?"

"Because you let this thing get in the way." Emily poked her index finger into my chest. "It's clear that you're not the only one. Rebecca was fooled, too. I'm sure there's a long list of others."

A glass fell off the counter, smashing as it hit the floor. A sigh escaped as I pushed my chair away from the table. "Good morning, Rebecca."

"Oh, shit. I forgot she was here." Emily came over and held the dustpan.

"I wish I could."

"It must be weird to know your husband's other wife lives with you." Emily snorted when she laughed.

"You're such a big help." My snort soon followed. It was impossible not to laugh when Emily was around, regardless of the subject.

"Sorry, too soon?"

"Ha-ha. To be fair, I didn't know she even existed until a few days ago."

"But you said you've been dreaming about her for months."

"Yeah, I was, but I didn't know who she was, or what it was

all about. Communicating with the dead is a new thing for me."

"No, it's not."

"What do you mean?" I tilted my head to get a better look at Emily's face.

"You don't remember?" She squinted her eyes at me. "When we were kids? You would always wake me up in the middle of the night after you had these dreams."

The memories crashed down on top of me. "Holy shit. I'd forgotten about that."

"Did you also forget about your invisible friends?"

"No, but what does that have to do with anything?"

"Tess, do I have to spell it out for you?"

"I guess so. I have no idea what you're talking about."

"Invisible friends?" Emily waved her hands around her and then rested them on her hips. "They weren't figments of your imagination."

"I still don't follow. All little kids have invisible friends. You're making it sound like I'm crazy."

"No, all little kids have tea parties with their invisible friends. You were always trying to help them. Don't you remember how mad Mom would get when you rummaged through the cabinets trying to find things?"

My hand covered my mouth as the memories returned. "You're right. I didn't know I was communicating with the dead. I would have been scared shitless if I'd known then."

"That's probably why you forgot. You have a gift Tessa. Ghosts don't just talk to anyone. You're like Gram."

"Gram? What do you mean?"

"What the hell, have you blocked our whole childhood out of your head? You don't remember the parties Gram had?"

"I remember. She had a lot of friends."

"You think it's normal for her friends to always leave crying and blowing their nose?"

A laugh spilled out. "I don't know. I guess I never thought much about it."

"Those weren't her friends. Those were her clients. Gram was a psychic medium. Why do you think Dad didn't want Mom to let us go over to her house? He thought she was working for the devil."

A vision of Gram's house came back to me. I remembered the windows and mirrors were covered with dark fabric at times, and the small, round table in her kitchen covered in pretty rocks. "Gram was a witch?"

"No. She was a healer. She did that work to help people. I bet she's the one sending Rebecca to you. She knows you're in danger, too."

"Why didn't she just come to me then? Why didn't she tell me what was happening when I was little?"

"Tess, Mom told her she couldn't."

"How do you know all of this? How come you know Gram so much better than I do?"

"I found her journal when I was going through her things a few years ago."

"And you're just now telling me?"

"I didn't want to bug you. You took losing Gram so hard, every time I talked about her you'd fall apart. I didn't think it was important."

"Gram being a psychic medium isn't important?"

"Would it have been before Rebecca started visiting you?"

"Hmm." I crossed my arms tight against my chest as more memories from the past settled around me. "Maybe."

"I didn't want to hurt you. I know you still struggle with her death."

"So, this means I'm not crazy." I closed my eyes as I pushed out years of self-doubt.

"Why would you be crazy?" Emily walked over to me and placed her hand on my shoulder.

"Because of the voices."

"Voices?"

"I never told anyone about them. I was afraid they'd lock me up."

"What are you talking about?"

"The voices in my head. I thought I was crazy. I didn't know they were spirits communicating with me." The warmth of my tears on my cheeks made me feel alive.

"You never told me about this. How long has this been happening?"

"I was scared. I thought I was schizophrenic."

"How long?"

"For as long as I can remember. They come and go."

"Has Mom…"

I shook my head as I wiped away the tears. "No. No one I know. At least, I don't think so. Like I said, I thought I was crazy."

Emily pulled me into a hug. "I'm so sorry, Tess. I should have been there to help you with this. I had no idea you were fighting a battle inside of yourself."

"I'm just glad to know a straitjacket isn't in my future." I took a step back to look at Emily's reaction. "Do you think Gram knew about me? Why doesn't she talk to me herself? Why wouldn't she help me with this thing?"

"I bet she didn't want to scare you."

"Oh yeah, because having a head full of ghosts bossing me around is a walk in the park."

"A walk in the park?" Emily tilted her head. "Tess, that's what Gram used to always say." Her smile grew. "Gram's probably been there the whole time, you just weren't listening."

"Me? Not listen?" I hoped she was right. I needed Gram more now than I ever had before. "Did Gram's journal explain how it all works?"

"No, they weren't like that. She was just talking about the sessions she had with people. There wasn't an instructional guide."

"Well, shit." Laughter erupted from both of us.

"Okay, so now we know you're not crazy, you've got to learn how to use this to your advantage. We need to find you a crash course."

"Yeah, let me type that into the search bar."

"Let's go back downstairs and see if there is anything else we can find before Keith gets back home." Emily took my hand and started walking to the basement door.

"I don't know, Em, I'm feeling overwhelmed."

"Don't crap out on me now. Obviously, Rebecca needs your help. We have to at least see if there is anything else down there."

"Maybe she doesn't need my help. Maybe she's the one helping me."

"Tessa, she's still missing."

My head dropped at the thought. "Fuck. You're right."

"Just think of this as an adventure. Try to take your emotions out of it."

"That's so much easier to say than to do. I love… I mean loved Keith. It's still hard to believe that he's this monster."

"I know. But, hey, next time listen to me?"

"Don't you dare say it."

"What? I told you so?" Emily laughed as she turned the doorknob. "Let's go find ourselves some answers."

"Rebecca, if you're here, just tell me what I need to know." I took a deep breath before I followed Emily down the stairs. "I can do this."

"Of course, you can. You can do anything." Emily squeezed my hand. "I love you, Tess."

"I love you, too. You don't know how happy I am to have you back in my life."

"Ditto, sis. Let's get to business." Emily winked as she returned to the box from yesterday. "I have a feeling there is more in here. I mean, we barely scratched the surface last night."

"What are you looking for?"

"I don't know. Anything."

"I doubt Keith would have kept anything incriminating. He's smarter than that."

"Yeah, like he was smart enough to get rid of the protection order?"

"I have a feeling he kept that for a reason. I mean, he's had plenty of time to get rid of everything. He must have needed it or something."

"But for what? Why would he need it for anything? I don't see how it could help him."

"I don't know. Maybe he was trying to prove his innocence. I could imagine he would want to tell people he didn't do what she said he did, especially since she was missing."

Emily nodded. "Yeah, I guess that makes sense." She took out a stack of papers and set them on the floor before she pulled out a shoe box. Her eyes widened. "What do you think this could be?" She gave the box a shake. A thud followed. "What the hell?" Emily picked at the tape wrapped around the box. "Do you have any scissors?"

"No. We can't open that. He'll know." My throat closed as I thought about Keith finding out we were snooping through his things.

"You think he'll notice? I hardly doubt he comes down here, let alone gets into this box."

"I don't know. But what if he does? I don't want him to know that I know anything. Rebecca made that clear."

"Okay, well do you have any tape? We can tape it back up after we take a look."

"I don't know, Em. I think he'll know." I twirled some hair around my finger.

Emily picked at the tape until it loosened. The sound of it ripping away at the paper under it was like nails on a chalkboard. "Stop. He's going to know."

"Calm down. I guarantee he won't know. You forget I'm an expert at snooping. I'll seal this thing back up and no one will ever notice."

I closed my eyes. "I can't watch."

The sound of the cover lifting off the box was followed by a gasp. "Oh my god. She was pregnant. That wasn't in any of the news stories I read."

My eyes shot open. "How do you know that?"

Emily held up a pregnancy test and an ultrasound picture. "Look, this has Rebecca's name on it. She was pregnant when she went missing. The date on this is June, that's three months before she was reported missing. In all the interviews I read, Keith never once said anything about this. Don't you think that's strange?"

"At this point I don't think there's anything that can be considered strange. I mean, we're in the basement while I try to communicate with my husband's dead wife."

Emily ignored my joke and pulled out a book. "Look at this Tess. It looks like it could be *her* journal." She held it to her heart. "Oh, Rebecca. I'm so sorry." She opened the cover and closed her eyes. "This feels kind of wrong."

"All of it does."

"I think we need to keep this. I'll take it back to my place and I'll let you know what I find out."

"I don't know about that, Em. What if Keith notices?"

"How would he? I'll tape the box up and he'll never know. I mean it's his fault for keeping this."

"I don't know about this."

"Tessa, we owe Rebecca at least this. Our mission is to find her, right?"

I nodded. "Yeah, I guess you're right. But make sure you put all that stuff back in the box just how you found it."

"Deal." She held her hand up as she placed the book to her heart. "I can't wait to see what Rebecca has to say."

"Do you really think it will be helpful? I mean, if he killed her she couldn't have written about it."

"I know that." Emily rolled her eyes as she flipped through the pages. "But she could have hinted to something."

"I guess you're right."

"Here, hold this while I keep looking." Emily handed me the journal.

When I opened the journal and saw Rebecca's handwriting, I felt a tear roll down my cheek. Conflicted by the love I had for Keith and the desire to help a woman I'd never met the emotions overwhelmed me. There was still a part of me that didn't want to find the answers Emily was so desperately searching for. Ignorance is bliss, or so they say. At least in this moment that was true.

"Look at this." Emily held up a piece of paper. "It's an email from Rebecca to a cop." She paused. "Whoa. It looks like they were having an affair."

My stomach dropped as the thoughts filled my head. "She was cheating on him?"

"I don't know, but does it really matter?"

"Well, maybe he's the one who killed Rebecca."

"I highly doubt it, but I guess anything is possible. I mean it could explain why Keith kept all this stuff. But it doesn't explain why Rebecca is haunting *you*. If she wasn't trying to protect you, why would she be coming to you in dreams?"

"I don't know, but at least it's a possibility, right?"

"I suppose, just promise me you'll stay alert to the danger."

"Yeah, I will." The idea that Keith might not be the bad guy that everyone was making him out to be did bring me some relief. Maybe Emily's gut was just overreacting. She had always been the protective big sister.

I found Emily some tape and watched as she closed the box up. She placed everything back in the box just as she found it. I was relieved this part of the journey was over. There was so much new information spinning around in my head I felt a headache coming on.

"Where else can we look?" Emily brushed her hands on the side of her jeans and rubbed them together.

"I think we've had enough excitement for today. Let's just

see what you find out after you read that thing." I held up Rebecca's journal before handing it back to her.

"Oh, come on, you can't tell me you're ready to stop looking now. There are so many boxes down here. There's got to be something else."

"Maybe, but I'm kind of tired. You'll just have to come back so we can do this again."

"But we're here now. Keith won't be home for a while. Just let me look around a little more." I couldn't decide if she was whining or annoyed with me. "Don't you want to know?" She crossed her arms while she pushed out her pouty lips.

"Honestly, no. I already have so much to think about." I rubbed my forehead and squeezed my eyes closed.

"I'm sorry, Tess. I'm just eager to find out the truth. I'll be patient. If Keith behaves like he did last night I think you'll be okay for a while. I just don't want anything to happen to you."

"I know you want what's best for me. I love that about you. I'm just really tired all of a sudden. Between figuring out my superpower and finding out Rebecca was pregnant, I'm exhausted. I just need to take a nap."

"I get it. Mandy is probably ready for me to come bug her anyway."

"I like her. She seems sweet."

"We're talking about the same person?" Emily laughed as she tapped the journal against her leg as we walked to the stairs. "She's pretty perfect. At least for me."

"I'm glad you're happy. I was worried about you."

"Ditto."

6

The dreams of Rebecca stopped. It had been a week since the last strange thing happened in the house, and I had to wonder if maybe we found out what we needed to. It felt like Rebecca wanted us to find out about her lover, and now we knew Keith was in the clear. The uncertainty of the future had been playing havoc on me. A headache took up residency for the past seven days, followed by nausea that wouldn't accept the eviction notice. The only time I felt okay was when I was sleeping. I just couldn't get enough. It was hard to believe everything could be over as soon as it began. There was something in me telling me there was more to come; but maybe it was just Emily.

Since having the journal, I hadn't heard much from her. I knew she was busy with a ton of projects, but I would have thought she would have started reading it on her drive home. Keith had been extra nice the last few days, too. Or maybe it was just me noticing what a great guy he really was. I had a feeling Emily was going to find out Keith was not who she thought he was.

"Good morning beautiful." The warmth of Keith's lips on my forehead eased the pain in my head for a moment. God, I hoped I was right about this.

"Good morning." I snuggled into his body and let him cradle me. "I love you."

"I love you, too. How are you feeling this morning?" He pushed the hair out of my face.

"I'm still not feeling well. I can't seem to shake this headache."

"Maybe you need to stay in bed all day and try to sleep it away."

"It feels like that's all I've been doing. I need to do some stuff around the house today."

"Oh, stop it. That stuff can wait. You need to take care of yourself."

"I'm sorry, I don't know what's wrong with me lately."

"Don't be sorry. I know you have a lot going on." His words took my breath away.

The beat of my heart throbbed in my head, intensifying the pain. "What do you mean?"

"You know." His hand rested on my back. I couldn't breathe. The pressure from the weight made me panic. "Are you alright?"

I swallowed hard to push down the lump taking over my throat. "Yeah."

"Tessa, I'm worried about you. I'm going to take the day off and get you to the doctor. This has been going on long enough." Keith swung his feet off the side of the bed and picked up his cell phone.

"I'm fine. Don't worry about me. I'll be fine."

Keith held up his hand and moved his index finger to his

lip as he stretched. His naked body standing before me, reminding me of some of my favorite parts of my husband. I couldn't look away. I loved this man.

He walked into the hall and shut the door behind him. I couldn't hear what he was saying any longer. I rolled over and fell back to sleep. The weight of the bed shifted, waking me back up. Keith stroked my hair. "You've got an appointment at 10:00, why don't you rest a little longer before your shower?"

"Stay here with me. I want you to hold me."

Keith stood up and walked back to his side of the bed and joined me. He pulled up the covers and pulled my body into his. The old feeling of safety he used to bring me returned. All I wanted was for him to take care of me.

For the first time in a week my headache was gone. I knew it wasn't a doctor I needed, but this. I just needed to love and trust my husband again. It was all I ever needed. He could always make things better. He wasn't the monster Emily wanted me to believe he was.

Keith had breakfast waiting for me when I was out of the shower. Buttered toast and coffee in my favorite blue ceramic mug. "I thought toast would be easy on your stomach." He sat next to me as I picked up the warm bread.

"Thanks babe, it's just what I needed." The bread melted in my mouth, reminding me of the breakfasts Gram made for me.

"How are you feeling? How's your head?" Keith sat on the edge of his seat watching as I set down my mug.

"Actually, I'm feeling a little better. I guess I just needed a little extra time with you."

"All you had to do was ask. I can see if they'll let me work from home for a while if it would be helpful."

"No, it's okay. You don't have to do that for me."

"I have a better idea. Let's go on vacation. We can get out of here, find some warm, tropical place and redo our honeymoon. We really didn't celebrate our anniversary yet."

The thought of soft sand between my toes and crystal-clear water was just what I needed. I needed to get away from here, from this house, from all of the outside influences. I needed time to just listen to myself and remember why I fell in love with Keith.

"Does that smile mean I should book something?" Keith put his hand on mine.

"Yeah, I think that's a great idea."

"Perfect. We can look online together after your appointment."

"Better yet, we can look now and cancel it. I don't need to go to the doctor. I'm fine."

"No, it's better to be safe. I don't want anything to happen to you." Those didn't sound like words from an abuser. The more he spoke, the more I questioned Rebecca's message. This wasn't a man that wanted to hurt his wife.

In the waiting room, Keith sat by my side, holding my hand as the minutes ticked by. The room was full of other patients waiting. I hated the doctors. Ever since I was a kid and they tried to tell my mom I needed to lose weight. The thought of stepping on the scale was enough to keep me away. It was not something I looked forward to. I'd rather suffer alone than be faced by the numbers on the evil contraption.

"Tessa Stevens." The muffled voice greeted me from behind a folder. The short, plump nurse in teddy bear scrubs held the door open as I made my way to her. Keith followed.

"You can wait out here." I turned to give him a smile.

"No, I'm coming in."

The idea of him knowing what the scale said pushed the headache back into place. I couldn't stand the thought of him knowing my darkest secret. No one knew what that number was. Even I didn't want to know. Sweat beaded up under my hair. "No, I'll be fine."

Keith shook his head. "No, it's okay, I'm coming."

There was no way out of this. He was going to know. Just when I decided things were going to be okay, he'd be the one to leave me when he knows. The nurse opened the file as she approached the scale, my breathing increased. The file closed and she flipped on a light in a small room. "The doctor will be right in."

Relief settled in when I realized I was in the clear. Keith would not find out, not today. When I sat down all the air I had been holding expelled from my lungs. I had forgotten how much power that device held over me. That would be the next battle I faced.

"You alright?" Keith put his hand on my knee and gave it a squeeze.

"Yeah." A sigh hung off the word.

"Are you sure? You seem tense."

"Yeah. I'm fine." I rubbed the sweat from my palms onto my jeans. "This is going to sound stupid, but I was really worried about you seeing how much I weigh."

"Babe, I see you naked every day. Why would you be worried about that?"

"Because once you see how much it is, you'll know."

"Know what? You're beautiful. Perfect in every way. A number isn't going to change that." He reached over and kissed me. "I love you."

"It's just… another one of those screwed up things about me." I forced a smile, trying to believe what he had said. Rebecca didn't look like she ever had to worry about the number on the scale. She was beautiful, and I knew he saw her naked, too.

The door opened and an older woman extended her hand. "Hi, you must be Tessa. I'm Dr. Harris." The stool squeaked as she sat down to join us.

I nodded and crossed my legs, pulling myself in as tight as I could.

"And you are?" Dr. Harris looked down her glasses as she waited.

"I'm her husband, Keith." He held his hand out for her to take.

She gave him a smile and looked down at the folder. "I see you haven't been feeling well for a week. Headaches, nausea, and exhaustion?"

"Yes, but I'm starting to feel better."

"Any other symptoms?"

"No."

"Hmm." Dr. Harris stood up and tapped the examination table. "Here, have a seat. I want to take a listen." She placed the stethoscope around her neck and waited for me to sit. "Take a deep breath." The coldness from the metal penetrated my shirt.

I inhaled and exhaled at her command.

"Everything sounds fine." She walked to the front of me and reached for a light. "Look straight ahead." She shined the light into my eyes before placing it on the counter. Her cold hands met my neck. "Can you look straight ahead for me?" Her fingers danced along my throat. "Anything hurt when I do this?"

"No."

"Well, everything looks fine. I'll have the nurse come back in to draw some blood. We'll give you a call when the results come back."

"What do you think it is?" Keith asked before she had a chance to exit the room.

"Everything looks fine. We're just going to run some tests to make sure we didn't miss anything."

"Miss anything? Like what?" Keith crossed his arms and leaned back in his chair.

"Well, that's what we're going to find out. Be patient, sir. Have a good day, Tessa." The door closed behind her.

"I don't like her." Keith's eyes went to the clock. "That nurse better hurry up. I don't have all day."

"I'm sorry." My head dropped with his mood shift.

The tapping of his foot intensified with each passing minute. "Where is that nurse?"

A knock at the door eased my worry and seemed to ease Keith's.

"It's just me again." The nurse set the plastic basket on the table behind me and put on rubber gloves. "It'll only take a second."

"What are you checking for?" Keith stood up and joined her at my side.

"Oh, just a few things. You know, the usual." She pressed her finger into my arm before rubbing it with an alcohol pad.

"Usual? What's that?" Keith placed his hand on my back.

"Sir, it would be a big help if you could take a seat. This is a small room. I'll be done before you know it."

Keith returned to his chair. "When will we get the results?"

"You should hear something by the end of the day. But like they say, no news is good news. Honey, this is going to pinch a little." She stuck the needle into my arm and blood began to fill the tube.

"No, we need to hear back either way. No news is unacceptable. Put that in your notes somewhere. I won't be able to relax until I know she's okay."

"You've got yourself a good man." She winked at me as she pulled the needle out of my arm. "All done. You're free to go. And I'll be sure to give you a call by the end of the day."

"Thank you." I pulled my sleeve down and stepped down.

"Thanks." Keith took my hand. "Sorry if I seem a little…"

"High strung?" The nurse laughed. "It's okay. I know you love your wife. The waiting is the hardest part."

Keith pointed and winked. "Was that a Tom Petty reference?"

"I'd be free falling if I said no." She laughed as we parted ways. "Have a great rest of your day."

"Tom Petty is everywhere, isn't he?" I squeezed Keith's hand this time. "I'm going to be fine. There's nothing to worry about."

"I'm sorry I got so impatient in there. I love you and I can't stand the thought of anything happening to you."

The concern in his voice was all I needed to know he wasn't a bad man. He just didn't want to lose anyone else he loved. Knowing Rebecca was pregnant before she went missing explains why Keith didn't want to talk about it. I can't imagine the pain that haunts him. It also explains why he was so eager to start our family.

7

The ringing of the phone jolted me out of the deep sleep I was in. I reached for my phone, knocking it onto the floor. I rolled out of bed to get it before the call went to voicemail. "Hello?"

"Is this Tessa Stevens?"

"Yes." The anticipation grew with each passing second.

"Hi there, this is Judy, your nurse from today."

"Oh, hi. Sorry, I ah…"

"No need to be sorry. I have the results back from your bloodwork."

I rubbed the sleep from my eyes. "Okay."

"And everything looked great. You're as healthy as a horse, and it looks like you're going to start eating like one soon, too."

"Excuse me?"

"Not funny? Sorry, it's been a long day. Congratulations, you're pregnant."

"Pregnant?"

"Yes. That's the only thing wrong with you. Get as much rest as you need, you're growing a tiny human."

I clicked off the phone unable to continue on with the banter. *Pregnant?* Unsure what to think, I let the news settle in around me. Keith and I were good now. I knew he was a good man, but the uncertainty of what happened to Rebecca kept me cautious. We'd been trying for a baby for the past year. It would be my luck that it would happen right when I was going to stop trying, at least until I could figure everything out. *Keith.* Where was Keith?

I stuffed my feet into my slippers and went into the living room. The light was on, but he wasn't around. A note met me in the kitchen. "Gone to pick up dinner. Be back soon. Love you."

Relieved I had a little more time to figure this out, I sat at the table and stared at the words on the piece of paper. "What the hell am I going to do?" The question I was thinking fell out of my mouth.

The light in the living room went out, causing my attention to focus there. "That's my answer, isn't it, Rebecca? I have to keep him in the dark."

The front door swung open and the light turned back on. "Hey there sleepyhead, are you feeling better?"

"Yes, thanks for picking up dinner." I stood up to give him a kiss. "The nurse just called, she said everything was normal, nothing to worry about."

"Well that's a relief. Guess we need to get you some more rest on that vacation."

"That sounds like just the cure." What the hell was I going to do? It wasn't like I could keep this from him forever. And he'd notice when I didn't have my usual glass of wine. I needed to talk to Emily; she'd know what I should do.

Keith and I enjoyed pizza together while we watched reruns of *How I Met Your Mother*. A good laugh was just what I needed to get my mind off the beautiful mess I was in the middle of. If only life were easy and made sense. I would figure out what I needed to do. I just needed to buy myself a little more time. Obviously, Rebecca wasn't done with me yet.

Insomnia made the swap with exhaustion while I wasn't looking. Since receiving the news, I couldn't stop my mind. The wrong decision wouldn't just cost me anymore, but my baby, too. I wondered if this was how Rebecca was feeling? The difference was Keith didn't hurt me. He never laid a hand on me. I couldn't even remember any fights we'd had. We just fit so well together. Imagining him as a father made my heart swell. I'd wanted this for so long. But if Rebecca was right, we weren't safe. I just didn't understand.

The clock seemed to have stopped working as I waited for each minute to pass. I just needed to get through the night so I could see Emily in the morning. I also wasn't in the mood to have a visit from Rebecca tonight. The week-long break had been nice.

I listened to Keith breathe as he slept, and an uneasy feeling washed over me. I was in Rebecca's spot. This was where she slept until she disappeared. Essentially, I had stolen her life, or at least her spot in it. I was sleeping in her bed, sitting on her couch, cooking dinner with her stove, feeding her husband. And the baby. I was carrying the baby that she was carrying, well not exactly, but I could be *her*.

I felt a tear roll down my cheek as the image of the beautiful redhead flashed before my eyes. *Where are you Rebecca?* I knew the thought alone was enough to summon her. What I didn't know was that I didn't have to be asleep to see her.

A flash of white light flickered in the corner of the room. I squeezed my eyes closed and opened them again. I saw her. Rebecca stood over me and motioned with her finger for me to follow her. A mix of fear and uncertainty held me in bed like a sack of bricks. A smile grew on her face as she put her finger to her lips to shush me.

I swallowed my tongue before getting out of bed and followed her. She led me into the bathroom and pointed for me to close the door behind us. "What's even happening right now?" I whispered as I sat on the side of the bathtub.

"He can't know about the baby." Her words floated to my ears.

"What am I supposed to do? He's going to find out eventually."

She shook her head. "No. He can't." Her hand went to her stomach. "He'll kill your baby like he killed mine."

"Where is your baby?" Unable to believe what she was saying, or even that I was talking to a ghost, I wasn't going to let her scare me.

"Oh, Tessa, my baby is in a safe place, but yours isn't."

"What will happen if I stay?"

"You don't want to find out." She disappeared as quickly as she arrived. I had so many more questions to ask. Maybe I was just crazy. It could all be a figment of my imagination. I walked back to the bedroom and slipped into bed. I snuggled next to Keith and lifted his arm to put around me. I needed to feel safe, even if by a monster. Morning couldn't come fast enough.

Confusion surrounded me more now than before. I knew I

had to listen to Rebecca, even if I didn't want to. I couldn't put our baby's life at risk. It was so much easier when it was just mine on the line. But he hadn't shown me any of the warning signs. If he were going to kill me, wouldn't I at least suspect something? If the documents were true, Keith and Rebecca had a violent history; but Keith and I were a perfect match. Not a single fight. Some couples just didn't work out. That wasn't a crime. But murder was. My headache returned as truth continued to be stranger than fiction.

8

As soon as Keith left for work, before his car even left the driveway, I called Emily. My call went straight to voicemail. I hadn't considered she wouldn't answer. I paced the kitchen and dialed her number again. Voicemail again.

Chills ran through my body when I relived the visit from last night. I just needed to get out of the house. I wasn't in the mood to talk to Rebecca today. Not yet anyway. I needed to know what Emily found in the journal. I needed concrete information; not paranormal activity brought on by stress. There was no way it was really her last night. Stress could play tricks on people. That was the only explanation. Dreams were one thing but having a full conversation with a dead woman was another. There was no way that really happened.

My phone vibrated in my hand before I heard the ring. I clicked it on before checking to see who it was. "Em?"

"Yeah, Tess, did the phone even ring? What's up?"

"I need to see you. Can you come by today?"

"Oh my god, is everything alright? Are you okay? Should I call the police?"

"No, everything is fine. I just want to talk to you, and I don't feel well enough to drive to the café today."

"You're sure? Everything is okay? You're safe?"

"Yeah, just get here as soon as you can, okay?"

"Okay, I'm leaving now." I heard her car keys jingle and the door close before she hung up the phone. I was glad she only lived thirty minutes away.

I took a quick shower to help the time pass by. The hot water beat down on my back reminding me how good the heat felt against my skin. I was also reminded that this was the room *it* happened in last night. The water no longer washed the stress away, instead it guided a panic attack to the surface. Between the steam from the hot water and the anxiety I couldn't breathe. I rinsed the remaining conditioner out of my hair and turned the water off, exiting the bathroom in a towel.

Now I wasn't only unsure about who Keith really was, but I was afraid to be alone in my own home. I rubbed the towel over my legs to dry off the remaining moisture and slipped my jeans on, my bra and shirt followed just as quickly. I slipped on my slippers and went to make a pot of coffee. My hand trembled as I measured the coffee grounds. "God damn it, Rebecca, just leave me alone." The anger behind my words made me question where they came from.

I wasn't ready to talk to ghosts, let alone see them. "Gram, it'd be really cool if you could stop by for a visit." Shit, maybe I was going crazy. "I'm past the point of talking to myself, now I talk to the dead. Are you even dead, though? I mean, you could still be alive living your best life somewhere." I shrugged my shoulders to my empty audience and watched the brown water drip into the pot.

A knock on the front door made me jump out of my skin. Saved by my big sister. "Thank God you're here." I ran to Emily and threw my arms around her.

"What's going on Tessa? You look awful." She took a step back to look at me.

"I'm not even going to fight you on that one." Uncontrollable laughter filled the kitchen. "Em, I think I'm going crazy."

She tilted her head and squinted her eyes. "Why? What's going on?"

"She was here last night." My eyes circled around the room. "Rebecca was *here*."

"Wait. Here? As in she's alive?"

I shook my head. "I saw her. She was in the bedroom and she made me follow her into the bathroom."

"Oh my god." Emily's hand covered her mouth. "You can see *them* now?"

"Don't say that like it's a good thing. I don't want to see them. I don't want to hear them. I don't want any of it."

"Okay, okay, I get it."

"You don't get it. Do you know how scared I am? I couldn't even take a shower. I mean, I don't want a bunch of people in there with me." I threw my hands in the air as I paced the kitchen.

"What did she say to you?"

"Well, that's a whole other story." I stopped pacing and held my face in my hands. "I went to the doctor yesterday and..."

"Oh my god, Tess, are you okay? Is everything alright?"

"I'm fine. But I don't think anything is alright." My hands rested on my belly. "I'm pregnant. I'm fucking pregnant."

"Oh shit."

"I know. I can't even be excited. I'm so scared."

Emily walked over to me and returned the hug from earlier. "We'll get through this, Tessa."

"Yeah, I don't know if *we* will. Rebecca came to warn me not to tell Keith. How the fuck am I not going to tell him? I mean, how do you hide a baby from your husband?"

"You know the answer to that." Emily took my hands and looked into my eyes.

"I don't. I don't know the fucking answer to that, or anything."

"You have to leave him. It's not just you anymore."

"But we don't know if Keith did anything. What if Rebecca was lying in that protection order? What if her boyfriend killed her? What if she's alive some place, hiding out? What if she doesn't even exist."

"You know none of that's true. Tess, you said you saw the hole in the wall. You said you saw the blood. I know you're confused. I know you love Keith, and this isn't how you wanted things to go, but you have got to get the hell out of here."

"What's in that journal? Is there anything in there that proves Keith is a monster? Do you have any proof?" The vein in my neck throbbed in sync with the pounding of my heart.

Emily shook her head. "No, there's nothing in there. Not yet anyway."

"So, you have no proof, and neither do I."

"Tess, you have all the proof you need from Rebecca. She's trying to save you."

"Did you ever think that maybe she's just jealous?" I crossed my arms against my chest. A glass fell off the counter and smashed onto the floor.

Emily's eyes widened as she looked at me. "Yeah, I don't think she's jealous. She seems pretty pissed off."

"Leave me the fuck alone." I pulled my hair and finished with a scream.

"Whoa, calm down. She's trying to help you. I bet if you listen to what she has to say, she will leave you alone."

"Oh, so now you're siding with a dead woman?"

"You seriously need to calm down. I just want to help, and by the looks of things, so does Rebecca." Emily took the broom and started to clean up the broken glass. "You of all people should know that people are not who they seem."

She was right. Our father was not who we thought he was. We didn't even find out the truth until after his death. My hero morphed into a villain, crushing everything I ever believed about him. Defeated by the truth, I fell to the floor.

Emily dropped the broom and rushed over to me. "Tessa." The fear in her voice couldn't be hidden. The reason she was so interested in finding the truth was the same reason I was running from it.

I curled into a ball and hid my head. "It's not supposed to be this way."

Emily sat on the floor next to me and cradled my head in her lap. "I know."

Memories from our childhood flashed before my eyes. We had the perfect life. The perfect parents. Everything was perfect. But everything changed in an instant. I don't want that for my baby, or for Emily. "Why is this so hard?"

"I don't know."

"Keith is just like Dad, isn't he?"

"I don't want to find out."

"Me either. This is why it hurts so much, isn't it?"

"Oh Tess, I'm so sorry. I know how much you love him."

"Loved. You mean loved. I can't love the man who murdered our mom."

"I was talking about Keith."

"Oh."

"Does he know what happened? With Mom and Dad?"

"Not exactly. I just told him they died in an accident."

"Hmm. Mandy knows. I told her right away. Why didn't you tell Keith the truth?"

"It was the truth. It was an accident." I sat up so I could look at Emily.

"No, Tess, a murder-suicide is not an accident. Dad planned it. He caused both of their deaths. That's not an accident. I always cringe when I hear you say that."

"I guess saying accident is a lot easier than admitting what a monster Dad was. I didn't want to remember him like that." And it all made sense. "Just like Keith." I dropped my head. "I need to put a plan together. I need to get out of here. Before it's too late."

"I'll help you. You can stay with Mandy and me. We can by a house somewhere far away from here."

"You want to run away with me?" I laughed at the thought of our childhood threat coming true.

"Honestly, Mandy has been after me to move out to L.A."

"As in California?"

"Yeah, but I couldn't go, not without you."

"Really? You stayed for me, even when we were fighting?"

She nodded. "You're my baby sister, and my only family left. I would never leave you."

I took her hand and gave it a squeeze. "How'd I get so lucky?"

"Seriously." Emily laughed. "So, do you want to start over? We can help you raise that precious little angel."

"I do like Mandy. She seems pretty cool. Kind of like a mom."

Emily hit my leg. "Oh, stop it. She's not *that* old."

After we got Rebecca's mess cleaned up, we went into the living room with our coffee and started to work on a plan. I had a little time before my belly started to grow, and if I could figure out a way to push through the exhaustion, Keith wouldn't even notice that I wasn't feeling well.

9

Keith handed me an envelope when he walked in the door. "Open it." He stuck his hand in his pocket as his smile grew.

"What is this?" I asked as I unsealed the envelope.

"You'll find out when you open it."

My heart sank as the contents reminded me of better days. "Oh, Keith. We can't afford this."

"Sure, we can. I sold the most cars this month so my bonus alone will cover the cost."

The trip was three months away. There was no way I would be able to hide my growing belly for that long, not in a bathing suit. My escape plan would have to happen before the trip. There was no way around it now.

"What's wrong? Why don't you look happy? This is what you said you wanted." Keith ran his hand through his dark brown hair.

"No, no, I am happy. I'm just shocked." I pushed up a smile. "This is going to be so much fun." I gave him a kiss and took his hand. "Thank you."

"I'm sorry it's so far away. I know you wanted to go sooner, but I can't leave during the busy season."

"No, it's great. Thank you. It will give us something to look forward to." The lie left a bitter taste on my tongue. The idea of getting away sounded delightful. I'd dreamed of a vacation like this since I was a little girl. A tropical paradise. It would have been perfect. Now, not only did I have to plan my escape, I had to plan for a vacation I would never get to go on.

Keith waited at the table as I served him dinner. Meatloaf and mashed potatoes, it was his favorite meal. I had it ready before his surprise. I guess it was my way of letting go of any of the lingering guilt I had. I wanted more than anything for him to be the man I thought he was, but as with my father, I knew that would never be possible.

"How's Emily?" Keith asked as he picked up his fork.

"She's good, I guess, why?"

"You guess, didn't you see her today?"

His question stopped me in my tracks. "Yes, I did. She came over today."

Keith smiled as he took a bite. "Mmm. This is good."

"How did you know she came over?"

"You told me."

"Oh." I didn't. I know I didn't tell him. Any sense of safety I had vanished. What else did he know?

"She's hanging around an awful lot lately."

"Yeah, it's nice to have her back in my life. I've missed her." The palpitation of my heart echoed in my head as I tried to imagine every possible scenario. Were there hidden cameras? My eyes circled the room without letting Keith see what I was doing. How long had he been watching me? They must have been here all along. *Oh my god.* What if there were microphones, too? What if he already knew I was planning on leaving? What if he saw me talking to Rebecca?

"That's nice." It was hard to read the smile on Keith's face. His energy did not match his mood.

"So, how was your day?" I pushed in a forkful of mashed potatoes to mask the fear.

"Same old stuff. Nothing to report back. How was yours? What did you and your sister talk about?"

"It was good. I felt a lot better today."

"What did you two talk about today?"

The question I evaded came back and slapped me across the face. "Oh, not too much."

"No?" Keith cocked his head. "She was here for a while."

I felt my eyes squint and tried to cover it with a smile. "How do you know that?"

"Know what?" Keith shrugged his shoulders.

"That she was here for a while. How do you know how long she was here?"

"You told me."

"No, I didn't. I don't even remember telling you she was here at all, but I know I didn't tell you she was here most of the day."

"You must have forgotten." Keith pushed his fork into his mouth. "Mmm. You've out done yourself with this one."

"No, but really. How did you know Emily was here all day?"

"Babe, you told me. You must have forgotten. It's no big deal, right? Let it go."

"I guess you're right. It's no big deal. I could have sworn I didn't mention it, that's all." I moved the meatloaf around my plate as I tried to pull the conversation we had today. Maybe he was right, maybe I just forgot. I looked around the room for any sign of a camera but couldn't find anything. I did have a lot on my mind. I guess I could have forgotten.

I pushed out the uneasy feeling from dinner and tried to enjoy some TV with Keith. I needed to get out of my own head. I was going to be the reason my escape plan failed. I never was any good at keeping secrets. As I sat in the chair across the room from Keith, I studied his face. He was so handsome. He looked like he could have been a *GQ* model. His jaw line jutted out just right, and his dimples were to die for. Even though he was older than me, he wore his age well. I should have known he was too perfect for me.

I was going to miss making love to him and feeling safe under the weight of his body on top of mine. And his lips. I was going to miss his tender lips as they kissed mine. I bit my bottom lip as I stared at the man I love. I needed to figure out how to make that past tense. He needed to just be a man I *loved*.

"What are you looking at?" Keith raised his eyebrow when he caught me staring at him.

"Oh, nothing." A flirty giggle left my lips, and I knew what was going to happen next.

"Oh, really?" Keith came over and kissed me. He picked me up out of my chair and carried me to our bed. He pulled off his shirt, exposing his muscles, making me melt. "You want a better look?" Keith unzipped his pants and slipped off his boxers. He pulled off my pants and started kissing the inside of my thighs.

I sat up enough to pull off my shirt and unhook my bra. My body pulsated for his. I needed to feel the warmth of his skin on mine. I needed him. "I love you, Keith." I meant the words as they slipped out of my mouth.

We made love. The man I needed was the man that was going to kill me. Unable to turn him into the same person, I let the pleasure take place of the confusion. How could I give up on him? On us? The thought of never making love to my husband again crushed me more than the thought of him being the monster deep down I knew he was. Sex with him was my weakness. Our bodies fit perfectly together, like we were made for each other. How would I ever find anyone like him? How would I raise my baby alone? The tears replaced the questions, falling onto Keith's chest as he held me.

"What's wrong, baby?" Keith moved the hair out of my face and saw the redness in my eyes.

"It's just… it's nothing." I buried my head into his chest and inhaled the scent of his cologne and skin.

"Come on, you can trust me. Tell me what's wrong."

"It's nothing, really. I guess I'm just emotional today."

"I don't like how upset your sister makes you. Maybe you should take a break from her."

"It's not her. I guess I just miss my family, that's all."

"But you were fine before you started spending time with her. It seems to me that she's making you sad. I don't remember you being like this when you two weren't talking."

"No. Emily isn't to blame. We were just talking about our parents today, and it made me miss them."

"See, I'm right. You need to stay away from her for a while. I want my happy, carefree wife back."

"Can we just stop? I want to enjoy this." I pulled his body close to mine and closed my eyes.

"I love you. I just want what's best for you. That's all."

"I know." Except I didn't. I didn't know anything anymore.

10

"There's more to it than you know." Rebecca's voice met my ears with a melody.

"More to what?" I followed Rebecca through the woods, dried leaves cracking under my feet with each step. Her pace increased. I could no longer see her. I followed the path, winding through the forest. The giant trees welcoming me with their arms of green pine needles. "Rebecca." My voice hung in the cold, crisp air as I looked for her. "Rebecca."

"Over here." Her voice pulled me deeper, my feet led the way.

A clearing in the distance, I could see her standing before me. She motioned with her finger for me to follow her. "Just a little bit longer."

"Where are you taking me?"

"You'll know when you get there." Her white gown bounced as she ran.

"I don't understand. Slow down."

"Any minute now, dear." Rebecca's red hair turned white, and when she spun around it was no longer her.

"Gram? Is that you?"

She placed her hand on her heart. "I've been expecting you, Tessa. My sweet girl."

"Grammy. It's been so long. I've missed you."

"Shh." She placed her finger to her lips and spread the trees open in front of us.

My mother and father laid together under the brush, the blood from the gunshot wounds made a perfect circle around them. Frozen from the sight, I could not move.

"Do you understand now?" Gram's hair turned back to red, and Rebecca stood in her place.

"No." The echo from my scream danced off the mountain tops. "No. I don't understand."

"We're more alike than you know. Keep digging, sweet girl."

The alarm clock pulled me out of my restless sleep. What was she talking about? More alike than I know? I closed my eyes to try to return to no avail. I wanted to talk to my gram. I wanted her to answer all of these unanswered questions. Where was she? Why wasn't she the one trying to rescue me? The fear from the dream morphed into anger, slowly slipping into rage. Where the hell was she?

I couldn't shake the image of my dead parents. I hadn't seen the crime scene photos, I was too young, and when I was old enough, I didn't want to. I knew they were found in the woods by a hunter, that was all the information I wanted. Why was Rebecca bringing my parents into this?

Keith rolled over and kissed me on the forehead. "Good morning beautiful. Did you sleep okay?"

"No." The answer surprised even me.

"Another bad dream?"

"Yeah." The word still hot with fury. "I'm so sick of this. I just want my life back."

Keith looked at me with concern. His usual response to get over it didn't fill the morning air. "Tell me about it."

I pushed out a sigh and threw the covers off of my sweaty body. "There's this woman that's haunting me. She won't leave me alone. She fucking brought me to see my dead fucking parents last night. How fucked up is that?" I grabbed my head, pulling at my hair. "She made me fucking see my dead fucking mother in a pool of her blood. I can't take this anymore." My heart dropped when I realized what I had said. I shared too much.

"Whoa. That sounds awful. But you know it's just a dream. You know that's not how your mom died." Keith sat on the edge of the bed, his feet in his sheepskin slippers.

"But it is. My dad fucking murdered my mom. He shot her and then himself. I never wanted to see her like that, to see them like that, but thanks to this bitch I had to. I can't take it anymore." I wasn't sure what was happening. I didn't want to say any of this. I sure didn't want Keith to think I was on to him.

Keith scratched his head. "What does she look like?"

"I've showed you her picture."

"No, not your mom, the woman?"

"I don't know." My eyes darted to the window as my nerves began to settle.

"Yeah, I think you do."

"She's, ah, she has short brown hair."

"Hmm, okay."

"Why?"

"Oh, no reason."

Was that a guilty conscience? Did he think it was Rebecca? How could it be if he didn't kill her? The dots began to connect in my mind. My anger and hormones raged inside of me. "Why do you want to know what *she* looks like, but you don't ask any questions about my parents?"

"What?"

"I just told you that my dad murdered my mom. You didn't know that before. Why didn't you say anything about that?"

"I knew about that. You told me."

"I know I didn't tell you about that. I don't tell *anyone* about that."

"Yeah, you did. You told me before. You must be so stressed out. It's okay if you forgot."

"I didn't forget. I *know* I didn't tell you that."

Keith stood up and stretched. "I don't know what to tell you." He came over to me and took me in his arms before kissing me. "I'm sorry you are having these nightmares."

My pulse beat against my neck as the vein in my forehead swelled. "I'm sorry. It was just a bad dream. I didn't mean to take it out on you." I said the words I knew he wanted to hear. I needed him to get to work so I could go to Emily's.

Keith lingered a little longer than usual that morning. It was as if he knew I was in a hurry to get out of the house. When I saw the taillights of his Toyota Tacoma, I grabbed my purse and keys and let the door slam behind me.

The adrenaline pumped through my body as my foot pushed the accelerator to the floor. My car hugged the corners as I followed the back roads to Emily's house. My head was pounding as everything around me spun out of control. The blue lights in my rearview mirror was the only thing that caught my attention. *Shit.* I banged my hand against the steering wheel as my car came to a stop.

The officer opened his car door and put on his hat. I

watched him in my mirror as he approached the car. I unrolled the window as I awaited his presence. "Hi Miss. Is everything alright?" He tipped his hat as he bent down to look into my window.

"No, not really." My sigh separated us.

"Are you running from something?"

"Not exactly. I'm just having a bad day."

"I'd say so. You were going pretty fast, thirty over the speed limit." He reached out his hand. "I'll need to see your license and registration."

I rolled my eyes as I opened the glovebox and pushed junk out of the way. "It's in here somewhere, hang on." I pulled out the envelope from the dealership and memories of meeting Keith flooded me. "Fuck. He's everywhere."

"Excuse me, Miss?"

"Oh, nothing. Sorry." I handed him the registration card and proceeded to open my purse to find my license.

"Blake? Any relation to…" His words fell short when he didn't know how to finish the question.

I tried to ignore the question and handed him my license. "How did you hear about that way over here?"

"I'm from Usher County. I went to school with Emily."

"Wait. You're Tommy?"

"It's Thomas now, but yeah." His bright white teeth popped out with his smile. His eyes went to my license and his smile faded. "Stevens? You're married?"

"Yes, a little over a year. Are you?"

"No." His eyes didn't leave the plastic card in his hand. "You married Keith?"

"How did you know?"

"A wild guess." His eyes met mine. "I'll be right back, okay?" His head hung as he walked back to his cruiser.

I watched him from my rearview mirror as he sat in the front seat and entered information into his computer. How did he know it was Keith? Stevens was a common name in Drakesville. I slouched back into my seat when I saw Thomas get out of his car.

He handed my registration and license back to me. "Tessa, you know, right?"

"Know what?"

Thomas dropped his head and kicked at the gravel with his boot. "About Keith?"

"What about him?"

Thomas looked up at me with a half-smile. "Just be careful, okay?"

"Tommy, tell me if you know something."

"Tessa, I don't really know anything. It's all just speculation at this point."

"Fuck, Tommy, just spit it out."

"I see you haven't changed." His somber mood lifted with a deep, belly laugh.

"Tommy... do I need to call your mother?"

"Tessa, people think Keith murdered his wife. She's still missing, so there was never any way to charge him with anything, but people from around here are sure he did it. She was dating one of the guys at the station while her and Keith were separated, and Rebecca told him if she ever disappeared to go after Keith."

"So why didn't he? Why didn't he tell anyone?"

"He did, but without any other evidence, there was no

case." Thomas put his hands into his front pockets. "Just be safe, okay?"

"I will. So, how much do I owe you?"

"For what?"

"For speeding?"

"Oh. It's on the house." He laughed. "Next time it will cost you a cup of coffee." Thomas tipped his hat as he walked away.

"I'll tell Em you said hi." I poked my head out the window before pulling back on to the road.

What are the chances that Tommy moved to Drakesville, too? I always had a crush on him when Emily would bring him over for study dates. They were almost an item, before we moved in with Gram. I hadn't thought about him in years.

I pulled into Emily's driveway, right behind her Subaru. I knocked on her front door before ringing the doorbell. I didn't want to be the obnoxious little sister, but I needed to get inside. My fist pounded the door as it swung open. "Oh, hey, Mandy. Is Em home?"

"Considering it's 8:30, yeah, my guess is she's here." Mandy's hair stood up all over her head, her ragged bathrobe hung off her shoulders. "Emily, you have company."

I pushed past Mandy and found Emily in bed. "Em, get up, I have so much to tell you."

"Whoa, slow down." She sat up and turned on the lamp. "Are you alright? Is everything okay?"

"I don't know. This morning started off awful, but it got better." I bounced from foot to foot as I waited for Emily to get out of bed.

Emily raised her eyebrow at me as she pulled on her hoody. "I'm intrigued."

"Do you remember Tommy?"

"Peters?"

"Yeah."

"How could I forget? We could never get any work done because you were always ogling him."

"No, I wasn't. I didn't do that."

"Come get some coffee, it's too early to remind you of your delusions." Emily laughed as she handed me a mug. "So, you were saying?"

"He pulled me over this morning."

"What? That's weird. How did he know it was you? Where the hell were you?"

"He didn't. I was on my way here."

"I don't follow."

"Tommy's a cop, he works in Drakesville."

"No shit." Emily took a sip of coffee. "Wait, why did he pull you over?"

"I was speeding. I was in a hurry to get here. I have so much I need to tell you, it couldn't wait."

"Tess, that's not cool. You've got a little one to take care of."

"Yeah, I know. So much happened, I wasn't thinking straight. I just needed to talk to you, but I couldn't do it at home, but then Tommy, and now I'm a mess."

Emily laughed. "Wow, Tessa, someone's smitten."

"Like a horny little kitten?" Mandy piped in from the living room.

"She didn't just say that, did she?" I whispered to Emily.

"She did. And she's old, not deaf." Mandy joined us in the kitchen. "Sorry if my sense of humor is a little… off. I'm an old lady who writes romance novels all day. What else do I have to do?"

"Yeah, her mind is *always* in the gutter." Emily shook her head as she took another drink.

"Oh, don't act like that's not why you love me." Mandy gave Emily a kiss and poured herself a cup of coffee.

"I love that you love each other so much. You know, that's all I ever wanted for my big sister. Hell, it's all I ever wanted for myself."

"You'll get there, honey. Give it time. Maybe you're playing for the wrong team?" Mandy raised her shoulders and smirked.

"Nope, sorry, no offense, but I'm team D all the way."

Emily covered her ears. "La-la-la, I can't hear you."

"Oh, stop it, not like you didn't root for the D back in the day."

"Jesus, Tessa, thanks for outing me."

I covered my mouth. "Shit, I didn't think it was a secret."

"Nah, it's cool. She's on team D-cell battery now." Mandy cackled from behind the computer screen. "Too much?"

"D-cell battery? Try double A, unless you're using heavy equipment." I snorted.

"Okay, okay, enough of this. So, tell me the rest of the story." Emily sat at the kitchen table and motioned for me to do the same.

"I don't even know where to start." I held the mug of coffee between my hands, letting the warmth take the chill out of me. "So last night, Keith asked me how you were. I told him I didn't know, or something like that and he said I should know since you were at the house most of the day."

"Okay. And?"

"And I never told him you were there. I know I didn't. If I

did, I at least know I didn't tell him how long you were there. How the hell did he know?"

"I don't know. You're sure you didn't tell him?"

"You were there, did you hear me say anything like that to him?"

Emily shook her head. "What about in a text?"

I turned on my phone and opened our conversation. "Nope, I didn't even text him yesterday."

"Shit, Tess, he probably has cameras up."

"I know, that's what I thought, too. I mean, how else would he know how long you were there? I looked around, but I didn't see anything."

"Some cameras are next to impossible to detect." Mandy shouted from the living room. "In this one book I wrote it was all about how easy it was to keep track of people with all the new technology. You know, nanny cams, and those tiny cameras can be in almost anything."

"You think he's spying on me?"

"I would almost guarantee it." Mandy joined us at the table. "Tessa, he's dangerous. Dangerous people do crazy things."

"What about microphones? What if he's listening to me, too?"

"Oh my god, Tess." Emily's hand went to her mouth. "Then he already knows."

"That's what I'm scared of. If he knows about the baby, or that I know about Rebecca he's going to kill me next. What the hell am I supposed to do?"

"I've got an idea." Mandy looked over at Emily. "Let's go on a little trip."

"What are you thinking?" Emily asked.

"Tess, you know how to shut the WIFI off at your place?" Mandy stood up and placed her empty mug in the sink.

"I think so, just unplug the router."

"Perfect. You get home. Go unplug it and then send Emily a text to let us know. We'll be waiting down the road. Once the WIFI is off we can start looking. Most of those cameras need WIFI to record, if it's offline it will give us time to at least see what you're up against. If it's just a camera without sound, you're probably much safer than one with a mic."

"How do you know all this stuff?" Emily and I asked Mandy at the same time.

"All that research I do for the books comes in handy sometimes." Mandy laughed. "The sooner we get there, the sooner we can either put your mind to rest or start panicking."

Mandy and Emily followed behind me in their car. I couldn't stop going to the worst-case scenario. What if Keith already knew? Was that why he was being so nice lately? Tommy crept back into my thoughts, too. Why couldn't I have run into him a year and a half ago, before I even met Keith?

If Tommy knew about Rebecca, it made sense that others in town did, too. Was everyone laughing at me? Did they all know who Keith was while he was busy fooling me? The thoughts played on a loop in my head. Over and over again, showing me right where I went wrong.

I pulled my car over and waited for Emily and Mandy to do the same. I rolled my window down when Mandy pulled in next to me. "You guys wait here. I'll go home and unplug the router. I'll send you a message once it's offline."

"Are you okay, Tess? You look awful." Emily leaned over Mandy and made sad eyes at me.

"Gee, thanks." I pushed the hair out of my face. "Oh my god. Fuck." I dropped my head. "Tommy saw me like this."

"Ohhh, someone has a boyfriend. Tess and Tommy up in a tree…" Emily hit her knee and laughed.

"Good lord, what are you, three?" Mandy shook her head. "We'll wait for your text, but if we don't hear from you in ten minutes, I'm coming over."

"Okay. See you soon." Back in my car I finished the short drive home. In the driveway, before getting out of my car I looked around the yard. Nothing looked suspicious, or out of place. It didn't appear there was a camera out here, which made the chances of Keith hearing what Emily and I talked about more of a possibility.

Inside, I went into the office and unplugged the router. As I sat at Keith's desk, I turned on his computer. It was not something I had ever done before. I'm not sure why, I guess I never had a reason to snoop around his stuff before. I trusted him. When the computer was on, I went to the web browser and tried to load the page. When it failed, I knew the internet was successfully turned off. I sent the text to Emily and waited for them to arrive. While I waited, I closed the browser and opened the file marked "important" on his desktop. It was empty. It's strange it would be labeled important and be empty.

Curiosity got the best of me and I opened more files. They were all empty. Why would he even keep this computer if all of his documents were gone? Without the internet, I wasn't able to look at his search history. He spent a lot of time in here for there to be nothing saved. I clicked on the photos and waited for them to load when I heard the front door open. My heart sank as I tried to turn the computer off before leaving the room.

"Tess?" Emily's voice reminded me what time it was and what we were doing.

"Just a minute." I stood at the desk and waited for it to turn off. When I got to the kitchen, Mandy was already snooping around. "It looks like you know what you're looking for."

"Not exactly. I've never done this sort of thing outside of a keyboard before, but what the hell, right?" Mandy took small calculated steps as she canvased the kitchen.

Emily opened the front door and poked her head outside. "Hey, what's this?"

I joined her to take a look. "Oh, that? That's just the doorbell."

"Are you sure? I've never seen a doorbell look like that before." Emily inched closer to the black ball next to the door. "Mandy, come out here for a second."

Mandy joined us, the crisp fall air rushed past us, into the house. Mandy adjusted her glasses. "What are you doing out here?"

"Take a look at this thing. Tess said it's a doorbell, but it's the strangest looking thing I've ever seen."

Mandy pushed her glasses back up her nose. "Oh, okay. I've seen this before. This is one of those doorbells with a camera. You know? Where it's linked to a monitor or an app so you can see who's at the door. You might have just solved the mystery."

"Really? This thing is a camera?" I hugged myself to keep warm. "You know how many times I've walked by this thing and never knew that?"

"Well, why would you? I mean, if it's always been there,

why would you suspect anything?" Mandy rubbed her hands together. "Let's get inside and warm up. I want to keep looking around the house."

"You think there's more inside?" I closed the door behind me and heard my phone vibrating on the counter. "Oh, shit, I forgot to turn my ringer back on." I picked up the phone and saw twenty missed texts and five missed calls. All from Keith. "Looks like he knows something's up." I held my phone out for them to see.

"What did he say?" Emily hovered over me to read the messages with me.

"I'm afraid to look." I pressed the message and they filled the screen. The first message was sent right after I left the house and the rest followed. "He really does know when I leave the house."

"Yeah, well, that camera can alert him to any activity." Mandy crossed her arms as she waited for my report.

"He wants to know what I was doing, and then why I wasn't answering him. He never mentioned he knew I wasn't home." Keith's picture took over my screen. "Shh, it's him. I've got to take this."

Emily and Mandy sat at the kitchen table to give me some space. "Hey, Keith." My heart rate increased with each passing second.

"Why haven't you answered my calls? Where have you been? Who are you with? What the fuck is going on, Tessa?"

"I'm sorry, I forgot to turn the ringer back on. I went to see Emily. You know how awful I was feeling this morning." I twirled a strand of my hair around my finger.

"I thought I told you to stay away from her. You know she's not good for you."

"I know. I just needed to talk to her after that dream."

"God damn it, I'm so sick of your dreams. How many times do I have to tell you, they're just dreams?"

"I know."

"What happened to the internet? Why is it off?"

"It's off?" I looked over at Emily and Mandy who were staring at me.

"You didn't know?"

"How would I know? It's not like I use it all the time. The better question is how do you know?" I surprised myself with an unexpected burst of bravery.

"I, ah, I get notifications when we lose power and stuff. I got one about twenty minutes ago and when I logged onto… oh, it's not important."

"Logged on to what? What did you log on to that told you we don't have internet?"

"It's not important. The provider said it's nothing on their end, it's something at the house."

"Well, it's not that big of a deal. I don't need it for anything."

"Stop being difficult. Go see if you can fix it."

"It's fine, you can fix it when you get home. I have enough stuff to keep me busy without needing to get online."

"Jesus Christ, Tessa, just go into the office and look at the router for me."

I rolled my eyes and looked over at the ladies. Emily was biting her fingernail. "Okay, I'll go check." I gave it a couple of seconds before responding. "Everything looks okay on our end."

"Are the lights on?"

"Yeah. It looks fine."

"What color are they?"

"Huh? I don't know, red?"

"Are you even looking at it? How don't you know?"

"Keith, it's fine. Everything is fine. Let me turn on your computer and I'll check if it's working."

"No. Don't do that. You're right, it's fine. I'll figure it out when I get home."

"He hung up on me." I tossed the phone on the counter. "I have a feeling he's on his way home."

"That's crazy, Tess, how can you think he's a nice guy? You don't see what a controlling piece of shit he is?" Emily stood up and pushed her chair in. "I guess we should get out of here."

"Not yet, let me look around a little more." Mandy returned to the living room where she had been searching. "I can't leave without knowing we checked everywhere. How much time do you think we have?"

"At least forty-five minutes. Thanks for your help, it means a lot. And Em, he's not usually like that. Don't you think I'd notice if he was always like that?"

"I don't know. I mean, from what I've seen it looks like he's always an asshole." Emily rolled her shoulders.

"Yeah, I get that. I'm seeing it, too. He just told me not to turn on his computer. He's never said that before. Like, what is he hiding?"

"Seriously, Tess? What is he hiding? Oh, I don't know? His dead wife?"

"Well, there's that." I reached for Emily's hand. "I know you just wanted the best for me. I'm sorry it took me so long to get it."

"I just hope you get out of here before you become his

second missing wife."

"I will. I'm working on my plan still."

"I don't see how it's that hard. Pack your shit and get the fuck out of here." Emily put her hands on her hips.

"Girls, enough." Mandy's voice shot in, reminding us we weren't alone. "Em, it's not like she can throw her shit in her car and leave. He would have seen her do it. She's being smart. It's not as easy as just leaving. Did you know it's more dangerous for a woman after she leaves?" Mandy appeared in the kitchen. "A friend of mine went through this shit with her boyfriend years ago. Thankfully she got out and she's okay, but her boyfriend did some crazy shit after she left."

"I didn't know that." Emily looked over at Mandy.

"Yeah, well, it's not a topic for everyday conversation. But trust your sister. She's the one who knows how he ticks. She will know when it's safe to leave. Stop being an overprotective big sister and let her be. We know she's in danger. We'll check in every day. But until she's ready, you can't push her."

"Yeah, what she said." I smiled at Mandy. "It does mean a lot that you care. I will leave. I promise. I just need to get all my ducks in a row first."

"I don't like the idea of you being here. I don't like anything about this at all. But if I don't hear from you every morning and night, I'll send Tommy over to check on you."

"Oh, that sounds like a threat to me." I laughed before looking at the clock. "He'll be here any minute."

"Okay, just a minute more and we'll get out of here." Mandy scurried back into the living room. "I don't see anything in here, either." She made her way down the hall into our bedroom and scanned the area. "It looks like everything is all clear inside the house. Just the doorbell camera. Those aren't that unusual, lots of people have them these days."

"Thanks again for rushing out here with me. It really means a lot." I grabbed Emily's hand and pulled her in to a hug. "I love you, Em."

"I love you, too. If that bastard does anything to you, you can bet your ass he's a dead man." She gave me a tight squeeze before letting go.

"I love you, too, Tessa. I know we just met, but I know how much you mean to your sister. If you need anything you can call us no matter what time it is. And we better hear from you at least twice a day."

"Thanks, Mandy. I promise you'll wish you never asked me to keep in touch." I laughed as they walked to the door. "I love you, too, Mandy. I'm glad Em has such a great woman."

"Who says I'm a woman?" Mandy winked before she got into the driver's seat.

"True, we know you're not a lady with a mouth like that." I waved before going back into the house. I watched from the window for their car to disappear. Once it was out of sight, I went back into the office and restarted the router. Within a minute it was back up and running. Looks like it was my turn to make Keith feel crazy.

I sent my evening text to Emily and Mandy, letting them know I was alright. When Keith arrived home, he was much calmer. I realized it was when he lost control his anger raged. My new game plan was to make sure he always felt in control. I couldn't let him know anything was out of the ordinary. Mandy knew what she was talking about, and I was glad to have her on my side.

I watched Keith closely when he got home. He did pay special attention to the doorbell and went straight to the office, where he saw the router was on and running. I followed close behind him to see if there were any other stops he made, but he did not. I thought Mandy was right, the only camera I needed to worry about was on the front door. I was relieved to know my secrets could remain just that.

When I left Keith's side to make dinner, I heard a door close. I took a few steps down the hall and noticed the office door was closed. He never closed that door before. My imagination ran wild as I tried to imagine what he was doing in there. Any trust I had in him was gone after finding out he had been spying on me this whole time. Luckily, I had never done anything to give him a reason to be upset, aside from spending time with Emily.

The sizzle of the chicken breast as it hit the hot pan brought me back to the present moment. I had a plan to form. The time ticked faster now that I was growing a tiny person inside of me. I made an inventory of the things I needed to take with me as I moved the chicken around the frying pan. I sold all my furniture before I moved in here, so I could fit most of my stuff in my car. I'd have to make one trip if I didn't want him to know I was leaving until I was gone.

He had no idea I was unhappy, though. That would be the hardest part. It was going to come as a complete shock to him. It would be a lot easier if we were unhappily married. He didn't know where Emily lived, but he wasn't stupid. A quick Google search would pinpoint her address. Staying with her and Mandy didn't sound like a good idea anymore. One of the main problems was I was dealing with a stranger. The Keith I knew wasn't the one I was running from.

"Hey, were you on my computer today?" Keith shouted from the hall, his head poking out of his office.

"No." I knew the lie was a mistake the moment it left my lips.

"It looks like someone was on it."

I closed my eyes as I stirred the carrots simmering on the stove. I knew I shut it down, there was no way he would know I was lying. The guilt faded when I remembered all the lies he fed me. "That's strange. Why do you think that?"

"It gave me an error message when I turned it on, you know when it gets shut down the wrong way?"

"Hmm, maybe we lost power or something?" I turned around when I heard footsteps. "Jesus, you scared me."

"Why are you so jumpy?" Keith put his hands in his pockets. "Are you hiding something?"

"What? What are you talking about? I just didn't know you were out here with me."

"Seems to me it's more than that. You're sure you didn't get on my computer? You told me you were going to on the phone."

"No, Keith. I didn't get on your computer. Sorry if I'm jumpy. I guess I've been like that since I found out my dad murdered my mom." The bitterness from my words mixed with regret.

Keith stood behind me and kissed my neck. "I'm sorry, baby. You're right. That must have been awful."

"It was. But it was years ago. I don't like to think about it." I put the spoon down and spun around, letting Keith embrace me. "Sorry I'm in such a bad mood."

"It's okay. I understand." He kissed the top of my head. "I'm going to take a shower. You want to join me?"

"I'd love to, but I can't. I have to finish this." I pointed to the stove. I never passed up a chance to shower with my husband. The thought of what I was missing out on filled me with regret.

"Alright." Keith pulled off his shirt. "You don't know what you're missing."

But I did. I knew exactly what I was missing. It was going to be the hardest thing to say goodbye to. I had to make my move before my desires held me prisoner. He was such an easy man to love. I hated how my own brain lied to me.

I pulled up a mental image of Rebecca. I needed to keep

what could happen in the front of my mind. Even Tommy knew who Keith was. I wondered how many people in town laughed at me knowing what they know. Why did it take a ghost to warn me? A whole town of people would rather laugh at me than help me? Even more reason to get the hell out of here.

I guess there was a possibility that no one knew about me. It wasn't like I ever left the house. The last year played back in my head. Was this the reason we never went out to dinner? Or to the movies? He was hiding me so no one could warn me? And why didn't he just move? That would have been the easiest thing for him to distance himself from all of this. Something didn't add up.

"Rebecca? Are you here?" I whispered the words and looked around the kitchen. "I need to talk to you."

I heard the water in the bathroom turn on. "You can come out now, he's gone." I wiped my hands on the towel hanging off the stove door. "Rebecca? Come on. Why do you only come when you want to?"

"Why do you think Keith never sold the house?" I sent a text to Emily.

"IDK. Why?" Her instant response lit up my screen.

"IDK, I was just thinking. Why would he stay here, where everyone knows?"

"Maybe she's there."

"Who?"

"Rebecca."

"No, I just asked her to come talk."

"No..."

"?"

"Her body."

"OMG."

The water turned off as this new thought haunted me. What if she was here? What if she was in the backyard? Or in the house somewhere? My phone buzzed. "Are you alright?"

"Yes. I got to go. Talk to you tomorrow. Love you."

Why hadn't this thought crossed my mind before? I could deal with sharing my home with a ghost, but there was no way I'd be able to sleep thinking there was a dead body here. A cold chill made my whole body shiver. "Rebecca, is that you?"

The bathroom door opened. "Who are you talking to out there?" Keith walked into the kitchen with a towel wrapped around his waist.

"No one."

"Really? It sounded like you were talking to someone."

I shook my head and walked over to the stove. "Maybe I was talking to myself. I do that sometimes."

"Do I need to get you a straitjacket?" Keith laughed and walked over to me.

I mimicked his laugh. "Maybe." My body tensed under his touch.

He kissed my neck and spun me around to face him. "Dinner can wait. Come with me."

"No." My cheeks burned. He had never heard me say that word to him before.

"Come on. You know you want it." He pressed his body into mine as I backed away from him.

"Keith, I said no."

"I can't hear you." He reached over me and turned the burner off. "Your husband has needs. Now get in the bedroom."

"No. I don't want to."

Keith picked me up and carried me into the bedroom. "I said I have needs. Don't be difficult."

"No. I said not right now." My words turned to cries as his towel fell to the floor. His naked body blocked the door. I tried to move him out of the way, but he pushed me back into the room. His cold hands lifted up my shirt and unbuttoned my jeans. "Stop it Keith."

"Come on, you know you want it." He pulled my jeans down until they fell around my ankles and pushed me against the bed. I felt his penis push into me.

"Stop." My face was pressed into the bed as he continued to penetrate me.

"Just how daddy likes it." The speed and intensity of his thrusting increased until he finished.

I fell to the floor as he walked away. I couldn't find any words as I folded myself into the smallest ball I could.

"Oh, stop it. You know you liked it. You were so wet. Just how I like it." Keith pulled on his sweatpants and turned off the light as he left the room. "Come on, I'm hungry."

What the hell was happening? Who was this man? I pulled my pants back up and went to the bathroom to clean myself up. I didn't want to have any part of him inside me. I stood at the mirror and saw my red eyes, swollen from crying. He'd never done anything like that to me before. Was this how it started? What was he going to do next?

1 2

Emily pulled into the Swiftwater Café. I asked her to meet me there because I wasn't ready to see Mandy yet. The shame from the night before hung on me like Keith's cheap cologne. As soon as I saw her, I couldn't hold back the flood of tears.

"Oh my god, Tess, what's the matter?" Emily pushed her purse up on her shoulder and pulled me into her. "What did that motherfucker do?"

"I'm just so happy to see you." I pressed my face into her hair and sobbed.

Her arms tightened around me. "I swear to God, I'll murder him."

"I'm ready to leave him. I just need a place to stay."

"I told you, you can stay with us." Emily took a step back to look at me. "Where did he hit you?"

"He didn't hit me." My words were swallowed by the tears that followed. Gasps of air made it harder to breathe. "He… he…"

"What Tess? He what?"

"He raped me."

"Oh my god. Let's go to the police."

"And what? Tell them my husband raped me?" I brushed the tears off my cheeks.

"Yeah. That's exactly what we tell them."

"No. I don't want to do that. I just need to get my plan together and get the hell out of there. I wasn't afraid of him before, but I see it now. He's changing and I'm afraid, Em."

"Okay, I'll do whatever you need. Let's get inside out of the cold."

At our regular booth, Emily returned with our drinks and handed me my coffee. "Thanks." My hand shook as I reached for my cup.

"You're in rough shape, huh?" Emily shook her head as she sat down. "I fucking hate that piece of shit."

"I'm alright."

"Come on, Tess, you don't have to pretend for me."

"I just can't understand how it even happened. He doesn't even think he did anything wrong."

"You don't know how bad I'd love to kill him."

"I know. I should have listened to you." I hung my head.

"No, I get it, Tess. He fooled you. Hell, I was even second guessing myself the other day. He's good at what he does. He's a conman."

"Well, he is a used car salesman." I laughed at the irony. "I guess I should have seen it coming."

"Good point. Maybe that's why I hated him from the start." Emily laughed as her drink met her lips. "Oh, yeah, that reminds me." She reached into her purse and pulled out a book. "I bought this for you."

"What is it?"

She flipped the book over and then handed it to me. "It's about your gift. Maybe you can learn how to use it. Maybe you'll be able to get Gram to talk to us."

"I don't know. This is all too much. I don't even know where to start."

"Do you want to go to the doctor and get checked out? Do you think he could have hurt the baby?"

"I don't think so. The baby is probably fine. I mean, people have sex all the time when they're pregnant."

"Yeah, Tess, but they're not raped all the time. I really think it would be best if you at least went for a checkup."

"Yeah, maybe, I'll think about it. You know what I can't stop thinking about? Rebecca. What if she really is at the house?"

"Do you really think he's that stupid? He was the prime suspect when she went missing. Do you think he'd want her body anywhere they could pin it on him? I hate the asshole, but I don't think he's dumb."

"Then why would he stay?"

"I don't know? He probably doesn't think he did anything wrong. He has no reason to leave if he didn't do anything."

"Hmm, good point. He's a psychopath. Who rapes their wife and goes about his business like nothing happened? Clearly I wasn't enjoying myself."

"Tess, he thinks he owns you. In his mind he didn't do anything wrong. There are some sick fucks out there who think just because they are in a relationship with someone, they have the right to do whatever they please to them."

"At least now I have a reason to leave, you know, other than him being a murderer and all."

"You really don't want to come stay with us? Mandy would love to have you."

"No, I know Keith would be able to find me there. I need to go somewhere he'd never be able to track me down."

"That seems smart. You'll need a new phone in case he has a tracking app on it."

I picked up my phone and looked and turned it on. "You think he did that?"

"I have no idea, but if you really want to get away from him with no chance of him finding you, it's worth thinking he did. At this point it's best to think the worst-case scenario in all situations. It's better to over-prepare than to under-prepare."

"True, that's why I can't stay with you."

"Okay, so you need a plan. Do you have any money?"

"No, not that Keith won't notice me taking."

"Mandy and I can give you enough to get you an apartment, but that's probably all we can spare right now."

"You don't have to do that. I'll figure something out."

"Tess, you don't have time to figure anything out. You need to get out of there, the sooner the better."

"Okay, but I'll pay you back every penny I borrow."

"Don't worry about that, it's more than worth it to get you out of there before it's too late. Do you know how much funerals cost?" Emily threw her head back with laughter.

"Wow, you've been spending too much time with Mandy, huh?"

"I guess so. I'm sorry, I know it's not funny."

"No, but it's true. I don't want you to have to worry about me anymore."

"Where do you want to go? Do you have any ideas?"

"No, not at all. I have no clue where to start."

"I'll start looking for an apartment for you. I'll rent it in my name."

"Do you think Mandy would be okay if you used her name? Keith knows your name, and I imagine he'd be able to figure it out."

"Good point. Okay, is Keith's name on your car?"

"Nope, I bought it before we got together, remember, that's how I met him."

"Gross." Emily stuck out her tongue. "Okay, that's good. Will you be able to get all of the stuff you want to take in your car?"

"I don't know. I'll have to make it work. I've only got one chance."

"Take inventory and if you need more room, Mandy and I can rent a U-Haul and meet you at your place. You can turn the WIFI off again while we load it up."

"That's a good idea, I never would have thought of that."

Emily pointed to the side of her head. "It's this big brain of mine."

"Thank you, Em, for everything."

"Hey, I'm always here for you. Don't ever forget it."

"Me, too, you know that, right?"

Emily nodded. "I know." She took a drink of her coffee. "When do you want this to happen? We need to set a date. If we have an end date in mind you can count down the days until your escape."

"Before last night, I would have never thought I needed to escape. I was doing everything I could to make him into a good guy. I could come up with every excuse I could think of to talk myself into staying."

"I'm sorry it had to come to that, but at least now you know how dangerous he is."

"I do. And the longer I stay the more likely it is that I will follow in Rebecca's footsteps."

"I don't want to even think about that."

"Me, either. How about we say I'll be out by December first. It will give me about six weeks to figure out what I'm going to take and give you time to find me a place."

"I don't know. Six weeks is a long time."

"It is, but I have to do this right. I can't make any mistakes."

"I'll try to be patient. But be prepared for a U-Haul to show up December first."

"I'm not backing out of this. I know this is what I have to do."

Back at home I did another walkthrough, with a notebook this time. When I left I would never be able to return. After walking through the entire first floor, the only place I needed to check was the basement. There were still a few boxes I hadn't unpacked. I left them down there so they wouldn't be in Keith's way. I guess there was always a part of me that knew this wouldn't last.

As I turned the corner to count how many boxes I was going to bring with me, I heard a crash behind me. When I turned my head, I saw a tote had fallen, papers and pictures sprawled across the floor. I picked up a piece of paper only to see a map under it. I bent down to look at it, it was for a hiking trail a few towns from here. When I opened it up I noticed there was a circle drawn on the trail, and then an X in Sharpie in the woods off the trail.

Keith never mentioned he liked to hike. He barely liked to be outside. That was one of the reasons we got along so well.

We were more of homebodies than anything else. I guess I made it easy for him to keep me prisoner.

I noticed a picture turned upside down by my foot. When I picked it up to have a better look at it, I felt my mouth drop open. "Oh my god, Rebecca, is that you?" A garbage bag with duct tape wrapped around it in the unmistakable shape of a body. "Why would he keep this?"

The light flickered. Sweat beaded up around my forehead as a cold breeze blew my hair. "Is this where you are?" The papers on the floor started to move in the breeze, uncovering another photo. This one was of Rebecca's body, it looked like she was still alive. She had two black eyes and blood all over her face. I got on my knees to get a better look at the contents of the tote. There were stacks of pictures of Rebecca. Some looked like they were photos of her beatings and others looked like they were taken when she wasn't looking. The more I looked into the pictures, the more I understood how dangerous the next few weeks were going to be. I picked up some of the papers and discovered they were more print outs of Rebecca's emails. I flipped through them to discover Keith had printed off every email she ever sent and received.

I gathered up the papers and photos and tossed them back into the box. Something shiny caught my attention and made me do a double take. It was a knife. I felt my body temperature rise as my attention fixated on the blade. Was this the murder weapon? I didn't dare touch it. I didn't want to contaminate the evidence. I finished picking up the mess and stood the tote back up. I needed to get out of here way before December first. I needed to get out of here today.

I raced back up the stairs and locked myself in the bathroom and turned the water on. "Rebecca, if you can hear me, I need to talk to you." I paced the tiny room as I tried to devise a plan to leave. I had to tell Emily, but I didn't trust my phone. Keith had to have it wired, or something. From the looks of the surveillance he was doing to Rebecca, I knew he was an expert at this game. "Rebecca, come on. I need to talk to you. I need you to help me."

She didn't answer. I knew she was there, who else toppled over the tote? I squeezed my eyes closed and thought of a way to get Emily's attention. Keith would be home soon, and I needed her to know what I knew; in case it was too late. What if Mandy was wrong, and there were cameras in the house, too? What if he already knew I was on to him? The questions fired off at me faster than my brain could absorb them. I took a deep breath and looked at my reflection in the mirror. "I need to get out of here." I noticed flowing red hair behind me. When I turned around, there was no one there. "Rebecca, I want to help you, but I need you to help me."

My reflection was blocked by hers. Relief washed over me. "The sooner you leave the better."

"Does he know what I know?"

"Not yet. You have a little time, but hurry."

"Was that you in that picture? The one in the... bag?" Bile rose as I heard myself speak the horrible truth.

"It is, but it's not what you think."

"What do you mean?"

"There's no time to explain. You have a little time, that's it."

My reflection reappeared in the mirror when she vanished. What did she mean? What else could it be? It was her body. I found the murder weapon. I was confident it was what I thought.

I left my phone in my car when I went to Emily's door. I couldn't risk Keith somehow being able to hear what we were going to talk about. I rang the doorbell and pounded my fist against the door. "Come on guys, open up."

"Good morning sunshine." Mandy's smile faded when she saw me. "Shit, sorry, I forgot."

"No, it's okay. Where's Em?" I pushed passed Mandy to get into the house.

"Well, it's nice to see you, too."

"Sorry, it's just… it's important."

"What's going on?" Emily ran into me as I was making my way to her room.

"Em, I got to get out now. I can't wait another day."

"What happened?"

"I found… I found…" I couldn't catch my breath.

"Whoa, slow down. What did you find?" Emily pulled her robe closed.

"Her body. The murder weapon."

"Holy shit. Did you call the cops?" Mandy's glasses raised with her eyebrows.

"No. I don't want to get them involved, not until I get out of there."

"That sounds fair." Mandy nodded. "Where's the body?"

"I don't know. It was just a picture, but there was a map, and all kinds of other pictures."

"Where did you find that?" Emily put her hand on my back, the warmth alone calmed my nerves.

"In the basement. I was making a list of the stuff I want to take with me, and the box fell over."

"Rebecca?" Emily asked.

"Yeah, she told me I don't have time to wait. I couldn't sleep at all last night. I knew I couldn't let Keith know I was freaked out, so I went to bed with a headache and just stared at the wall until the alarm went off this morning."

"Holy shit, Tess, that's fucking scary." Emily turned on her phone and started scrolling through pages. "I wasn't able to find you an apartment yet."

"I didn't think it was going to be that easy. I don't know what to do, but I know I've got to get out of there and take that box with me."

"Why don't you call that hot little cop? What's his name? Timmy?" Mandy nudged me with her elbow.

"Tommy? Why would I call him?"

"Oh, I don't know." Mandy winked at me. "He could come by while you get your stuff, just in case Keith shows up."

"That's not a bad idea, Tess. Why don't you give him a call?" Emily shut the bathroom door behind her.

"I don't have his number."

"Just call the police station and ask for him. It's not rocket science." Mandy sat at the kitchen table to put her shoes on. "My brother has an extra bedroom at his place. I'm sure he wouldn't mind letting you crash there until you get your own place."

"I don't know. Isn't that weird? He doesn't even know me." I joined Mandy at the table.

"Don't get your panties in a bunch, he's gay. He won't try to get in your pants. Besides, he's a nice guy and his place is on the lake. You can take some much-needed R and R."

"Well, it doesn't sound awful. You don't think he'd mind?"

"No, he'd probably like it. He could use some company. He just broke up with his boyfriend, so he's been down in the dumps." Mandy picked up her phone and sent a text.

"Tess, are you going to call Tommy? Or should I?" Emily was pulling her hoody on over her head.

"I don't think that's necessary. I don't want to get the whole town involved."

"Oh, come on. I'd love to see him. It's been years. Besides, what happens if Keith comes home while we're loading up your stuff?"

My cheeks burned at the thought of seeing Tommy again. I didn't get a chance to shower before I left this morning. "I don't know. I look like absolute dog shit." I pulled at my shirt.

"When have you ever looked like shit? You're the pretty one." Emily laughed. "Isn't that what you used to say?"

"No. I never said that."

"Yeah, you did. All the time."

"No, I don't think that's something I would ever say to you."

"Yeah, you did." Emily put her hands on her hips.

"Girls, girls, enough. Do I need to put you two in timeout?" Mandy stood between us with her arms out. "Look, I think you're both the pretty one. How's that? Did I fix it?"

"Yes, Mother." Emily and I answered at the same time.

"Good, now would you like some cookies?" Mandy brushed her hands together. "Randy said he'd love to have you. You're welcome anytime."

"Oh, that's sweet of him. He's such a good boy." I could tell Emily meant it by her smile. "I love that kid."

"Kid? How old is Randy?" I looked over at Mandy for her answer.

"He's twenty-five. Why?"

"That's not a kid." I raised my eyebrows and looked at Emily. "I'm only twenty-seven."

"To us old ladies he is. Besides, your sister's right, he is a good boy. You'll see." Mandy grabbed her keys. "Em, why don't you bring your car, too, that way Tessa will have more room for her stuff."

"You're so smart. That's why I keep her." Emily giggled as she took her keys off the counter.

"That and many other reasons." Mandy winked as she opened the door.

"TMI." I shook my head to get the images out of my brain. "Can you guys wait like you did last time? I'll send you a text when it's safe to come?"

"You're the boss." Mandy got into her Volvo wagon and shut the door.

Mandy and Emily followed behind me as we made the last trip to my house. The finality of this event hadn't sunk in yet. This was going to be my last time pulling into my driveway.

My life was going to start over, just as it was getting good. I never understood why everything had to come to an end. At least it wasn't going to be my life.

I saw Emily's directional signal turn on as she pulled into the parking area, and Mandy followed. My heart dropped at the thought of what was to come. I wished I hadn't been such a jerk and let Emily call Tommy.

I pulled into the driveway and looked around. Keith wasn't here, but an eerie feeling lingered. I knew we didn't have much time. I let the front door swing open before I stepped inside. A heaviness was in the air. I couldn't put my finger on what it was. I pulled the door closed and went into the office to unplug the router. I didn't want Keith to see Emily and Mandy's car, or us moving my stuff into them.

"All clear." I sent the text and took out the box of garbage bags. In my room I opened my bureau and stuffed the contents into the bags. I had two bags full before I heard the front door open. "I'm in my room." I yelled while still stuffing my belongings into the trash bags.

"Whoa, you're not messing around." Emily popped her head in the doorway. "What can we do?"

I tossed her the box of bags. "Can you empty my closet?"

Emily started unhanging my clothes and shoved them into the bag. "No, wait a minute." Mandy took the stack of clothes from her. "Here, load me up." She held out her arms. "I'll put these in my car, save the bags for the other stuff."

"Seems like you've done this before." Emily stacked the clothing on Mandy's arms.

"I told you, one of my friends went through this. This will make it easier for Tessa when she's unpacking."

"Smart. You're such a genius." Emily gave Mandy a kiss

before piling the clothes higher than her face. "Do you need help?"

"Nope, just get packing." Mandy made her way out of the bedroom and I heard the front door creak open.

"I'm going to get my stuff out of the bathroom." I turned down the hall as Emily was on my bedroom floor stuffing my shoes into a bag.

Mandy came back in and started hauling the bags out to the cars. When I filled a bag, I left it on the floor and made my way into another room. "I know I'm going to forget something."

I heard the rustling of the plastic behind me. Emily was dragging a bag full of my stuff. "Don't worry about stuff, it's all replaceable. I'll buy you whatever you leave behind."

"I feel like we need to hurry." I pushed the hair out of my face as I filled a bag from the linen closet. "I don't know what it is, but there's this uneasy feeling I can't shake."

"Yeah, I feel it, too." Emily paused and locked eyes with me. "Where's the tote you found?"

"Down there." I moved my head in the direction of the basement.

Emily and I dropped what we were doing and started for the door. When we got downstairs, I went to spot the box had fell. "It's not here." I swallowed the lump forming in my throat. "It was right here." I spun around in a circle to make sure I was in the right spot. "It's gone."

Emily's and my mouth dropped open.

"He knows. We've got to get out of here." I grabbed a box of my belongings and headed for the stairs. Emily followed me.

"How could he?" Emily panted as she followed behind me.

"I don't know. I didn't say a word."

"Ladies, there's someone here to see you." Mandy stood in the doorway.

"He knows. We've got to get out of here." Emily ran past her, bumping into her with the box she was carrying. I followed, my head down.

"Emily? Is that you?" The familiar voice brought comfort with the words.

"Oh my god, Tommy, I'm so glad you're here." Emily set the box down and gave him a hug. "I don't think I've been happier to see you in my life."

"Mandy called and asked me to meet you guys here. When she told me what was going on, I knew I had to come."

"See, you really are a genius." Emily picked up the box and pushed it into the back seat.

"When you ladies were arguing I knew one of us needed to call him." Mandy crossed her arms. "What makes you think he knows?"

"The box is missing." I drew in as much fresh air as I could before I ran back inside. "We've got to get out of here."

"Tess, calm down, Tommy's here. Nothing is going to happen to you. We can take our time now."

"No, we need to get out of here before he gets home. I don't have a good feeling." I ran back down the basement stairs and grabbed another box. I ran into Tommy on my way back up.

"What can I do?" Tommy put his hands on my arms to keep me from falling.

I pointed to the stack of boxes in the corner. "Can you get one of those?"

"Sure. Are you okay?"

"Not really." I ran out of the house to put the box into my car before returning to the basement. Tommy was still down there. "What are you doing?"

"I wasn't sure I had the right pile." Tommy held up an old journal of mine.

"Jesus Christ." I pulled the book out of his hand. "Of all the fucking things you could find." I flipped through the pages.

"Is it true?" Tommy smirked. "Does Tessa love Tommy?"

"Oh my god, that was from ages ago." My cheeks burned.

"Yes, but you kept it." Tommy picked up the box. "It's cool, I get that I was irresistible."

"My god, how much did you read?"

"Just the cover, but give it back, now I want to see what's inside." Tommy laughed. "I didn't know you liked me like that."

"Don't flatter yourself, I was a kid."

"Ouch."

"No, no, that's not what I meant." I grabbed a box and followed him back up the stairs. "I may have had a huge crush on you, but Em told me you were off limits."

"Why would she say that? I thought you were pretty cute, too." Tommy set the box on the backseat.

"You were my older sister's best friend. I wasn't allowed to annoy you."

"Okay, so how about now?" Tommy stuck his hands into his pockets.

"Does this really look like the best time to try to hook up? I'm running away from my husband before he murders me."

"Yeah, not my best work. I'm sorry, Tess. Are you okay? Has he hurt you?"

I nodded and went back into the basement. "Just a few more boxes down here and I think all my stuff is out."

"Tess, what did he do to you? Do you want to press charges?"

"No, just help me get the rest of my shit."

"Okay, but if you ever change your mind, you know where to find me."

"Thanks." I picked up the last of the boxes and looked around to see if I could spot the tote before I left for the last time.

"Here, I'll take that." Tommy took the box out of my hands. "Is this everything?"

"Yeah. I was just looking for something, but it looks like Keith took it."

"He took your stuff?"

"No, it was his stuff."

Emily and Mandy met us outside, all three of our cars were full, with just enough room to put the last box on Mandy's front seat. "Don't forget to leave your phone." Emily came over to my car and peeked in. "Are you sure you got everything?"

"Yeah, I'm pretty sure." I pulled my phone out of my back pocket. "I just need to put this inside."

"Did you grab your birth certificate and social security card?" Mandy looked down at her watch.

"No, I didn't even think about that."

"Make sure you have all your important documents." Mandy's words fell behind me as I raced inside to the safe. Footsteps behind me made me freeze in place as I turned the lock to the last number of the combination. I closed my eyes and pushed the fear out of my lungs.

"Hey, it's just me." Tommy's voiced calmed my nerves. "I just wanted to make sure you remembered to leave your phone."

I reached into the safe and pulled out the folder with my name on it before closing it. "Thanks, I probably would have forgot."

"Are you ready?" Tommy reached out his hand for me to take. The warmth of his hand in mine made my body quiver.

"Yeah, let's get out of here. Thanks for being here today."

"Anytime." He pulled out his business card. "Call me, anytime."

"Thanks, but I won't be living in this town after today."

"Tess, that's not what I'm talking about. My personal cell is on there, too. Give me a call when you get your new phone." He gave my hand a squeeze before letting go as we joined the others outside.

"I guess this is it." The world started to spin as I opened the door to my car. I closed my eyes to try to regain my balance and pushed the air out of my lungs. "Thanks for all of your help, I couldn't have done it without you."

"Are you up for meeting Randy or do you want to wait until tomorrow?" Mandy asked.

"Who's Randy?" Tommy zipped up his jacket.

"Calm down Casanova, he's my brother. Nothing to worry about." Mandy chuckled.

"I think it's for the best that I get there today. I don't want to give Keith a chance to find me."

"Okay then, follow me." Mandy got into her car and Emily did the same.

"I'll see you later, Tommy." I smiled at him before following the parade of cars out of the driveway.

We made it out of town without Keith driving by. We were in the clear now.

The winding road lined with pine trees was longer than I anticipated. Mandy pulled her Volvo into a driveway and the path of trees continued until we reached a cabin. The road was not visible from where we parked our cars. This was going to be the perfect escape.

Mandy got out of her car and stretched, forming an arch with her hands above her head. "So, what do you think?"

"This is not at all what I expected. It's perfect. I don't think anyone will ever find me here."

"That's the idea, right?" Mandy laughed. "I'm getting old. I guess I haven't highjacked anyone's life in a while."

"Yeah, it was a first for me, too." Emily joined us. "How are you holding up?"

"I'm okay. I know it's only just begun, but I don't want to think too far ahead right now."

The door to the cabin swung open. "Are you all going to come inside, or am I going to have to come out there to get my hugs?" A man, the same height as Mandy with a red plaid shirt tight around his round belly stood in the doorway. His spikey brown hair had a sheen to it, likely from hair gel.

"Ah, yes, so this is Randy." Mandy started toward the jolly looking fellow. "I've missed you, too, baby brother."

"Easy now." Randy held his hand to his mouth and pushed out his hip. "I'm no one's baby anymore. Come on, give me some sugar."

"Who are you, and what have you done to my brother?" Mandy scooped him into a hug. "So, this beautiful little lady is Tessa and you know Emily." She motioned for us to join them.

I held my hand up to wave. "Thank you so much for letting me stay here for a while."

"Hey girl, I got you." Randy held his hand to his heart. "I've been around a time or two, I know how it is to need an escape."

"You'll soon find out that Randy is the sweet one." Emily gave him a kiss on the cheek as he held the door open for us.

"Yeah, Mandy can be a real bitch." Randy cackled and shut the door.

"Do I need to give you a knuckle sandwich?" Mandy held her fist up.

"No ma'am." Randy held his hands up. "Can I interest you in a peace offering? I made lunch if you're hungry." He pulled out a tray of sandwiches and placed them on the table with five different types of chips in unopened bags.

"I forgot to tell you he's going to smother you with love. This poor guy needs a baby." Mandy tapped his chest before she picked up half of a tuna sandwich.

"Aw, how sweet of you." Emily picked up the other half of the sandwich. "You're such a good boy. Tess is going to be in good hands."

"You did tell her, right?" Randy held his fingers to his lips.

"Tell her what?" Mandy asked with her mouth full.

"You know." Randy batted his eyes. "That I'm…"

"Gay? Queer? Yeah, she knows." Mandy took another bite and pointed to the stack of remaining sandwiches. "Help yourself Tess."

"Okay, as long as we get that awkward elephant out of the room." Randy opened a bag of sour cream and onion chips and crunched into one.

"I'm pretty certain she would have figured it out honey." Mandy took the bag of chips out of his hands. "Thanks for remembering these are my favorites."

"Anything to keep my elders happy." Randy laughed. "Don't worry Tessa, I'm harmless. Mandy and I just like to tease each other."

"I think it's nice you two are so close. Emily and I are pretty close, too." I smiled and looked over at my big sister. I was thankful she was always there for me when I needed her.

"Take good care of her and her little one, Randy." Emily patted my back.

"Oh my god. I forgot to call my doctor." Nausea crept up as I imagined Keith answering my phone. "I've got to give them my new number." I paused as the reality took hold. "I don't have one." Panic took my breath away as my escape plan began to crumble around me. I was out, but I was far from free.

"Take a deep breath." The crinkle of a shopping bag brought me back to the room. "Here, Mandy told me to pick you up a disposable phone. I thought we were going to do something fun with it, you know like murder people, but I guess you need it now." Randy set the bag in front of me.

"I knew you were going to need a phone as soon as you got here, so I asked Randy to have one waiting for you." Mandy sat across the table from me. "You're in good hands now, Tessa. You have a team around you. You don't have to go through this alone."

"I know it all feels overwhelming right now, but it will get easier. Just one day at a time." Emily put her hand on mine and gave it a squeeze. "Thanks, Mandy, for taking such good care of my baby sister." Emily took the phone out of the bag and started to set it up.

"We're all family. We have to stick together. I know you'd do it for Randy." Mandy stood up and started helping clear the table. "We might not be everyone's cup of tea, but I'm okay with that. We're just a couple of misfits."

Randy rolled his eyes. "You can't just leave it at a compliment, you've got to start the name calling." He jabbed Mandy with his elbow. "And now I'm excited for Christmas. Guess I'll start decorating now."

"It's not even November yet." Mandy and Randy continued their bickering in the living room.

"Here you go." Emily handed me the phone. "It's nothing special, but you can get online and get calls. We'll hook you up with a better phone soon." She sent me a text. "Here, so you have my number."

"What's my number?" I laughed as I opened the message. "Oh, you're smart."

Emily tapped the side of her head. "See, I'm good for something."

After a quick Google search, I dialed the number to my doctor's office. "Hi, this is Tessa Stevens, I need to change my number."

I heard the clicks of a keyboard on the other end of the phone. "Again?"

"What? I haven't ever changed my number before."

"Yes, it says in here you just did last week."

"What's the number?"

"Umm, let me see, it's 802-555-1243."

"That's not my number. That's my husband's number."

"Hmm, well, that's the one we've been calling."

"Calling? Why have you been calling me?"

"To set up more testing. You have an appointment tomorrow for blood work."

"Do you know if there was any mention of the pregnancy on these calls?"

"I'm not sure, but I would imagine so."

I hung up the phone and felt my heart racing. "He knows."

"Oh my god, Tess, you got out just in time. I can help you find a new doctor."

"How long has he been spying on me?" I felt a rock forming in the pit of my stomach. "He was going to kill me."

"I know. It's scary."

"No, but, like soon. He never told me about that appointment. And the tote was missing. He was planning something. He knew I knew."

"Shit Tessa. I'm so glad you got out. You have angels looking out for you."

"Yeah, I'm not sure crazy, pissed off ghosts classify as angels."

"I don't care who or what they are, I'm just glad they helped you get out."

"Me, too. I hope they stay with Keith and haunt the shit out of him."

Emily let out a sigh. "I hope so, too. It would be a shame if he were to come up missing, wouldn't it?"

"Yeah. Wouldn't that be ironic?"

"Right." She threw up her hands. "I bet someone could make that happen."

"Do you have connections with the mob I don't know about?"

"No. A girl can dream, though, can't she?"

"Remember when we used to dream about growing up and living together on the beach?"

"I do." Emily smiled. "You know, we still can. Come to California with us."

"That's sounding better and better by the minute."

Mandy, Emily and Randy helped unpack our cars and moved me into a guest room overlooking the lake. The trees around the water were bare, leaving my imagination to paint the picture of the beauty it must hold in the summer and early fall. I couldn't see any other houses from my view. Randy said he was the only one on the lake that stayed year-round.

I fell onto the bed and sank into the luxurious fur comforter. The glow of the lamp made me feel like a little girl waiting for my gram to cook dinner. I could get used to this. I drifted off to sleep as the safety of my new surroundings lulled me to dreamland.

15

The smell of bacon, eggs, maple syrup, and coffee tickled my nose as I looked up at the clock in the shape of a log cabin. My short nap lasted all night. I jumped to my feet and straightened my sweatshirt before joining Randy in the kitchen. "I'm sorry I fell asleep last night. Do you want any help?"

"Why are you sorry? I'm surprised you're awake now. You've had a rough few weeks. Let Uncle Randy take care of you."

I felt my top lip curl up and tried to push it down before he noticed.

"I crossed a line, didn't I?" Randy wiped his hands on his apron.

"No. You do know I'm older than you, right?"

"Hush. Don't you worry about the calendar. Just let me take care of you, at least until you get on your feet."

"Thanks again, for everything." I wrapped myself into a hug. "Did Mandy tell you what's going on?"

"Kind of. But it's none of my business."

"I don't mind if you know. You're practically my brother."

"Brother's okay but uncle's too much?" Randy shrugged his shoulders. "I'll never understand straight women. Why don't you go get washed up and I'll have breakfast ready when you're done?"

In my room I dug through the bags until I found my clothes. I pulled out a pair of jeans and a clean sweater and went into the bathroom. My toothbrush and toiletries were lined up around the sink. Emily must have done that before she left. There was a fluffy green washcloth and towel on the side of the bathtub with a brand-new bar of soap. This was better than staying at a resort.

The hot water hit my skin and I let it soak in. There was so much I needed to do. My to-do list was strangling me. I rubbed the rose shampoo into my hair and was transported back to my childhood. This was what Gram always had in her shower. Emily must have bought this for me. The fragrance alone was enough to squash the crippling thoughts. I was right where I needed to be.

At the table Randy had a plate of food waiting for me. The steam from the coffee danced out of the cup. "This smells amazing." I pushed my chair into the table.

"I do know a thing or two around the kitchen." He sat across from me and stirred honey into his cup.

"Did you just put honey in your coffee?"

"No, that would be gross." The clank of his spoon against the ceramic as he stirred was mesmerizing. "It's tea. Coffee really gets me going, if you know what I mean." He waved his hand at his side.

"Well, thank you for making me a cup." I held the mug

against my mouth and let the warmth fill me before I took a drink.

"Emily told me about your favorites. I wanted to make you feel at home."

"So, you're the one I should thank for the rose shampoo?"

"You don't have to thank me." He took a sip of tea. "Dig in before it gets cold."

The bacon crunched under my teeth. "Mmm, this is so good. I don't remember the last time someone made me breakfast."

"Well, honey, get used to it. I love to cook." Randy set his mug down. "You know, I was in an abusive relationship, too. Did Mandy tell you about it?"

"No, she really didn't say much."

"Well, when I was nineteen, I was with this older guy. He was in his forties. Don't ask… I guess I have daddy issues." He picked up his fork and moved the scrambled eggs around his plate. "He was super-hot, and a pro in the sack so I was instantly smitten. He was everything I thought I wanted in a partner. I moved into his place and he slowly started controlling me and everything that I did. There was even a period of time he wouldn't let me talk to Mandy, or any of my family."

"That's kind of what happened to me, too."

"He was so good at it, I didn't see what he was doing. He used to call me names, but not like outright. He would call me dumb for not knowing about something from his generation or call me ugly because I wasn't as handsome as his ex, or he'd joke about my weight." Randy patted his belly. "He'd just do anything to beat me down. I still didn't see it. I didn't know I was in an abusive relationship until the night he hit me." Randy pushed a sigh out of his lips. "I didn't have dinner done right when he walked through the door and he punched me right in the face. There was blood everywhere. And you know what I did?"

I shook my head.

"I told him I was sorry and made sure he had a hot plate of food in front of him, and then I gave him the best blow job my mouth could handle. I was so in love with him, I didn't even think him hitting me was that big of a deal."

"Oh my god, Randy, I'm so sorry."

"Don't be. I'm not telling you so you pity me, but so you know I'm not pitying you. I've been through the wringer, so if there is anything I can do, don't hesitate to ask."

"How did you leave?"

"It took me another year before I clearly understood what was going on. But I called my big sister and she came and moved all of my stuff out while the dickhead was at work."

"Ah, now I understand why she knew what she was doing."

"Yeah, she's good at coming to the rescue."

"Big sisters are the best."

He nodded. "They really are." Randy took a sip of tea. "So, let me help you learn from some of my mistakes."

"Okay, I'd appreciate that."

"You're going to need a new email, social media account, pretty much anything that he knows about. You'll want to change all of your passwords to something he'd never think of. Don't use birthdates, nicknames, anything that he might guess."

"That's a good idea."

"And don't trust anyone you know mutually. I know it sounds ominous, but if your safety is at risk you can't be too careful."

"We didn't know anyone mutually. We didn't have friends, and I never even met his family. I guess that should have been my first sign."

"Hey, like I said, it can take a while for everything to become clear. Don't beat yourself up over it now."

"Thanks. It makes it easier knowing you've been there before."

"Us younger siblings have got to stick together. We're the badass bitches no one is ever going to mess with again." Randy held his fist up for me to bump.

"I can get on board with that."

After breakfast, I started to log onto my old email account. I caught myself before I completed the sign in. I wasn't sure if there was a way for Keith to find out where I was from doing that, but I didn't want to find out. Mandy and Emily worked too hard to get me to a safe place I didn't want to risk it by being careless.

I logged onto Gmail and created a new account. It was going to be like I was starting over. I had to leave everything behind. The only person I needed in my life was Emily, and I knew I could trust her. Keith didn't like me on social media, so I deleted my account when we met. I hadn't even been on Facebook in almost two years. I wasn't missing anything; it was probably better to stay off it all together.

After I had my new email address, I sent Emily an email. On the nightstand in my room, I noticed the business card Tommy had given me. I held the piece of paper between my fingers and closed my eyes. Everything in me told me to rip the card up and forget about him. I wasn't ready for a relationship, hell, I was still married. I really could use a friend, though. A friend from my past, that knew who I was and everything I'd been through.

My fingers led the way and entered Tommy's number onto the screen. "Hey, thanks for all of your help yesterday." I tossed my phone down and hid my head in the pillows.

The ping of an incoming message penetrated the barricade of feathers and cotton. When I couldn't hold myself back any longer, I picked up the phone. "I've been waiting to hear from you all day!"

"I think I have the wrong number."

"Tessa, don't mess with me!"

"LOL. Sorry, I couldn't resist. You know I'm a married woman, right?"

I dropped the phone when it rang. "I'm aware. You do know that I'm a patient man, right?"

The excitement the conversation triggered inside me was unexpected. I felt like I was fourteen all over again. "I just wanted to let you know that I was safe and sound. I'm being well taken care of."

"I'm glad to hear that. Has he been in contact with you at all?"

"No, he doesn't know where I am or how to contact me. That was kind of the point to all of this."

"I know. I was just worried. He filed a missing person's report. I had the Sergeant drop it. I told him you left of your own free will."

"Did he tell Keith?"

"I don't think so, not yet anyway."

"Thank you."

"You keep saying that, but when are you going to show me your gratitude?"

His boldness threw me off. I didn't want to have to owe him. It took the fun out of things.

"Tess, you know I'm joking, right?" Tommy cleared his throat.

"Sorry, I guess I have a hard time telling the difference right now. I'm a little stressed out."

"Yeah, of course you are. I'm sorry. I was trying to be funny. I do that when I'm nervous."

"Nervous? Why are you nervous?" I rolled the bottom of my jeans up to keep my hands busy.

"Oh, I don't know. Maybe because I have to live up to the cover of that old notebook." He laughed and cleared his throat again. "Sorry, being funny again."

"I don't remember you being such a comedian."

"Yeah, I guess that's what old age does to a person. We either get fat or funny."

"Wow, Tommy. You better work on your humor."

"I'm sorry. I'm real glad you're safe. I was worried about you."

"I like that. You can protect me."

"You bet I will. I'll do whatever it is that you need. Don't hesitate to call, okay?"

"Okay. Thanks again."

"You're welcome. Will I talk to you later?"

"I'd like that. Have a great day Mr. Peters."

"You, too, Tess."

I laid back on the bed and stared at the ceiling. If only we'd run into each other two years earlier. Life always had to throw a kink in it somehow. I rubbed my belly. "I need to get to the doctors and see how you're doing, little one."

16

Emily met me at the clinic in town to meet with my new doctor. I hadn't been back to the doctor since I found out I was pregnant. "I'm so glad you're here with me."

"Are you kidding me? I'm so excited that you asked me to come with you." Emily took my hand and led us into the building.

After checking in, we found our seat in the waiting room. The chairs were filled with women with round bellies and husbands looking anxious. A tinge of sadness settled over me when I thought about the family I was about to start on my own. This was not how it was supposed to be.

A young nurse came through the door and called my name. I stood up and reached for Emily's hand. "Come on."

"Are you sure? I don't mind waiting out here."

"I'm sure. I need you in there with me."

After leaving a urine sample the nurse opened the door to a big examining room and flipped the lights on. "You ladies can have a seat in here. I'll be back in a few minutes." The door shut behind her, leaving Emily and I alone.

"This is a nice place. A lot nicer than the place I was going in Drakesville."

"Are you nervous?" Emily tapped her foot as she looked around the room.

"No, not really. I'm not sure I feel anything right now."

"I'm nervous. I feel like something is going to happen."

"What do you mean?"

"I don't know. I just have this uneasy feeling I can't shake."

"You were fine before. At least, you looked like you were."

"I was. I don't know what's wrong with me." Emily cracked her knuckles before sitting on her hands. "Sorry, bad habit."

"Yeah, I remember. Gram used to hate it when you did that."

"I know. I only do it when I'm really stressed out."

"It's okay, Em, everything is going to be alright."

The door swung open and the nurse stood in the entrance of the room. "You said your previous doctor said you were pregnant?" She tilted her head.

"Yes, why?"

"Well, that's strange. Maybe it's nothing."

"Maybe what's nothing?" Emily asked the question I wasn't able to form.

"It's just that the pregnancy test came back negative."

"Maybe it's a faulty test."

"Yeah, I thought that, too, so I dipped another two. All three came back negative. Ms. Stevens, have you been experiencing any symptoms? Sore breasts, nausea, tiredness?"

"I was nauseous a few weeks ago, and I've been tired a lot."

"Hmm, okay. I'll have the doctor come in and talk to you." She closed the door behind her leaving us alone again.

"What do you think that's about?" I looked over at Emily. She was still sitting on her hands fidgeting in her chair.

"I don't know, but I don't have a good feeling about this."

The door swung open again and a woman in a white coat came in. "Hi, I'm Dr. Johnson." She extended her petite hand for me to shake. Her blue eyes enlarged by her glasses. "Nurse Sam tells me your pregnancy test came back negative." She glanced down at the computer screen. "She said you had been seen by your doctor a few weeks ago?"

"Yes, they did a blood test and said I was pregnant."

"I'd like to talk with them and see what they found. Would that be alright with you?"

"No." Emily blurted out before I had a chance to answer. "That's not a good idea."

Dr. Johnson raised her eyebrows and looked at Emily and then back at me. "Why's that?"

"I just left an abusive marriage. My husband doesn't know where I am, and I don't want to give him any chance to find out."

"I see. Are you safe right now?"

"Yes. I just want to be as careful as I can."

"I understand. I'd like to run some blood tests then but first, I'd like to take a look at you. Could you get up here?" She stood up and pointed to the table. "How long ago did your doctor give you your results?"

"Hmm, it was about three weeks ago." The paper crinkled under me as I sat down.

"Okay. The test should have been positive here then. Even if you miscarried the test should have still read positive. When was the date of your last menstrual period?"

"It was about three weeks ago. I guess it was about the same time they told me I was pregnant."

"I see." Dr. Johnson let out a deep sigh. "Can you lay back?" She pressed her fingers into my belly and felt around. "Does that hurt?"

"No."

"I'd like to do an internal examination." She pulled out a sheet and handed it to me. "I'll step out while you undress from the waist down. Just let me know when you're ready."

I jumped off the table and slipped out of my jeans and underwear and wrapped the sheet around my waist before returning to the table. "Ready."

"She's ready." Emily got her attention when my voice didn't reach her.

I laid on my back, with my feet in the stirrups and closed my eyes. I fought back the tears as I felt Dr. Johnson's hands poke around inside of me. The cold metal against my skin was the least of my worries. "It doesn't appear that your cervix is closed. If you *were* pregnant it would be closed. Had you been to the doctor since they called you?"

"No. I hadn't gotten around to it. Everything happened so fast."

"From everything I can see, and the negative tests, I'd guess you had a false positive."

"What does that mean?" I covered myself up with the sheet and sat up.

"Well, sometimes results can get altered in the lab, or human error can cause the results to read positive when they are actually negative."

"So, I was never pregnant?"

"I don't think so. I'll run some tests and see if there is

anything else we should be concerned about. I'll call you if we find anything alarming."

"Alarming?" Emily cracked her knuckles again.

"Yes, we'll call if Ms. Stevens needs follow up care."

I was never pregnant. The weight of those words haunted me. It was the only reason I needed to leave as fast as I did. It was the only reason that led me to the basement, where I found the box of evidence. It was what made me stop waiting and take action. I wasn't sure who was behind this pregnancy scare, but I owed them my life.

I danced between sorrow and gratitude. I had already gotten used to the idea of being a mother, and now it was stolen away from me as fast as it was handed to me. But still, I was grateful. No matter how bad I could prove Keith was, there was always a possibility that no one would believe me. The chance that he would have had visitations with our child was not something I was ready to consider. The loss of the baby that never was became one of the most precious gifts I had ever received.

17

"Hello?" The ringing phone pulled me out of bed.

"Tess, I need you to meet me at Swiftwater as soon as you can."

"Wait, who is this?"

"Tess, it's me, Em."

"What time is it?" I squinted my eyes to look at the clock, but the room was too dark to see.

"Stop messing around. I need you there as soon as possible."

"What's going on? Is everything okay?" Silence met my words. I sat up and rubbed the sleep from my eyes. It was six in the morning. Emily was never up this early. I switched on my lamp and got out of bed. I pulled on my jeans when I heard it.

"Don't go." The voice wasn't like Rebecca's, it was familiar, but I hadn't heard it in years.

"Grammy?" There was no answer.

I scanned the room, but there was no one there. I must just be tired. I threw on the sweatshirt I had tossed over the chair the night before and slipped my Bearpaw boots on. A quick trip in the bathroom I ran my fingers through my hair and swished a mouthful of mouthwash. I found my keys and grabbed my purse.

Something told me to look at my phone. The number that had woken me up was from an unknown caller. I scrolled through the call history and noticed that Emily's name came up with her number. A lead sinker sank to the pit of my stomach. I dialed Em's number and counted the rings until it was sent to voicemail. She *was* sleeping. I sent her a quick message and asked her to call me as soon as she got up and returned to my bed.

I pulled myself back out of bed and went to the front door to make sure it was locked. It was. I walked the perimeter of the house and checked to make sure all of the windows were locked, too, before I went back to my bedroom. Who could have been calling me? How did they have my number? I went through the list of people who had my new number and couldn't imagine who it could have been.

Tommy and the clinic were the only people I had given my number to. Emily already had it, and I was sure Mandy did, too. None of them would be playing tricks on me. Unless someone at the clinic gave it to Keith somehow and he had someone call me. He knew that Swiftwater Café was where Em and I would meet. No one else knew that.

I closed my eyes to try to fall back asleep as I waited for Emily to call me. There was no way I was going to fall asleep without knowing who it was. Without that voice telling me not to go, I might have gone. And then what? I couldn't even think about what might have happened to me.

As I waited for Emily to call me, I remembered the book

she had given to me at the café the last time we were there. I rolled over and pulled it out of the drawer of the nightstand. "How to Communicate with the Dead." This was not a skill I ever wanted to develop, but the voice of my gram was all it took to make me consider it.

There was so much on my mind, learning a new skill seemed as good as any to occupy my thoughts. As I turned the page to chapter three, my phone rang. I looked down at the name before answering. This time it *was* Emily. "Hey, I'm so glad it's you."

"What's the matter? Are you alright?" From the scratch in Emily's voice, I knew she had just woken up.

"I am, but only because I listened to Gram."

"Wait. What?"

"I got a call earlier this morning, they were pretending to be you and told me to meet them at the Swiftwater. They told me it was an emergency, so I was in a hurry to get there. As I was pulling on my jeans, I heard Gram tell me not to go."

"Holy shit, Tess. Who was it?"

"I have no idea. The number came up as an unknown caller."

"Oh my god, I'm so glad you didn't go."

"I know, me, too. It could have been bad."

"How did he get your number?"

"I have no idea. I've only given it to Tommy and the clinic. That's it."

"You gave it to Tommy? Oh la-la."

"Would you stop it? We're just friends."

"Uh-huh, sure you are."

"Em, stop it. I'm really scared."

"I'm sorry, I bet. Do you think someone at the clinic called Keith?"

"I don't know, I mean, why would they?"

"I don't know, why wouldn't they? People suck."

"That's for sure. What if they gave him my address, too?"

"You put mine down, remember?"

"Thank God you talked me into that."

"Yeah, it was a moment of brilliance. We'll have to get you a new number. Mandy and I are going to the mall later today, we'll just add you to our plan."

"You don't have to do that."

"Yeah, I do. I don't want you dead."

"Thanks. I don't want to be dead." I laughed. "Speaking of the dead, I'm reading that book you gave me the other day."

"Is it any good?"

"I think so. We'll see if I can get Gram to come back to talk to me."

"That would be amazing, wouldn't it? To be able to talk to her anytime you want?"

"It would be. I don't think it works like that, but I'm ready to find out."

I joined Randy for another hearty breakfast. Blueberry pancakes was on the menu today. "These are so good, Randy."

"You like?" He poured me a cup of coffee.

"Yes, they are way better than any I've ever had before. What's your secret?"

"If I told you then I'd have to kill you."

"You and everyone else." I shoved the warm pancake into my mouth.

"Whoa, what's that supposed to mean? Who's trying to kill you?"

"Oh, you know, the usual."

"What's going on?"

"I got a weird call this morning. Some woman pretending to be Emily told me to meet her at the café we always go to. I almost went."

"Jesus Christ. Why didn't you wake me up?"

"I didn't want to be a burden."

"Newsflash, cleaning up your dead body is the only burden you'd ever be. Seriously, tell me this stuff. I have a gun, I can take them, but only if I know about it."

"You have a gun?"

"Of course, I wouldn't live out in the middle of the woods without one. You never know what danger might be out there. And when the word gets out that a sad, lonely little gay boy lives here I want to be prepared to blow their redneck brains out."

"Wow, that was specific."

"Yeah, well, you know how it is growing up in the country. All the other boys at hunting camp and here I am at dance class." Randy laughed. "But seriously, if that ever happens again, please wake me up. Hell, you can come sleep with me if you want. I don't bite."

"Thanks, Randy. I do have to admit I was scared."

"I would have been, too. That's a new number, right?"

"It is."

He shook his head. "How in the hell did he already get it?"

"I have no idea. My only guess is that someone at the clinic gave it to him."

Randy curled up his lip. "I'd find that highly unlikely. Could he really have a connection to someone in this town? He's a car salesman, right?"

"He is."

"That doesn't add up. I can't imagine he gave some nurse a good enough deal that she would be willing to risk her license for him." Randy held his cup of tea in his hands, blowing into the water.

"I don't know who else it could have been."

"The clinic is the only place, besides your sister, that has your new number?"

"Well, no. I did give it to an old friend."

"Does this old friend happen to have a penis?"

"I'd bet money on it, although I've never seen it."

Randy hung his head. "Tessa, Tessa, Tessa, when will you ever learn?"

"What? He's a cop and a friend from our childhood. He knows what Keith did to his first wife. I highly doubt it was him."

"But you can't be certain, can you?"

"No, I guess not."

"Don't ever trust anyone with a penis. That's the first rule they should teach you in school."

"You have a penis."

"Exactly." Randy winked. "And I know how to use it."

"Oh my god. You need a man."

"That I do. But if there is one thing I've learned in life, it's that your heart can fool you. Just be careful, okay?"

"I will. I won't give my number out again."

"That's smart, at least until things calm down a little."

"Do you have any idea how long that will be?"

"No clue. The only reason my ex stopped harassing me was because he's dead."

"Great." Maybe I didn't want to learn how to talk with the

dead after all. Death wouldn't stop Keith from trying to control me.

"You'll get through this. Just give it some time."

"Thanks for listening and being honest with me."

"That's what family is for."

Randy was right. I had to be more careful. I had no way of knowing how Keith got my new number. I needed to be more careful, especially if he thinks I'm carrying his baby.

Emily and Mandy arrived just in time to have lunch with us. Randy made a giant pot of corn chowder and egg salad sandwiches for us to share. "Here, we got you one just like ours." Emily handed me an iPhone box.

"This is too much. I can't take this." I pushed the box to Emily.

"Knock it off, would you just be grateful? You're our daughter now." Mandy laughed.

"Daughter? I mean I'm not objecting, but aren't I a little old to be your daughter?"

"See, Em, this is why I love her." Mandy set down her sandwich and wiped her mouth on her napkin. "It was the only way to get you on the plan. You had to live in the same household. I don't know, I didn't read the fine print." Mandy lifted her shoulders.

"Thank you. I'm not giving this number to anyone."

"No, not even Tommy?" Emily scrunched up her nose and smiled.

"Oh, please, let the girl breathe before you put her back in the saddle." Randy rolled his eyes. "How do you know Tommy is a safe person?"

"He was one of my best friends growing up. He's a cop, and he helped us move Tessa. I think he's as safe as they get."

Emily looked over at Mandy to get her approval. When she didn't respond she looked to me.

"I know, and I think he's safe, too, but Randy's right. I can't be too safe right now. If Tommy is as great of a guy as we think he is, then he'll understand." I hoped I was doing the right thing. I didn't want to upset Emily or Randy.

"I guess I understand. You just looked so happy with him. I just want to see you happy, but your safety is more important." Emily took her phone and went into the bathroom.

"Should I go after her?" I asked Mandy.

"No, let her cool down." Mandy clenched her teeth. "Randy, you don't always have to be such a dick. Emily doesn't want anything to happen to Tessa, she was just trying to help."

"I know, so was I. You forget that I've been in Tessa's shoes. I know what it's like to not be able to trust anyone. I'm just trying to protect her. I wasn't trying to be a dick."

"Thank you, Randy. I know. I appreciate your help, all of it. I don't know what I'd do without you. Without all of you."

Mandy got up from the table and went to the bathroom door and gave it a little knock. "Hun, are you alright?"

"Yup. I'm fine. I'll be right out." The toilet flushed and the door opened soon after. Emily's face was red, her phone shoved in the front pocket of her jeans.

"I'm sorry. I wasn't trying to be an asshole." Randy pushed up a smile.

"I know. I'm sorry I overreacted. It's just a lot to have to worry about Tessa's safety. I wasn't thinking clearly." The look on Emily's face told me she had already given my new number to Tommy. She was in the bathroom telling him not to use it. I could read her like a book.

"So, how about this chowder? It's delicious, isn't it?" I

guided a spoonful to my mouth half excited that I'd be hearing from Tommy later.

"He missed his calling." Mandy snickered. "I tried to talk him into culinary school, but he refused."

"Yeah, I wanted to be like my older sister. Besides, my hatred for humankind wouldn't have worked out well. A little too much arsenic in the rice and…" Randy held his hands up in front of him.

"Wait, you're a romance writer, too?" I felt my eyes cast a judging look at him.

"Not exactly." Randy picked up his mug and took a drink.

Mandy tossed her head back. "Well, go on, tell her what it is that you do."

"I'm a writer."

"But what kind of writer?" Mandy could hardly contain her laughter.

"I write horror stories."

"Like Stephen King?" I couldn't find the humor in this.

"Go on, tell her." Mandy gave Randy a nudge.

"No, like R.L. Stine."

Mandy erupted with laughter. "He's always been a little wussy, when he told me he was going to write horror I about pissed my pants. I knew he wouldn't be able to handle it."

"Shut up. It's not like anyone else has an issue with my writing." I couldn't tell if Randy was upset or enjoying the teasing.

"I don't like being scared, either. I think it's cool that you're a writer." I gave Randy a smile, then focused on Mandy who was snorting.

"R.L. Stine is being generous. His books are more like

Scooby Doo. Lots of mysteries and pesky kids. Isn't' that right, D.L. King?"

"D.L. King?" I felt my brow furrow.

"Yes." Randy sighed. "That's my penname."

"Penname? What's that?" I asked.

"It's the name I use to write the books, that way no one knows who I am."

"Oh, okay. That sounds like a good idea. Why is it so funny?" Mandy's howling made me turn my attention to her.

Randy hung his head. "Because I thought I was being clever, mixing R.L. Stine and Stephen King's names together that I would be guaranteed success."

"But… go on. Tell her." The contents of the table shook when Mandy slapped it.

"But I got the nickname Dick Loving King."

"Okay, that's not upsetting, though, right? I mean you do love the dick." I raised my eyes with my smile.

"Yeah, it would be cool, except I write children's books, but people think I'm a giant pervert. It's not exactly great for business."

"Hey mommy, I'd love you to read me one of the Dick Loving King books to me, please." Mandy bobbed her head as she spoke in a high pitch voice.

"Is that still your penname?" I asked.

"Yeah, it just kind of stuck. It's hard to explain. The good news is I'm a best-selling author, that bad news is I'm not sure the right audience is reading my books. I'm pretty sure conservative Christians buy them just to burn them."

"Hey, a buck is a buck, right? I think it's cool you two are authors. Who cares what people think?" I looked over at Emily who was scrolling through her phone.

"I knew I liked you. Thanks for sticking up for me." Randy winked at me.

After lunch, Emily brought me into my room and closed the door behind us. "Hey, I don't know how to tell you this, but…"

"You gave Tommy the new number?"

"Yes. How did you know?" Emily leaned against the wall and crossed her arms.

"I know you. I knew that's why you went into the bathroom."

"Yes and no. I had asked Tommy to try to get the surveillance footage from the café to see if he could figure out who it was."

"That was smart. Was he able to get it?"

"Yeah. It wasn't Keith. It was a woman."

"Okay, so he put someone up to it."

"Tess, it was a woman with red hair."

"And?"

"And Tommy thinks it could have been Rebecca."

"How is that even possible? She's dead. I talked to her ghost. I saw pictures of her dead body."

"I don't know." Emily pulled her phone out of her pocket and turned it on. "Here, look at this." She handed me her phone.

"Holy shit. This looks just like her." Chills encased my body. "How is that even possible?"

"I have no idea. Tommy is baffled, too. He showed it to some of the other guys, and they were pretty certain it was her, too."

"Why would Rebecca want to help Keith? I mean if she were still alive?" I closed my eyes and shook the images out of my mind. "There were so many pictures of her covered in bruises. Why? How?"

"I have no idea, but I think you need to be even more careful."

"I will. Randy told me he has a gun, so there's that."

"As much as I hate guns, I'm kind of glad to hear that."

"Yeah, same." I pulled my hair back into a loose ponytail. "Do you think it's her ghost playing games with us?"

"I did consider that, but how would a ghost drive a car?"

"Your guess is as good as mine."

"Hey, Tess, don't tell Randy about this, okay? I don't want Mandy to know. She'd be pissed at me if she knows I got Tommy involved."

"No problem, it's our little secret." I held my finger up to my lips.

18

"It's not what you think." Rebecca stood over my bleeding body.

"What's happening to me?" I wiped away the blood as it ran down my face.

"It's not always what it looks like. They're using me to get to you."

"What do you mean? Who's using you?"

Suddenly we were in a field by a cabin. "Don't look down."

I gasped when my eyes looked to the ground. Rebecca's and my dead bodies were stacked on top of each other in a hole. A man with a black mask on threw dirt on top of us. "What's happening?"

"He's going to kill you."

"Who is?"

"Keith."

"Like he killed you?"

Rebecca shook her head. "He didn't kill me. I'm not dead."

I pointed to the hole. "But look."

"Look closer."

Rebecca morphed into Emily. It was Emily I was on top of in that hole.

"You have to get out. You have to fight." Rebecca gave me a kiss on the cheek. "Silly girl."

"Who are you?"

"You know the answer to that question. To all of the questions you are seeking. Listen to the answers."

The sheets were soaked in sweat when I sprung to my feet. "What does this mean?" I pulled my hair and screamed a silent scream, not wanting to wake up Randy. Rebecca hadn't visited my dreams since I left Keith. And then the picture of the woman at the café who called me, I wasn't even sure she was dead anymore, or about anything else.

I found my phone and sent a message to Emily. "I need to figure out this whole talking to the dead thing. I can't stand being haunted by Rebecca... or whoever she is anymore. Help!"

I threw my phone on the bed and fell back into the pile of soft blankets. My tears soaked the pillows I buried my head into. My mind kept taking me back to the beginning of my relationship with Keith, when everything was perfect. Why did life have to be so cruel? After my gram died, I thought I was going to be alone forever. Everyone in my life always left me, but now I was the one doing the leaving. Even Emily left me for a while.

The more the thoughts came, the more I questioned everything I thought I knew. Was Emily who I really thought she was? Was she really trying to help me? Or was she in on this, too? Was I going crazy? Was mental illness responsible for the voices I was hearing? Maybe Gram never had a gift, but a sickness.

I felt myself fall deeper down the rabbit hole. *Trust no one.* That was the one constant message. But Emily would never hurt me. I hit the sides of my head to try to drive the crazy making thoughts out. "Who's doing this to me? Who's trying to destroy me?"

"Is everything okay in here?" Randy's voice penetrated my bedroom door.

"No, not really."

The door cracked open and Randy poked his head in. "Here, come get some cocoa with me."

I pushed the tears off my face and followed Randy into the kitchen. "I'm sorry if I woke you up."

"You didn't wake me. I was working on my book. I heard you talking in there and it didn't sound good." He put the kettle on the front burner, the flame lighting up the dark kitchen. "Do you want to talk about it?" Randy took two mugs out of the cabinet and set them on the counter.

"I don't know. It's crazy. I'm crazy." I rested my head in my hands.

"No, you're not. The world is crazy, but you are not. You can tell me anything. You can trust me."

"I had a bad dream. It was my husband's missing wife. She was telling me it's not what it seems. Then she took me to a cabin in the woods and showed me Emily's and my dead body, stacked together in a hole."

"That sounds awful. I'm sorry you had a nightmare, but that's all it was. No one is going to hurt you here."

"I just can't get the idea out of my head that Rebecca, his missing wife, isn't really dead."

"Did they ever find her body?" Randy poured the hot water over the packets of cocoa and carried the cups to the table, handing me a spoon.

The clack of my spoon against the glass brought enough normalcy to comfort me. "No, she's never been found."

"So, the possibility is still out there that she could be alive?" Randy blew on his cocoa before taking a sip.

"Yes, but I don't think she is." I held the mug between my hands, not wanting to look at him.

"Why not?"

"This is going to sound crazy." I paused to gauge his reaction.

"Hey, I'm a chubby, single children's horror author who lives alone in the woods, who am I to judge?"

"You have a point." I covered my mouth to hide the laugh. "I've seen her, talked to her."

"To her ghost?" Randy took a drink of his cocoa and set it back down.

"Yeah."

"And?"

"And, who sees and talks to ghosts?"

"Lots of people."

"Really? You don't think I've lost my mind?"

"Not at all. One of my good friends is a psychic medium."

"Are you messing with me?"

"No. I'm serious. That's her job. She talks to dead people for a living."

"Can I meet her?"

"I can probably arrange that." Randy took another drink of his cocoa, leaving a chocolate mustache on his face.

"Oh my god, that would be amazing. I just really want to talk to someone who can tell me what's going on, you know, and not throw me in a looney bin."

Randy's roaring laugh made me jump out of my skin. "Looney bin. I haven't heard that term in ages. Sara is cool, I think you'll like her. I'll give her a call in the morning. She lives about an hour away, but I'm sure she'd love to come for a visit. I mean who doesn't want to have dinner at Chef Randy's?"

"I'll give you that, you are one hell of a cook. You're almost too good to be true. You seem to be able to solve all of my problems."

"I am pretty great, aren't I?" He wiped the chocolate off his mouth with his shirt sleeve.

"I was going to agree until I saw that."

"What? I didn't have a napkin. It's two in the morning."

"I'm just teasing you."

"Will you be able to get to sleep now?'

"I think so. Thank you for listening to me. It gets over-whelming when I get lost in my thoughts."

"I know how that is, trust me. Sweet dreams, Tessa."

"Back at you."

Back in my bed I snuggled into the blankets and let the warmth ease me back to dreamland. Answers were on the way. I knew they were. They had to be.

19

I woke up to the sound of messages pouring into my phone. I stretched before picking it up. Twelve missed messages from Emily. I had forgotten I sent her a message last night before I talked with Randy. "False alarm. Everything is fine."

In anticipation of what was to come next I held the phone and waited for it to ring. "Good morning, Em."

"Jesus Christ, Tess, you can't send messages like that and then ghost me."

"Funny choice of words."

"What? Are you sure you're okay? If you didn't answer me I was on my way over there."

"You could have called Randy."

"Hmm. Good point. Anyway, you freaked me out. I was worried something else happened."

"It did, kind of. I had a nightmare. Rebecca was back for a visit. It's too awful to tell you over the phone, but Randy helped me through it."

"Oh, well, I'm glad he was there for you."

"Yeah, me, too. I thought I was going crazy. Did you know he has a friend who talks to dead people for a living?"

"No, I can't say that I did. But he always has a surprise up his sleeve, just like his sister."

"I almost wish he wasn't gay."

"Oh, Tessa." I could hear her shaking her head. "You've got a one-track mind."

"Oh my god, you're such a pervert. I meant that he takes such good care of me, he gets me."

"He is a good guy. I knew what you meant."

"Sure you did. I think you spend too much time with your romance writing girlfriend."

"What is that supposed to mean?"

"I have no idea." I dropped my head into my pillow and laughed. "But I'm excited to meet Randy's friend. I hope she can help me understand what's going on. Maybe she'll be able to tell me what I'm supposed to figure out."

"I want to meet her. I want to talk to Gram and Mom." Silence filled the space between us. "And Dad. I want to know what the hell he was thinking."

"I don't know, Em. I'm not sure I want a family reunion. I kind of just want to figure out what I'm supposed to do."

"You don't even want to talk to Gram?"

"I do, but only her. At least for now. I don't want to deal with the afterlife drama. I don't have it in me right now."

"I get it. Can I come if I promise not to talk?"

"Okay, but do you really want to make a promise you can't keep?"

"Oh, knock it off. I just want to understand what's going on. I'll keep my mouth closed. I want to be there for you."

"Thanks. That means a lot. I have a feeling I'm going to need your help sooner than later."

"What does that mean?"

"I'm not sure, it's just a feeling I have."

It was a feeling I couldn't shake, and it was growing with each passing day. It was becoming something I could no longer ignore. There were too many possibilities for me to figure anything out on my own. Was Rebecca alive? Was she dead? Who was the woman in my dreams? Or the woman at the café? There was no way she could be alive and dead at the same time. That was too much for even me to wrap my mind around. Could she have a twin? But why would she be working with the man who killed her sister? I shook my head to clear the banter I was having with myself. This was not going to be easy.

"Hey. I've got good news." Randy's muffled voice broadcast through the closed door.

"Come on in and tell me." I sat up in bed and pulled the covers up to my neck.

"I just talked to Sara, and she's on her way over. Isn't that exciting?" Randy closed his teeth together and gave me a big smile.

"Wow, that was fast. Holy cow."

"Yeah, she kind of owes me."

"How long before she gets here?"

"She should be here within the hour."

"Oh shit, I got to get up and get dressed."

"Oh, don't worry about what you look like, she doesn't care."

"Yeah, but I do. I don't want to look like I've been sleeping all day."

Randy held his index finger to his chin. "Oh, you mean, this isn't what you normally look like?"

I threw a pillow at him. "Oh, shut up."

"Breakfast is waiting when you decide to join the living… that is until you join the dead." Randy paused holding the doorknob on his way out of the room. "Wait, I don't think that's what I meant."

"Okay, okay, get out of here so I can at least get dressed." I bounced off the bed and locked the door after he left the room. "Wait, Randy?"

"Yes?"

"Do you think it would be okay if Emily joined us?"

"Sure, I don't see why not."

I sent Emily a text inviting her over and grabbed clothes before taking a shower. I needed to wash the remaining pieces of last night's dream off of me. Excitement ran through me as I thought about what Sara was going to tell me. At the very least I was hopeful she would know who the woman from my dreams was.

When I finally made it to breakfast Emily was waiting for me at the table, drinking coffee out of a to-go cup from Swiftwater. "How did you get here so fast? I just sent you a text like ten minutes ago." I ruffled my hair to shake out the remaining water.

"I had a feeling." Emily smiled as she took a drink from her cup. "Here, I brought you one, too." She nodded her head in the direction of the iced coffee waiting for me by the plate of bacon and eggs.

"A girl could get used to this." I took a sip from the straw. "That hits the spot."

I noticed a plate in front of Emily and knew Randy had

already tended to her. I cleaned my plate just in time. The rap of the knocker on the mahogany door rang through the cabin. "Coming." Randy yelled and ran for the door. "Oh, Sara, it's so nice to see you." He took her hand and pulled her inside. "Ladies, this is Sara, Sara, this is Tessa and Emily."

"Hi there." Sara took off her deep purple scarf and unbuttoned her black wool coat before Randy took them away. Her short wavy black hair bounced around her face and her green eyes almost twinkled when she smiled. "It smells like Randy's been up to his old ways." She closed her eyes as she inhaled the lingering smell of breakfast.

"Would you like some? I'm sure there's some left." I stood up to shake her hand.

"Oh, no, I've already had breakfast." She pulled out the chair and joined us at the table. She sat with her hands folded in front of her. "So, Randy tells me you've been having some problems."

"Yes, I guess you could call it that. What else did he tell you?" My inner skeptic was creeping out.

"Nothing, really, just that you've been having nightmares and are looking for some answers."

"That's true, too." I looked over at Emily, who so far was keeping her promise.

"Do you want to ask any questions, or do you just want me to tell you what I'm getting?"

"You're already getting something?" My eyes squinted with the question.

Sara closed her eyes. "There's a woman here that needs you to listen to her. She said it's a matter of life and death." Sara opened her eyes. "She said she's been trying to tell you. Did you already talk to her?"

"That's kind of part of the reason I wanted to talk to you. I'm not sure."

Sara's eyes looked through me as she stared straight ahead. "She says you are sure. You just don't want to believe it. You know things, and what you think you know, you actually do know. She's telling me to tell you not to doubt yourself." She pulled her focus back to me. "You do know this woman, don't you?"

"Not exactly. I know who she is, but I didn't know her before she died. It's kind of a long story." A sigh I couldn't hold back filled the space between us. "Did she tell you her name?"

"It's an R name. Rena. Reba. Rebecca."

"Shit." My hand covered my mouth. "It *is* her. Her name is Rebecca."

"She wants to know why you aren't listening to her. You need to take it seriously. He's dangerous. Don't let your guard down."

"I am listening." Frustration shadowed my words.

Sara shook her head. "No, you're not. She's been talking to you and you've been ignoring her. She wants to make sure you watch your back."

"But I left him. I don't know what she means that I'm not listening. What else does she want me to know?"

"Does she know who was in the car the other day?" Emily sank back into her chair. "I'm sorry, I'm not supposed to interrupt."

"No, it's okay. I do need to know that." I leaned forward and rested my body on my hands on the edge of the table.

"She doesn't know. You only know pieces of the story. There is much more to it all."

"Okay, I'm listening."

"No, it doesn't work like that. You'll have to figure it out yourself." Sara opened her eyes. "She just said it's too much for you to handle right now."

"What does that mean?"

"I don't know, she didn't say. Hold on." Sara closed her eyes again and held her hands out, cupping the air. "She said when you find her you will find the answers."

"Where is she?"

Sara scrunched up her nose. "There's a map."

"Where? Where do I find the map?"

"You've seen it. She's already showed you." Sara rolled her head between her shoulders. "She's gone now." She stretched out her arms and shook them. "She's powerful. I can see why you've been able to hear her."

"Wait. What map? I don't understand. I don't remember a map."

"I don't know what to tell you, I told you everything she said."

"Tess, remember that tote? You said there was a map in there." Emily's voice was so soft I could barely hear her.

"Oh my god. I forgot about that. But it's gone. When Keith took the box, the map went with it." I closed my eyes and rested my head in my hands, trying to bring back the image of the map.

"So, do you think the only reason Tessa has been able to communicate with Rebecca is because she's so powerful? Or do you think she could have a gift?" Emily's question wasn't one I had considered. I lifted my head to hear what Sara had to say.

"It's hard to say. Everyone has the ability to communicate

with the dead, but most people are too afraid to do it, or they can't open themselves up enough to really listen. When a spirit is stuck here, especially due to tragic circumstances, they try harder to make people listen. I think it's a mix between Tessa being open to her gift and Rebecca needing to have someone listen to her."

"What if I'm not open to my gift? I mean, I wasn't before Rebecca. I didn't really understand what was happening."

"Then that would mean Rebecca *really* needs your help. It also means you won't have to work as hard as others to fine tune your gift, if that's something you want to do." Sara gave a sympathetic smile. "I can help you if you would like. I remember how scary and confusing it can be."

"Thanks." I rubbed the bridge of my nose to try to stop the headache from forming. "I really just need to try to remember what was on that map."

"You said it was some hiking trail." Emily pulled out her phone and turned it on. "I don't know how many of those are around here, but maybe we can narrow it down."

"I just wish I'd paid closer attention to it or taken the tote with me before I left the house."

"Don't beat yourself up now, let's just try to figure this out. It sounds like you won't have any of the answers you're looking for until we find her body." Emily's attention remained focused on the screen of her phone.

"Try to relax your mind, maybe take a walk, or a hot bath and it might come back to you. I have a feeling Rebecca is going to do everything in her power to get you the information you need." Sara reached over and patted my back.

"Tess, I'm not finding anything here. I'll keep looking. I'll have Mandy help. She's good at researching." Emily shut off her phone and turned it over. "We'll figure this out, I know it."

"If she wants me to know so badly, why couldn't she just tell me where she is? Or better yet, why can't she just take me there?"

"Unfortunately, it doesn't usually work like that. They can only give us so much, especially if you're supposed to learn some sort of lesson along the way."

What kind of lesson was I supposed to learn from this? My mind couldn't even take me down that road. All I knew was I needed to find Rebecca if I wanted to get my life back to normal. What else was I going to find out? Wasn't it enough that I had to marry a murderer? I couldn't let fear keep me from figuring this out.

I took Sara's advice and ran a hot bath. It had been a while since I had done anything to relax my mind. The rushing sound of the water as it filled the tub washed out the thoughts filling my head. The sweet smell of lavender and vanilla encased me as I let the water reach my neck. I closed my eyes and tried to let the image of the map come to me.

My body and mind felt light and free under the weight of the water. "Rebecca, please show me the map again. I know you did before, but I wasn't paying close enough attention." I waited for the image to appear. Nothing came.

The only image my mind could pull up was of a box of books. My focus couldn't pull up what I needed. Water splashed around me when I sat up, the bubbles no longer covering my skin. "This is impossible."

Why could I only see a box of books? What part of my mind thought that was helpful? Disgusted by my lack of ability to concentrate, I used my big toe to unlatch the drain. There was no use in relaxing when frustration had hold of me. Why couldn't I have kept the map out? It wasn't like Keith would have noticed.

After I slipped into my nightclothes, I took myself to bed. There was nothing else to do. I had no friends, and I was sure Emily was sick of hearing from me. She had a life of her own, after all. It was just poor, pitiful Tessa all alone for eternity. Self-pity was a shade I wore often. I knew it didn't look good on me, but it was what I always fell back on.

The dreams I had as a girl of having a happy family taunted me. I was so close, and yet lightyears away from my dreams. What lesson was I supposed to learn from all of this? It was the question I couldn't let go of. I was certain other people with far less shitty lives didn't have to learn this crap. Why me?

The self-pity train was rounding the corner when my phone pinged. I rolled my eyes expecting to see a message from Emily, reminding me of my only contact with the outside world was my older sister. My body heat increased when I saw I was wrong.

"Hey beautiful, do you want to go get dinner?"

"Sorry, you have the wrong number." It had to be. Who else would send me a message like that? This old spinster was going to die alone.

"It's Thomas, silly."

Shit. I had forgotten Emily gave him my number. I promised Randy I'd be careful, and after talking with Sara, I knew more than ever I needed to keep that promise. But Tommy did have my number this whole time and I hadn't received any life-threatening messages. Maybe he was safe.

"Oh, hey. I'm actually in bed right now. Lame. I know."

"Raincheck?"

"Sounds good." What the hell. What else did I have to lose? "Can I call you?"

"No, sorry. I'm exhausted." Which wasn't a complete lie. I never thought I'd have to keep my relationship secret from a gay man. I guess there was a first time for everything.

I drifted off to sleep feeling more confident about the status of my future. Maybe I wouldn't have to die alone. I had a good feeling about Tommy. About *us*.

The box of books from my bath filled my dreams. A box of books in a room. Nothing else. The box grew and grew, taking up all of the space in the room, and then it tipped over. The contents of the box were familiar. They were books I owned and had stored in the basement at Keith's.

I popped out of bed and rummaged through my closet. I moved the stack of boxes until I found *the* box. I pulled it out and got on my knees next to it. I pulled the books out and fanned through the pages before making a stack on the floor next to me. With only one book left in the box, the anticipation grew as I shook it open. There was no map. I kicked over the stack of books in front of me. "I don't understand what you're trying to tell me. Why can't you just fucking say it?"

Frustration fueled my anger as I threw the books back into the box. "I don't even know why I keep these things anyway. Once you've read it, what's the point in keeping it?" I knew the answer to that question. I kept them because they were the last thing of my mother's I owned. I kept them because having them around me made me feel at home. They made me feel at home and they were stored in the basement for over a year. I never felt at home with Keith. Why didn't I see this earlier?

Sadness replaced the anger as memories of feeling out of

place rushed back. I never belonged with Keith. These books being hidden away was more than just a box of my belongings, it was *me*. It was the same thing as not having Emily in my life for a year. He was slowly killing who I was. "Was that the whole point of me going through the books? For me to realize how screwed up things really were?" I buried my head in my knees and felt the warmth of my tears hit my legs.

"Screw it." I crawled back to my bed and picked up my phone. "Do you want to go grab a coffee?" I stared at the screen of my phone as I waited for Tommy to reply.

"I'd love to. Where do you want to meet?"

"Swiftwater Café?"

"Sure, I love that place."

"Great, see you in an hour."

"Can't wait."

I walked past the box of books to get to my closet and picked out my favorite sweater. If Tommy wanted to be with me, he was going to get me. Not some made up version of myself that I think he'd like. I was done wasting time being who everyone else wanted me to be. Take me as I am or leave me alone. No more pretending.

I pulled on the most comfortable pair of jeans I owned and my favorite warm boots. I ran the brush through my hair and put it up in a ponytail. Confidence I hadn't felt in years settled inside me. My reflection in the mirror smiled back at me. I thought I was going to like this.

Randy was just starting breakfast when I walked into the kitchen. "Hey, I'm going into town to run a few errands. I'll grab something to eat there. Do you need me to pick you up anything?"

"No, I'm all set." Randy put the pan back in the cabinet. "I guess it's just tea for me this morning. I have a deadline I have to meet anyway. Have fun in civilization."

"Thanks. Have fun writing." I closed the door behind me and walked to my car. Butterflies filled my stomach as I thought about seeing Tommy. The excitement was quickly replaced with fear as I remembered the call from the unknown woman. Why had I suggested Swiftwater? What if she's there? What if Keith's there? The possibilities began to pour in.

I slammed my hand on the steering wheel. "No." The sound of my voice pulled me out of the rabbit hole I was falling into. I couldn't let Keith keep me prisoner in my own life. If I couldn't live, then I didn't want to. I turned on the radio and let the music take me away.

I pulled into the parking lot and saw the Drakesville cruiser parked in the back. I couldn't keep the smile off my face when I got out of my car. Fuck Keith.

"Well, don't you look beautiful." Tommy's dimples lit up the greyness of the sky.

I looked down at my choice of outfit. "Really?" I tugged on my sweater and smiled. "Thanks. You look pretty cute yourself. I've always had a thing for a guy in uniform."

"That's what they all say." Tommy laughed and held out his hand. "I'm so glad you suggested this."

With my hand in his, the butterflies returned, along with my red cheeks. "Me, too."

In the café, instinct kicked in and I tossed my purse in the booth Emily and I always share. "Sure, we can sit here." Tommy's smile hadn't left. "Do you want to get our coffee before we sit down though?"

"Oh my god, I'm sorry. This is just where Em and I always sit. We don't have to sit here."

"No, no, it's fine. This looks like the best spot in the place. You girls have good taste." Tommy took off his jacket and placed it on the seat. "What would you like?"

"I'll come with you." I reached down to pick up my bag.

"You don't need that. It's on me."

"Oh, you don't have to do that."

"Stop it. Let a guy get some brownie points."

I went with Tommy to the counter and waited with him until our order was ready. It felt strange being here without Emily. Tommy was the first person other than her that I had come here with. Maybe this would become *our* place, too.

Back at the booth, Tommy sat in Emily's usual spot. "I know this is going to sound crazy, but I've missed you."

"That doesn't sound crazy. I've missed you, too." The heat returned to my cheeks. "How crazy is it that we both ended up in Drakesville?"

"I know, right? Like they say, it's a small world." Tommy placed his mug to his plump, pink lips.

"What brought you here?"

"Well, after police academy, I knew I didn't want to stay at home. You know, too many people I know there. I didn't want to have to give my friends a ticket or something. So I started looking online for jobs and I found the one here."

"How long ago was that?" I held my cup between my hands, letting the coldness from the ice help cool my body temperature.

"It's been about seven years."

"You must like it here."

"I guess. It's close enough that I can go home whenever I

need to, but far enough that I don't have to get tied up in the old drama from home. How about you?"

"I've only been here about a year. I moved in with Keith and have been here ever since."

"Do you like it here?"

"I don't love it. But I don't hate it, either. I don't really have a place to call home. Not since…" I hung my head and focused my attention on my coffee.

"I'm sorry to bring that up, Tessa. You know I always felt terrible about what happened." Tommy reached over and placed his hand on mine.

"Thanks." I looked up and saw moisture in his eyes. "It's still hard to believe sometimes. Our whole world was ripped out from under us. And when Gram died, it was just Em and I."

"I can't even imagine." Tommy rubbed the top of my hand with his thumb.

"But, enough of that." I picked my eyes up to look into his. "So, have you been married?" I regretted the question as soon as I asked it.

"Nope. Work has kept me busy. I haven't really had time to date much."

"So, you're telling me you've been single this whole time?" I raised my eyebrow and tilted my head.

Tommy's cheeks turned as red as mine had been. "Well, not exactly single. But it was never anything serious."

"Ah, so a lifetime bachelor?" I closed my eyes and dropped my head. "I'm sorry. I didn't mean that."

"That was a little harsh." Tommy laughed. "Well, it's not my choice. I just haven't found the right girl. I'd love to settle down, get married, and have a family."

I bit my bottom lip as I imagined a life with Tommy. "Yeah, same."

"Not exactly, though. I mean, you're still married."

"Yeah, well there's that. But to be fair, I didn't know I was married to a murderer." I shrugged my shoulders and pushed the straw to my lips.

"I guess you're off the hook." Tommy winked at me. "I'm just happy you're not with him anymore. I'm glad you got out alive."

"Me, too. I still don't understand how he could have had me so fooled. I literally had no idea that he was even married before me."

"Really? How is that possible? Don't you have to write that in on the marriage certificate or something?"

"I don't know. I don't think so."

"Yeah, I think you do. I'm pretty sure you have to produce a death certificate or something to prove that you are legally able to be married."

The wheels started spinning in my head. "Hmm. I wonder if I was even legally married. That might make this divorce thing way simpler."

"Seriously, though." Tommy took a sip of his coffee. "I'm sorry, I didn't mean to bring him into this. I'm sure he's the last person you want to think about right now."

"True, although, I can't stop thinking about him."

"Ouch."

"No, no, not like that. I just mean I'm terrified that he's going to find me. I know if he finds me, he'll kill me."

"Why do you think that? Do you really think he's just a murderer?"

"He knows I know things."

"What things?"

I closed my eyes as I tried to come up with the right answer. "Ah, well, it's complicated."

"Try me."

"It sounds crazy. I mean, I feel crazy."

"Tess, I'm not going to judge you. It's okay to tell me anything."

Against my better judgement I took a deep breath and clenched my cup. "I've talked to Rebecca."

"What? So, she's alive?"

I shook my head. "No, I've talked to her ghost." My words trailed off into a whisper as I looked around the café.

"Whoa."

"See, it's crazy."

"No, I mean, it is, but you're not. I've seen shows where detectives use people like you to solve homicides."

"It started off as dreams. This woman came to me and told me I needed to leave Keith. She was coming almost every night. At first, I just thought it was because Em and I had been fighting over us eloping. Then Em showed me the articles about Rebecca online and it was *her*."

"What do you mean?"

"The woman in my dreams was Rebecca. When I saw the pictures online, I knew it was her. After I figured that part out, it all kind of escalated."

"So, you're saying a ghost saved your life?"

"Yes."

"And that means she's really dead. She's not just a missing person, but an unsolved homicide."

I nodded. "And now I have to find her."

"How? Do you know where she is?"

"No. I have no idea. All I know is she told me I'd find out the truth about a lot of things when I found her."

"Well, shit. Looks like we need to find her."

"I wish it were that simple."

"It can be. I can look at her file and see if I can get them to open her case back up."

"No, don't do that. She wants me to find her."

"Well, you would be, in a roundabout way."

"No. I have to be the one to find her. Please don't do anything."

"Can I at least help you?"

"I guess. But I need you to promise that you won't tell anyone about this. I really feel like she doesn't want me to tell anyone, not yet."

"Okay." Tommy held up his hands. "I promise."

"Thank you. I really don't have any idea where to start looking for her. And, now with winter settling in, I'm not sure I'll be able to find her this year."

"We have a little time before the ground freezes, if that's where she is." Tommy scratched his head. "Shit, you know she could be anywhere."

"I know. I'm hopeful she'll give me some more clues. I mean if she wants to be found, she can at least help me out."

"Hmm. So, you're hot and you're a witch." Tommy licked his lips.

"Easy buddy. I'm not sure calling a girl a witch is a good idea, especially if she is one."

"Good point. But for the record, I've always had a thing for Samantha, the good witch."

"Too bad for you we missed Halloween."

"There's always next year. That is if you don't turn me into a toad before then."

"Very funny." My cheeks lifted and I dropped my head to hide my face.

"I'm just teasing, you know that right?"

"I know. It's just been a while since I've been able to be myself. It's been fun today."

"It has been. I hope that means there will be a next time."

"Me, too." It was going to be a challenge to wait until next time. The love I had for Tommy was rekindled without effort. He was who I was supposed to be with. Now to find Rebecca so we could live our happily ever after.

Randy was still working on his novel when I returned home. It was just as well. I wasn't ready to tell him about Tommy just yet. I knew he had the best of intentions for me, but not everyone was out to get me. I knew there was still a chance Tommy wasn't who I thought he was. I learned that lesson the hard way with Keith.

The rainy afternoon seemed like as good a time as any to read up to try to figure out how to contact Rebecca. On the way to grab the book, I tripped on the box of books I had left out in my room earlier. I landed on the floor. *Fuck.* I could feel the bruise already starting to form on my knee. I steadied myself on the box to stand up, in the process I heard something scratch the hardwood floor. I pushed the box onto its side and saw something stuck to the bottom. I tugged at the paper to free it.

Holy shit. It was the map. The dream was right. I took the piece of paper to my bed and pulled out my laptop to search the location of the trail. I took a picture of the map and sent it to Emily. There was no way I was going to lose this thing again. The search results loaded on the page painfully slow. My heartbeat echoed in the quiet room as I waited to see where the directions would be taking me.

The paper crinkled in my hand as I studied the page in front of me. Who would keep a map of where they hid a body? Without this thing the chances of her ever being found were slim. When the webpage finally loaded, a message scrolled across the top of the page. "Webster's Trail is closed until further notice due to recent bear attacks." *Great.* Now I have to deal with psychopaths and bears. What could possibly go wrong?

My phone rang causing me to jump out of my skin. Just as I was about to answer it, I remembered I needed to look to make sure I knew who I was talking to. "Thank god it's you."

"That's what I was going to say. Wait, who else would it be?" Emily sounded as breathless as I felt.

"Did you see it? I can't believe I actually found it."

"See what?"

"The map. I sent you a picture of it."

"When? I didn't get anything from you."

"Really? Then what made you call?"

"Tess, make sure all the doors are locked. The windows, too."

"What's going on? Why do you sound so upset?"

"I just got a phone call from Keith, he said he knows where you are and that he's on his way to get you. He said if you don't go with him there will be hell to pay. I'm scared Tess. He didn't sound like himself."

"Oh my god. How does he know where I am?"

"I don't know if he knows or not. He could be on his way here, I don't know."

"Shit. What the hell do I do? I don't want him to hurt you. Should I just call him?"

"No. Are you out of your mind? Don't you dare contact him. Maybe you need a protection order."

I walked to the front door and turned the lock and then the deadbolt. "Are your doors locked?"

"Yeah. Mandy has her gun loaded just in case."

"Holy shit, she has a gun?"

"Yes, but I'm glad. I know I hate them, but it does make me feel better knowing we have a fighting chance."

"Wait, you're sure you didn't get the picture I sent you?" The adrenaline surged through my body. "Hold on." I pulled the phone away from my face and checked my messages. "Oh my god, I sent the map to Tommy."

"Tommy? You two have been talking?"

"Yeah, someone gave him my number, remember?" The mood of the conversation changed.

"Oh, I have a feeling I want to hear all about it, don't I?"

"You might. But before you get all up in my business, what do I do? He can't have that. He's a cop. How do I make him not do something with this?"

"What did the message say?"

"Just 'look what I found,' and I sent a picture of the map."

"Why are you freaking out over that? Just tell him it was meant for me and that it's a place we used to go or something. He doesn't have to know anything else."

"You're right. What would I do without you? Oh, I know, I wouldn't be sending shit to the wrong person, because he'd never have had my number."

"But you also wouldn't be talking to Tommy."

"Good point. But what do we do about Keith? I'm scared he's going to hurt you."

"Why don't you call Tommy and ask him what to do?"

"I guess it couldn't hurt, but you and I are both out of his jurisdiction. There's nothing he can do."

"I know that, but Keith is. He could swing by Keith's place or at least tell you what you should do."

"I guess. It just feels weird involving him, you know? What if Keith finds out we're dating?"

"Wait, dating? You and Tommy are dating? Already?"

"Not exactly, not yet anyway."

"Then there's nothing to worry about. You said Tommy knew about Rebecca, that means the other cops know about it and they all think Keith did something, so there is every reason Keith should be on their radar, right?"

"Good point. Okay, I'll see what Tommy says. Just make sure you're safe. Don't let him in if he comes by."

"I wouldn't. I might let Mandy have her way with him, though."

"Better her than me." I laughed as I hung up the phone. What else could I do? Fear for my life? I already was.

The call to Tommy went straight to voicemail. I hung up before leaving a message. He didn't respond to the picture I sent, either. Maybe he was busy with work. I went into Randy's office and sat in front of his desk. I waited for him to look up at me before I started talking. "Yes?" Randy peered over his computer screen. "Can I help you?"

"I'm sorry to bother you. I just got off the phone with Emily and she said Keith told her he was on his way to get me."

"That's crazy. Did you tell him you're here?"

"No. I haven't talked to him since I left. He could have just been trying to scare her, or follow her to me."

"Those do sound like possibilities. Is Emily on her way over?"

"No, she said they are staying put, but Mandy has her gun loaded in case he shows up there."

Randy threw his head back and laughed.

"What's so funny?"

"Mandy loves any excuse to get that thing out."

"Well, this seems like a good one."

"It does. Don't worry, your sister is in good hands. If Keith shows up there you'll never have to worry about him again."

"That doesn't sound like a bad thing. I just don't want anyone getting hurt because of me."

"Tessa, the only one who is going to get hurt is Keith. You and Emily are safe. You're both in great hands. Don't you worry, okay?"

"Thanks, Randy. I'm glad you're here."

"Hey, what can I say, I'm God's gift to man… I just need to find one now."

"I hope you do. You're going to make someone very happy." I got up and let myself out and returned to my room. I shut the door and locked it behind me. I did feel safe with Randy, but that extra layer of protection wasn't something I was ready to give up.

I picked up my laptop again and did a search to see how far away Webster trail was. It was only an hour from here, and forty-five minutes from Keith's house. What made him pick this place? I held the map and studied it. The X was off the trail in what looked to be a bunch of trees. How would I ever find her? And what would I do if I did? How do you explain to the police that you found the body of your husband's missing wife? I rested my head on the stack of pillows and drifted off to sleep.

"Not much longer." Rebecca's red hair swayed behind her as she walked down a path.

"Where are we going?" I ran to keep up with her.

"You'll see." Her stride turned into skipping.

"Wait, I can't see you." She vanished out of my sight.

"Over here." Her voice sang in the breeze. "Just a little bit further."

The path turned to a thick patch of trees. So dense, I couldn't see where to walk. "Wait for me. I don't know where you are." I pleaded for her to stop.

"I can't stop, or he'll know. I've got to keep going. Come on slow poke." Rebecca laughed as her voice became quieter.

Out of breath, I stopped and leaned against a tree. The tall pine began to move, and I fell to the ground. Leaves and branches covered me. "Help. Rebecca, help me." My voice echoed in the distance. "Help me."

Rebecca didn't answer me. No one did. The growling of a bear was all I could hear. I covered my eyes and hid my head between my knees, trying to become as small as possible so the bear wouldn't see me. The crunching of the twigs became louder, until it was all I could hear. Panic riddled my body. The heat of someone near me replaced the coldness of the ground. Something or someone was prying my hands off my eyes.

"Don't look away now. Keep your eyes open at all times." The familiar voice filled the rest of my body with warmth. The leaves and twigs turned to luscious, green grass and daisies. I sat up and saw my grandmother's gray curly hair walk away. "Don't give up now. You know where you need to go."

"Gram. Come back." I pleaded with her as I had with Rebecca, but she continued to walk until I could no longer see her. Back on my feet the ground turned back to the forest I had been in. A ramshackle cabin was at my fingertips. I turned the doorknob, and the high pitch screech of the door opening stung my ears. The floorboards creaked under my feet as they met the floor. A layer of dust covered everything inside. A plate on the kitchen table still had moldy bread crusts on it, a mustard-stained napkin next to it. A chair was turned upside down and a pool of blood began bubbling up around it.

The sound of a gunshot rang in my head as the walls around me started to fall to the ground. The floor under my feet disappeared and a hole opened up in the earth, swallowing the contents of the cabin. I held on to the side of the hole, digging my fingernails in to keep myself from falling.

My body jolted when I heard a knock at my bedroom door. "Tessa, are you hungry? I baked us up some peanut butter cookies."

I shook the memory of the dream out of my head before crawling out of bed. I looked down at my phone. Tommy hadn't responded to my message yet. Maybe the picture didn't actually go through. With my hand on the doorknob, the details of the dream came back to me. Keith never ate the crust, but he hated mustard. What was this trying to tell me? I already knew Keith was the one who murdered Rebecca, so what was with all the nonsense clues? Half in a daze I joined Randy for warm cookies and milk.

"What the hell happened to you? You look like you've seen a ghost."

"You could say that." I rubbed my eyes. "I just took a nap."

"Rainy days always make me sleepy, too. And look, no sign of Keith." Randy held his hands up in the air at his sides.

"I think he was just trying to get to me, hoping Emily would tell him where I was. He's all talk." Except I knew he wasn't. I knew I'd have proof soon that he was more dangerous than anyone realized.

"Sorry about that picture I sent you yesterday." I said to Tommy as we shared another morning coffee at Swiftwater.

"Picture? What picture?" Tommy raised his eyebrows.

"The strange one I sent you."

Tommy picked up his phone and turned it on. He clicked on the messages and showed me. "Look, no picture."

"That's weird. It said it was delivered. I guess maybe it was too big to go through." I held the straw between my teeth before taking a sip.

"I want a do over. If you sent me a picture, I'm going to have to ask you to send it again." His smile spread across his face.

"Oh, no, it's not what you think. It wasn't *that* kind of picture." I felt my cheeks start to burn. "I was sending it to Em, but when she told me she didn't get it, either, I checked and saw that I accidentally sent it to you."

"Accidentally, huh? Bummer." Tommy snickered as his cup went to his lips. "But I guess if it was meant for your sister it can't be that much of a bummer. At least you didn't accidentally send it to another guy."

"You're the only guy I text, well, besides Randy, and I doubt he'd want to see that any more than Em would."

"Ah, come on, I bet you'd be surprised."

"Nope. He's not into me at all. I like it that way."

"Well, it's his loss." Tommy turned on his phone. "Ah shit, I've gotta run. We have our monthly staff meeting today." He stood up and took our cups to the counter. "If you're feeling generous, I'd love one of those pictures." He winked at me as he held the door open.

"Nope, sorry, not that kind of girl. Besides, what happens if someone else got it, accidentally?"

"Hmm. I guess I could settle for the real thing. That's always better than pictures any day."

"Slow down Mr. Peters. Don't you have a meeting to attend?"

"I do." He turned his phone on again and checked his calendar. "Today is my early shift. Do you want to have dinner?"

"I don't know. Seeing you twice in one day? That can't lead to anything good." As I laughed Tommy bent down and kissed my cheek.

"Think about it?"

"I will."

"Great. Text me later what you decide."

Instead of going back home I turned the other way out of the parking lot and went to see Emily. It had been a couple of days since I'd seen her, and I wanted to talk things over with her in person. There was only so much I trusted to send through messages.

The door opened before I knocked. "Oh, hey."

Mandy met me on the other side. "Hi. I was just on my way to the grocery store. Emily is still sleeping."

"What a bum." I laughed as I let myself in. "Is everything okay? You look… I don't know… sad."

"Yeah, I'm fine. I've just got a deadline to meet but I don't have an ounce of creativity left."

"You sound like Randy."

"Yeah, I'm afraid we're more alike than any other normal pair of siblings."

"If there is anything I can do, just let me know."

"Thanks, Tessa. It was nice seeing you."

In Emily's room I switched on the light and saw her cover her head with a pillow. "I said I don't need anything."

"Hey, what's the matter? Are you okay?" I stood by the edge of her bed and waited for her to emerge.

"Tess? What are you doing here?" She poked her head out from under the pillow.

"I just wanted to talk. It's been a while. What's wrong?"

"Oh, nothing. Mandy's just a beast when she can't write. It's the only time she drives me crazy."

"So, everything is alright? You two are good?" I sat on the edge of her bed and played with her hair.

"Yeah, we're good." She sat up. "So, tell me about Tommy."

"What about him?"

"Stop it. I know things." Emily winked.

"How do you know things?"

"Tommy and I text."

"You do? Since when?"

"Since the other day. Don't worry, I'm not going to steal your man."

"Speaking of my man, do you know that I might not even be legally married?"

"What are you talking about?"

"Tommy told me Keith should have had to show proof that his first marriage ended before he was able to get married again."

"Does that mean you don't have to file for divorce?"

"It might. I need to go to the courthouse and see if I can figure it out."

"That would be nice. Save you a step, and you wouldn't have to count the marriage."

"Count the marriage?"

"You know, when you and Tommy get married, he can be your first husband." Emily laughed. "Sorry, I couldn't help myself. He's the kind of guy I want for my baby sister."

"I feel the same way. I just worry that maybe I'm wrong about him, too. I was certain Keith was a great guy. I'm scared that I don't know who I can trust."

"I can understand that, but remember, we've known Tommy forever."

"I know, that's the only thing keeping me interested."

"What is it now? Twenty years since the flame's been burning?"

I tossed a pillow at her face. "Very funny."

"I just want you to be happy, and I know Tommy will make you happy." She held her hand up. "I won't say anything else."

I pushed out the sigh that had been building as I avoided the real reason I was there. "So, are you up for a hike?"

"Are you crazy? It's freezing out there."

"I know, but it's only going to get colder, and I'd like to get my life back."

"Do you really think she's out there?"

"I don't know, but I had another dream, and I think I have an idea where she might be."

"But what if Keith planted that map to trick you? He must have known you found the box, or it wouldn't have been missing. He could have been the one to put the map in your stuff."

"Hmm, I hadn't thought about that. But he didn't know I was leaving him, either." I tried to get into Keith's head and think like him. "What would he gain from sending me to the trail?"

"He could get you into the forest and kill you, too."

"How would he know when I was going? I could have given the map to the police. What normal person would go to a closed trail to hike with hungry bears?"

"You've got a point. So, you think Rebecca put the map where you could find it? Do you really think ghosts can do that kind of thing?"

"I have no idea, but you heard Sara, I need to find her."

"Looks like we're going to go freeze our asses off." Emily climbed out of bed and went to the bathroom.

I wondered if this was as good of an idea as I thought. What if Keith was waiting for me out there? What if we ran into the bears? "You better keep us safe, Rebecca. We're doing this for you."

After Emily was dressed, she found an extra pair of gloves and a hat for me to wear. "Have I told you how much I hate being cold?" Emily tied the scarf tight around her neck, covering every part of her face, except for her eyes.

"Em, it's not *that* cold out."

"It's November in New Hampshire. That's all I need to know."

"California is all making sense to me now." I laughed as we left the house.

"You're the only reason I'm here still. Whenever you're ready I'll rent the U-Haul." Emily pulled off her gloves and scarf before getting into the driver's seat.

"Do you think Tommy would move?" I shut the car door and struggled with the seatbelt.

"He might if he knew you were." Emily blew her warm breath into her hands. "Do you know where we're going?"

"Not exactly." I turned on my phone and entered the address to Webster trail into Google maps. "Just listen to her, she knows how to get there."

"Perfect. We're being sent into a bear infested forest by a ghost and a talking device thingy."

"Welcome to the wonderful world of technology." I laughed and looked out the window, watching the naked trees dance in the light wind.

"How come we never went hiking when we were kids?" Emily turned her directional signal as ordered by the talking phone.

"Because you refused."

"I don't remember ever being offered."

"You don't? Dad always tried to take us with him, and you'd freak out about the snakes."

Emily nodded her head and smiled. "Oh yeah, it's all coming back to me." She tapped her thumbs on the steering wheel. "Wait, do you think the snakes are out there today?"

"Nah, it's too cold for them. They're probably fast asleep in the trees."

"What?" She whipped her head around to look at me. "You better be kidding."

"I am. I think."

"You think? Or you know? I love you, but there is no way in hell that I'm going hiking in a forest with trees full of snakes."

"Look on the bright side, if I'm right, then they're sleeping."

"There is no bright side when it comes to snakes."

"You do know there are snakes in California, right?"

"God damn it, Tess, don't tell me things I don't want to know."

"Do you remember going for vacations with Mom and Dad?" I looked out the window to try to hold back the storm of emotions brewing inside me.

"I do. It was fun, wasn't it?"

"Yeah. My favorite was the time we stayed at the ocean campground."

"Oh my god, I remember that. Remember how hard the ground was?"

"Yeah." I laughed as the memory played back like a movie in my mind. "And we thought it was supposed to be soft because we were sleeping on sand."

"We were dumbasses."

"Hey, speak for yourself." I closed my eyes and heard the crashing of the waves. "That was probably my favorite trip."

"Mine, too. I miss the ocean. Another reason to move to Cali."

"Do you ever think about what life would have been like if Dad didn't..."

"All the time." A tear ran down Emily's cheek. "You look like Mom."

"No, I don't." I looked over at my reflection in the mirror.

"Yes, you do. The older you get, the more I see it."

"You really think so?"

"Yup."

I pushed the breath out of my mouth. "I was almost just like her."

"Stop it, Tess. I don't even want to imagine that."

"I wonder what she's doing?"

"She's probably reading and drinking wine."

"You think God allows you to drink wine in Heaven?" I looked over at Emily and couldn't hold back the smile.

"I don't know, but if it's all they say it is, I imagine you can do whatever you want. Within reason though."

"Em?"

"Yeah?"

"Do you think Dad is there, too?"

Emily released a sigh and shook her head. "I don't know, Tess. I'd like to think he is, but then I'd like to think he's not."

"I know. Me, too. Do you think Mom knew it was coming?"

"I don't know. Would you have? If you didn't know who Keith was, would you have known it was coming if he had killed you?"

"No, I don't think I would have. I loved him. Just like Mom loved Dad. Dad was just as perfect as Keith was in my eyes."

"Mine, too. He never yelled at us. Not even when we should have been. I'll never understand why it happened."

"Do you think they fought when they were alone?"

"I've tried to remember a time they were mad at each other

and I can't. I'd had thought there would have been a time or two we would have seen them fighting."

"It drives me crazy, too. The perfect little family turned upside down without warning."

"Yup. That's why I have trust issues." Emily turned on the radio.

"Why don't I? I mean, I do now, but why didn't I?"

"I don't know, maybe you're more like Gram and you want to see the good in people."

Thoughts of the life we missed out on with our parents crashed down around me as we finished the journey to find the body of the other woman whose life was cut short. What does it all mean? Why was it so important to Rebecca that I find her? What was with all the hidden meanings in the dreams? The questions flooded me, saving me from the sorrow of the life we'd never have again.

"This is going to sound crazy, but I think there's a reason it's us who is going to find Rebecca."

"Yeah, because you married her husband." Emily maintained her concentration on the road.

"No. There's more. There has to be. I feel like there's a bigger meaning behind it all. There's a reason I fell in love with Keith so quickly. Just like there is a reason I have the dreams and find the clues that need to be found."

"What do you think it all means?"

"I don't know, but I know we'll figure it out when we find her."

"Tess, you know there's a good chance we'll never find her, right?"

"No, we'll find her. Maybe not today, maybe not on Webster trail, but we'll find her."

"How are you so certain?" Emily took her eyes off the road long enough to show me the doubt she held.

"Because there's no other choice."

"Well, for your sake, and hers, I hope you are right." Emily slowed the car down to turn into the empty parking lot. "You said this place was closed, right?"

"Yeah, due to the attacking bears." The snort followed the laugh I couldn't keep in. "I can see the headline now." I held my hand up in air quotes. "Two crazy sisters eaten alive by bears. Remains found inside their tummies."

Emily rolled her eyes. "That's sick, you know that, right?"

"What, we've got to have some fun with all of this."

"I suppose it doesn't hurt." Emily put her Subaru in park and looked over at me. "Hey, have you Googled Rebecca?"

"No, have you?"

"No, which is strange, because I Google the shit out of everybody."

"Hmm, what do you think that means?"

"That you might be on to something. Maybe I never did it because I wasn't the one who was supposed to find out."

We locked eyes and nodded our heads in unison.

"If we survive, looks like I've got some research to do."

"Well, I want to help you. I'm an old pro at cyberstalking."

"Cyberstalking? Is that even a thing?"

"I think so." Emily shrugged her shoulders before reaching into the backseat to get her scarf, gloves and hat.

With our winter gear on there was nothing stopping us from starting our search. I pulled the picture of the map up on my phone and tried to match our location to where the X was on the map. "I think it's that way." I pointed to the trail.

"Gee, what gave it away?" Emily laughed as she gave her coat the final zip to cover up her face.

"Knock it off." I smacked Emily on the side of the head. "I won't let you Google with me if you don't stop being a smartass."

"Okay, okay, let me see the map." I handed her my phone. "Yup, I think you're right. Let's follow the trail until we see a bunch of trees. Oh wait, we're already there."

"Em…" I took my phone back from her. "It looks like it's about a mile in. If you were going to murder and then bury someone in the woods, why would you do it so close to the trail?"

"Beats me." Emily held her head down as she entered the trail. "Why do people kill the people they love?" She lifted her gloved hands over her head. "None of it makes sense, if it did, she'd still be alive."

"True." I followed behind Emily trying to listen to the land around us. Goosebumps covered every inch of my body. I wasn't sure if it was from the mountain air, or Rebecca. The possibility that this was the last place she was alive made the walk even more haunting. With every step I took, I couldn't help but wonder if she were under my feet. Here? There? Over there? There was so much ground for us to cover. How had no one else found her before? The trail looked like it was heavily used. In the past ten years, no one stumbled upon something out of the ordinary. It just didn't add up.

Raindrops started to fall. Within a few minutes, the tree branches started to bend. "Was there even rain in the forecast?" Emily huddled into her coat.

"I don't think so. Maybe someone doesn't want us out here?"

"You're not serious right now, are you? Why the hell are we out here then?" The look in Emily's eyes when she turned around told me all I needed to know.

"You're right, but we should come back another day, before this shit turns to ice."

"Fuck. I hate winter. We came all this way just to turn around?"

"You're so hard to read. One minute you act like you don't want to be out here and when I give you a pass to go home you fight me?" The rain fell into my eyes as I stood under a tall pine tree.

"What can I say?" Emily threw her arms above her head. "You know how much I love to snoop. I feel like we have to keep looking."

"I want to stay, too, but I don't want to get stranded here. If this turns to ice, we might not be able to get off the trail unless we slide down it on our asses."

Emily bent over and started slapping her leg. She gasped for air between belly laughs. "What a sight that'd be."

"I know. Let's just go to Swiftwater and warm up."

"Really? You're ready to give up?" Emily dropped her head and turned around. "If you insist."

"I'm not giving up. I just don't want to die out here. Besides, now we know what it looks like out here. Next time we come, we can be better prepared."

"Make sure you invite me next time. I don't want you out here alone."

"Scout's honor." I held two fingers up.

"You know that doesn't mean shit if you're not a scout, right?"

"You know what I mean. I'd pinky promise, but it's too

cold to take my gloves off. I swear you can come back with me. I sure as hell don't want to come out here alone."

I couldn't help but wonder if the rain was a way to keep us out of the woods. I knew Rebecca wanted me to find her, but who didn't want us here? There was more to the picture than we were seeing. But wasn't that the case with everything in life? Nothing was ever as it seems. Nothing.

23

I couldn't believe I hadn't thought about Googling Rebecca before now. It felt like I knew her, although how couldn't I after dreaming about her for so long. Entering her name in the search bar only produced articles about her disappearance. To really get to know her I needed to know her maiden name. Who was she before she became Rebecca Stevens?

My mouse hovered over a picture of her. She was striking. There was something in her eyes that looked familiar. It felt deeper than just sharing my nights with her. It felt like a connection, one I couldn't put my finger on.

"Who are you?" I stared back at her piercing green eyes. I'd seen them before. But where? I closed my eyes and tried to pull up the memory. Nothing came. I typed her name in the search bar again, hoping for different results. None came.

How do people do this? Emily would know, she was an old pro at finding out information. I dialed her number and waited for her to answer. My patience grew thin as I counted the rings. Where the hell was she?

Without Emily's help I was at a standstill. *Dig deeper.* The voice filled my head. "What does that even mean?" I muttered as I clicked through the pages of the search results. I felt my fingers go to the keyboard and watched "Keith and Rebecca Stevens marriage." I hit enter and saw the Drakesville Town Report for 2003 on the top of the page. I clicked on the link and waited for it to load.

I scrolled through the pages. There were one hundred and thirty to go through. Page after page there was no useful information. This was going to take forever. As I was about to lose hope, page number seventy-three turned out to be the motherload. "Drakesville Marriages." Jackpot. I scrolled through the names. At the bottom of the page, "Keith R. Stevens married Rebecca S. Hayes on May 3, 2003." *Hayes.* Why did that name sound familiar? I laid back on my bed and tried to pull the memory up. I'd heard that name before. Not just Hayes, but Rebecca Hayes. Why? Where? I squeezed my eyes tight trying to drum up the lost details. All it produced was a migraine.

The shrill ring of my phone penetrated my head. "Em, who's Rebecca Hayes?"

"We're calling with important information about your car's extended warranty." The robotic voice on the other end infuriated me.

"Fuck off." I tossed the phone onto the bed and closed my eyes. The pain from the headache was too intense to look at the computer screen. Why was everything an obstacle? When it was so close it was pulled out of reach.

The phone rang again. Irritated by the sound I answered as quick as I could. "I said fuck off."

"Whoa, nice to talk to you, too." Emily snickered.

"Oh, it's you. I thought you were trying to sell me

something."

"Nope, just saw that you called. What's up?"

"So, I Googled Rebecca, like we talked about the other day."

"What did you find out?"

"Well, I was calling you because I couldn't figure it out. All that was coming up were the news articles about her missing. I figured you'd know what I needed to do."

"What do you need help with?"

"Nothing, now. Something told me to search for Keith and Rebecca's wedding certificate so I could figure out her maiden name."

"Well done grasshopper. I'm impressed. What did you find?"

"Hayes. Her name was Rebecca Hayes."

"Shut the fuck up."

"Excuse me?"

"Tess, do you know who Rebecca Hayes is?"

"No, but I feel like I should. Who is she?"

"This can't be the same one."

"Same one? What are you talking about?"

"Dad's sister. Becky. Aunt Becky."

"No way. How would her last name be Hayes when Dad's was Blake?"

"You don't remember anything, do you?"

"No, I guess not. Enlighten me."

"After Grammy Blake left her husband, she had a baby with a different man, Howie Hayes, if I remember correctly."

"Why didn't we call her Grammy Hayes then?"

"Because she never married Howie, it was a short-lived affair. A wham bam thank you ma'am type deal."

"Gross." My gag reflex stopped me from vomiting in my mouth. "So, why did she give Becky his name?"

"I don't know. Maybe she wanted them to have a relationship. How old was Rebecca when she went missing?"

"She was twenty-eight."

"So, she'd be thirty-eight now?"

"Yeah. It can't be the same person."

"Yes, it could. Aunt Becky was a lot younger than Dad. She was closer to our age. Don't you remember going to Grammy Blake's and playing with her when we were kids?"

"Yeah, but she was older."

"Older than us, but she was a kid. We played Barbies together for Christ's sake."

"I just thought that's what aunts do. I didn't think that was because she was a child."

"Is your whole life a delusion? You seriously don't remember her being around our age?"

"Em, we didn't see Grammy Blake enough for me to remember anything. After she moved away, we didn't see her again, and then after Dad died, we never heard from her again. I always thought she was mad at us for picking Gram."

"Tess, she wasn't mad, she died. She had cancer. This is all news to you?" Annoyance bounced off Emily's words.

"I guess I blocked a lot of that out. After we lost Mom and Dad, I shut everything off."

"I can't believe you didn't remember Aunt Becky."

"I remember her, I just didn't think about her. I'm not convinced they're the same person. Aunt Becky wasn't as pretty as Rebecca."

"True, but the last time we saw her she was a gangly

teenager. People grow up, Tess, remember how hideous you were as a kid?"

"Yeah, about as ugly as you were."

"Touché."

"It can't be her. The articles we read about Rebecca said her family was looking for her. If Grammy Blake died, who was left to look for her?"

"Rebecca went missing in 2005, Grammy Blake died in 2006. It adds up. There was no one left to look for her after Grammy died."

"Oh my god. That's why she needs me to find her so bad. Because we're the only family she has left."

"Do you know how crazy this is? I mean, if Rebecca really is Aunt Becky. This is the type of thing you see in the movies."

"Horror movies, maybe. I married my uncle." The magnitude of that thought alone made everything more complicated.

"Gross, but I guess if she is her, then you did. At least he's not a blood relative."

"That's why he wanted to be with me. I was just like Rebecca. I don't have any family that would have looked for me, either."

"Um, hello. What am I?"

"I mean when we were fighting."

"Tess, if you went missing, I would have done anything to find you."

"But how would you have known I was missing? We didn't know Rebecca was missing."

"We were kids, we had enough on our plate. Besides, how would we have known it was her? Her name was different, and this whole thing didn't happen in our town."

"How did we not ever see Grammy Blake on the news? How come we didn't connect the dots when we saw the news articles?"

"I don't remember seeing a picture of her mom, only Keith. I also don't remember seeing her name, I think it just said her family."

"This just became a hell of a lot more personal. The bastard murdered my aunt." I paused as the thought came crashing down. "Do you think he knew who I was?"

"I doubt it. I mean he didn't seek you out, you found him."

"She led me to him. Fuck. She had this whole thing planned all along. Did she want me killed, too?" Disgust turned to anger. "Why wouldn't she have wanted to keep me safe? This is bullshit."

"Tess, I don't think she wanted you to get hurt. I think she just wanted you to find her. Now we need to."

"I needed to before. This just makes it all so much more confusing. I feel like I'm in a bad dream. Fucking Aunt Becky."

"You know, every time I saw the pictures of Rebecca I felt like I knew her, but I couldn't figure it out."

"Yeah, me, too. Her eyes were so familiar."

"Oh my god, Tess, she had Dad's eyes."

"You're right."

"I knew I hated that fucker."

"I know. I hate him now, too." The idea that Keith killed my aunt made my desire to make him pay for what he did even stronger. He'd never be held accountable for what he did without a body. Snow was about to fall. We had to find Rebecca before the ground froze. We were in a race against New Hampshire's changing seasons. "So, want to go look for her again tomorrow?"

"You read my mind."

"I'm getting good at that, huh?"

"Tess, what do you say we bring other people with us? The more help the better the chances are that we find her."

"I don't know. I guess it couldn't hurt. We can't tell anyone about this twisted backwoods shit yet, though, okay? I'm not ready to tell the world I slept with my uncle."

"Okay, besides, we're not sure anyway." Emily's attempt to talk me off the cliff failed. I *knew*. It was the only thing I was sure of.

24

Emily and I gathered up as many people as we could for our makeshift search party. It consisted of exactly five people. Emily, Mandy, Randy, Tommy and me. Times like these I was reminded of how alone I really was, but also how lucky I was to have this many people that cared about me in my life.

The forecast called for morning sunshine, so we met at Webster trail at 8:00. This might have been the earliest Emily had been up since she graduated high school. She never was a morning person. Chances were she didn't fall asleep last night after our discovery. I know I didn't.

Emily took the blame for inviting Tommy so Randy would stay off my back. There was only so much I could handle, and a lecture from him wasn't one of them. At the trailhead, Randy took a backpack and a shovel out of the trunk of the car. "What are you going to do with that?" I asked sounding more afraid than I should have.

"This is a search party, no?"

"Yes, but do you really think we're going to need a shovel?"

The thought of that made my heart drop. I knew we were searching for her remains, but I hadn't connected the dots completely.

"If we're lucky, yes. I've watched every episode of Dateline. I know we're going to have to do some digging."

"How will we know where to dig, though? I mean she's been missing for over ten years. Won't everything be grown over?" I asked him as I slid on my gloves.

"I don't know. This is my first time at one of these things. I do know I don't want to have to walk all the way back here in case we need one." Randy shrugged his shoulders. "Maybe we should have invited Sara."

"Has she ever found anyone before?"

"I don't know, but if this chick wants to be found, I'm sure she'd lead the way." Randy slung the backpack over his shoulder.

"What's in there?"

"Probably a picnic." Mandy joined us at the car, Emily was right behind her.

"Really?" Randy kicked at the loose gravel. "I don't want to see you eat any of these tasty sandwiches. Never mock the chef."

Tommy pulled into the lot, completing our party.

"Oh, if it isn't captain hotty pants." Randy rolled his eyes.

"Be nice little man." Mandy cuffed her brother upside his head. "But not too nice." Mandy noticed Randy's mouth drop when Tommy got out of his Dodge Ram.

I stayed in the circle and watched Emily go over to greet Tommy. She leaned in and whispered something. Tommy's face lit up with a smile and they walked over to join the rest of us.

"At least one of us men came prepared." Randy put his other arm through the backpack strap.

"Should I have brought something with me?" Tommy ran his hand through his hair before pulling down his winter hat.

"It is a search party." Randy held out the shovel for Tommy to carry. "Here, in case we need it."

"I don't know if we'll need this." Tommy took the shovel. "But, hey, better to be safe than sorry, right?"

"That's my motto." Randy winked and Mandy lifted her hand to threaten him.

"Okay, so we all stay on the trail and just look around. The map shows an area where there's dense trees, I think that's where we should veer off course and start the real search." I handed a photocopy of the map to each of them.

"Tessa, this looks like one of those tourist maps. I don't think this is accurate at all." Tommy held it up to show me the marketing logo on the bottom of the page.

"So, why would there be an X right here?" I pointed on my map.

"To throw people off? I don't know." Tommy adjusted his hat.

"Tommy, what do you think we should do? We have to find her." Emily looked over at me in an attempt to keep me calm.

"Let's start looking. It could mean something. We'll never know until we try." Tommy showed his teeth as his smile grew. "Why don't you lead the way?" He pointed to Randy.

"I don't mind if I do." Randy held the bag by the straps and marched into the woods.

Tommy lingered behind, waiting for Randy to get out of

sight. "Em told me to keep my hands off you. Little does she know how hard that is." He winked at me.

"Yeah, Randy doesn't want me getting involved with anyone right now. He doesn't think anyone is safe to trust."

"So, are you two a thing?" Tommy tilted his head, his dimples making him irresistible.

"Don't be a jackass. If I piss him off, I'm homeless. Besides, you'll be sorry if you piss him off."

"Why's that?"

"Because he won't give you one of his famous sandwiches."

"Seriously?"

I nodded and held out my hand. We held hands on the way to the path. I gave him a squeeze before letting go. "Thank you for coming."

"You know I'd do anything for you and Em, right? All you have to do is ask and I'll be there."

"I know." We continued along the trail, Randy and Mandy were out of sight. Emily waited back for Tommy and me to catch up.

"Did Tess fill you in?" Emily asked out of breath.

I widened my eyes and gritted my teeth to try to get her to stop talking.

"No, she didn't." Tommy looked over at me.

"It's nothing really. I just really have to find her, so she'll leave me alone. I guess I'm like the real-life *Ghost Whisperer*."

"I used to love that show." Tommy smiled.

"Really?" I looked over to see if he was being serious.

"Yeah, Melinda Gordon was so hot." Tommy tossed his head back and laughed.

Emily joined him. "She really is."

"This is cool, Em, now you and I can compare ladies together."

"Easy now, there's no way I'm going to tell you how hot my baby sister is." Emily snorted.

"You two are unbelievable." I shook my head and continued on the trail.

Up ahead, Mandy and Randy were sitting on a large stump eating trail mix. "I think we're getting close. Look at all those trees." Randy pointed down the path.

I took a closer look at the trees ahead of us before closing my eyes to try to pull up the images from my dreams. The only thing that came back to me was the cabin, the crust, and the napkin with the mustard stain. "This is useless."

"What is?" Mandy asked.

"Nothing." I hung my head. "It's just that I thought I'd know. You know, like really know when we were close to where she was."

"Honey, we've only just begun. You might know. You might not. That's the chance you've got to take. I know how important this is to you." Mandy stood up and took my hand. "Here, let's go together."

"Thanks, Mandy." I felt safe with Mandy. I knew Emily would hate to hear this, but she reminded me of our mom. "Did Em tell you?"

"She did. I promise I won't tell anyone, not even Randy."

"Thanks. I'm just not ready for the world to know our family's dirty little secret."

"You're incredibly brave. You know that, right? What you're doing for Rebecca isn't something most people would do."

"I don't know, I bet they would."

"Nope. My guess is they'd start drinking and pretend it didn't exist."

"Shit, is that all I needed to do?"

"I'm serious though, you've been through so much and you still want to help. You and Em are such good people."

"You and Randy seem alright, too." I tripped over a tree stump and fell to my knees, still hanging on to Mandy's hand.

Mandy pulled on my hand to help me up, instead I shook my hand free. "Shh." I leaned my head to the ground and listened.

"Keep going." The voice lingered in the air. It was the first thing I had heard since we started walking.

"We've got to keep going. I have a good feeling about this." I brushed my knees off and took off ahead of Mandy, leaving everyone else behind me. My pace increased, leading me deeper into the trail. She was close, I could feel it.

I pushed my way through the trees. Branches full of pine needles swung back to hit me in the face. I brushed the sting away with the sleeve of my jacket. My eyes went to the ground. "Guys, get over here." My throat stung from the cold air as I tried to catch my breath. "Hurry."

Mandy was the first to arrive. "What is it?"

I pointed to the ground. "I think it's her. I think she's here."

"Who has the shovel?" Mandy turned around and pulled the trees open.

"Mr. Wonderful does." Randy hunched over, his hands on his knees.

"Em. Tommy. Get your asses over here." Mandy cupped her hands around her mouth to yell.

The rustling of branches snapping alerted us that they were on their way. Mandy kicked at the dirt pile with her foot while we waited for them to catch up. "Stop that." Randy swatted at Mandy's arm. "Don't kick a dead woman."

"It's not like she'll feel it." Mandy continued to move the earth with her hiking boot.

"Maybe he's right. I don't think it's a good idea." My eyes fixated on the disturbed ground.

Tommy and Emily emerged through the trees. "What did you find?" Tommy pushed the shovel into the ground to lean on it.

"Careful." I scolded him as I pointed to the pile of dirt.

"That's strange. That looks fresh." Tommy bent down to take a closer look.

"He's right." Randy joined him. "How long did you say she's been missing?"

"It's been about ten years." I looked over at Emily.

Tommy pulled the shovel out of the ground and started to remove some of the dirt. When he made a hole, I walked over to examine it. "It doesn't look like there's anything here." I pulled my gloves off and took the map out of my back pocket. "This looks like we're in the right place."

"Who would've moved her? How would they have known we were going to be looking for her after all this time?" Tommy leaned against the shovel. "This has obviously been disturbed recently. You can tell by the color of the topsoil."

"Tess, do you think Keith knows you found the map?" Emily put her hand on her hip.

"He did know I found that tote, maybe he noticed the map was missing."

"What tote?" Tommy and Randy asked at the same time.

"Ah, I, ah… I found a tote in our basement before I left. That's where I found this thing." I held up the map. "There was other stuff in it, so I doubt this thing was really cause for alarm. Besides, Keith never would have expected me to venture out into the woods."

"Wait, evidence? Like what kind?" Tommy squinted his eyes as he looked at me.

"Like pictures."

"Tess, tell him what else you found." Emily exposed the secret I hadn't wanted to share just yet.

"What is she talking about, Tessa?" Tommy crossed his arms.

"A murder weapon. Well, at least I think it was used to kill her." I closed my eyes and took a breath before I continued. "I wanted to take the tote to the police, but it was missing."

"Shit, Tess, he really murdered her? I just thought we were on a wild goose chase here." Tommy dropped his head. "I can't be involved in a search party for an actual murder. Do you know how much trouble I could get in if anyone found out?"

"Isn't that your job?" Randy crossed his arms. "What *do* police do?"

"It's not like that, man. I mean if they find out I'm pawing around a cold case without getting permission I could get fired." Tommy pulled off his hat and scratched his head. "Holy shit."

"You didn't believe me before?" The sting of his words pierced my heart. "You thought I was just some crazy person trying to dig up ghosts?"

"I never thought you were crazy. I just didn't think there was any evidence. I thought we were going on a hunch."

"But you didn't believe me. You're just here to mock me." I couldn't shake the shock off my face.

"Tess, I'm not mocking you. I honestly didn't know how

serious this is. I didn't know you had a map until this morning. I swear, I'm not making fun of you." Tommy started to walk toward me.

I held my hand up. "No. Why don't you just go? I wouldn't want you to get in trouble."

"Tess, don't be like that. Tommy's not being a jerk. He really could lose his job. This is serious shit. To be fair we weren't honest with anyone here." Emily looked around the circle and stopped with a sympathetic look for me.

"That's bullshit, Em, I know you told Mandy."

"Wait, told Mandy what? What am I missing?" Randy uncrossed his arms and let them fall to his side before he recrossed them.

"Come on guys. Now is not the place to start a fight. Let's just fill in this hole and get out of here." Mandy started kicking the dirt back in the hole.

"No, I think it's important for Tommy to know why this is so important to Tess, to us." Emily held her hand out for me to take. "Tess, come on. We're all friends here. More like family. You can trust everyone who's here."

"I'm not ready for this." I left her hand outstretched in front of me.

"Tess, no one here is going to judge you. You did nothing wrong." Emily took another step closer and put her arm around me.

"Fuck." I hung my head and exhaled all the anger and hurt I had been holding. "Okay, well, long story short I married my uncle." I threw my hands up. "So, there you have it."

"Hold up." Randy cocked his head. "Your uncle? How?"

"After doing some research, Em and I discovered that Rebecca was most likely our Aunt Becky."

"Fuck me." Randy's eyes widened. "That's some twisted shit."

Mandy kicked Randy in the shin. "Enough."

"It's not as messed up as it sounds." Emily pulled me closer. "Our Grammy Blake had a baby with a guy she was dating after our dad was grown. Becky was much younger than our dad, and she moved away with our gram when we were kids. We rarely saw them after they moved, and after our parents died they pretty much stopped communication altogether."

"Why do you think Rebecca is... I mean was your aunt?" Tommy focused his attention to Emily.

"When Tess found out her maiden name, it was the same name as our aunt. She would have been about the same age, and our gram, her mom died in 2006. With Grammy Blake out of the picture there was no one left to look for her. Tess and I are her only living family members."

"Wow, I'm so sorry. I had no idea." Tommy hung his head. "I'd never make fun of you about that."

"Yeah, it's not as creepy as you made it sound at first." Randy nodded and smiled. "It would make one hell of a book though."

"Randy." Mandy shrieked.

"So, now finding Rebecca means even more to us."

"Yeah, and more than ever I want Keith to pay for what he did to her." I lifted my head to look at the group. "Please don't tell anyone else about this."

"It's nothing to be ashamed about. Don't you think it'd be good to get the police involved? Especially if there's evidence?" Randy asked.

"No, I have a bad feeling about that. I can't explain it, but it feels like this is something I need to figure out without their help."

"Our Gram, the other one, taught us to listen to our gut. You know that inner voice?" Emily placed her hands on her stomach. "If Tess doesn't want to get the police involved, we have to listen."

"I take back what I said before. I want to help you two." Tommy placed his hand on Emily's back.

"We don't want you to get fired." Emily moved away and placed Tommy's hand on my back.

Tommy's hand rubbed the top of my shoulder. "I don't care. Helping you is worth more than my job. As long as I'm not doing anything illegal, it's fine." He lifted his shoulders. "Hell, even if it is and it'll help, count me in."

The five of us left the trail after we filled in the hole. The thought that we were that close to where Rebecca had most likely been resting for the past ten years gnawed at my heart. We were so close, and now she could be anywhere. "We won't stop until we find you, Rebecca. I always loved you Aunt Becky."

"This way, follow me." Rebecca's hair flowed behind her as she ran through the tall grass. I followed her laughter until we arrived at an open field of wildflowers. "Come play with me." Rebecca transformed into the girl I knew and held her hand out for me to take.

I looked down at my hand in hers and saw I was a little girl, too. "Wait for me, Auntie." Hand in hand we ran barefoot through the flowers.

"I love you Tessie-bean." Aunt Becky bent down and kissed me on my cheek. She held my hands and started to spin. My tiny body swung in a circle. We both fell to the ground when she stopped.

I rested on her gangly body and she played with my hair. "You're a good girl, Tessie. Don't ever change."

"I love you, too, Auntie. You're my favorite."

"Shh, don't tell anyone, but you're mine, too." We fell asleep under the sun. The safety of her arms around me made everything alright.

The knock at my bedroom door pulled me out of the comfort of Aunt Becky's arms. "Tess, breakfast is ready, if you're hungry." I heard Randy rest his head on the door before I heard the floor creak under his feet as he walked away. Since he found out about my secret, he increased the attention he gave to me. Fresh baked cookies, the fridge stocked with my favorite iced coffee, fluffy, clean towels after every bath.

I stretched my arms above my head as I tried to capture some of the love from the dream he had pulled me out of. I had forgotten how close Aunt Becky and I were. She was like a mother hen. I was young enough that I soaked in all of the love she was willing to give. Emily was older and hung back at the house with Dad and Grammy Blake. It hurt so bad when they disappeared from our lives after Mom and Dad died. It felt like everyone I loved just walked out on me. She was still just a kid herself. I imagine losing her brother the way she did was just as hard for her as it was for us.

"Where are you Aunt Becky?" I closed my eyes to wait for her response. Silence hung in the air. "I have no idea where to even begin to look for you now. Where could you be?"

I slid on my slippers and put on my robe before joining Randy for breakfast. Chocolate chip waffles and whipped cream waited for me at the table. "Yummy, these are my favorite."

"A little birdie might have told me that." Randy wiped his hands on his apron. "Can I get you some iced coffee?"

"No, I'm all set. You know you don't have to wait on me."

"I know. I just want to." Randy tilted his head and smiled.

"I appreciate all the special attention you're giving me. What did I do to deserve all this?" I shoveled a forkful of waffle into my mouth.

"You're a special girl, Tessa. I just want you to know how loved you are."

"No offense, but that's a little creepy." I couldn't hold my giggling back.

"Creepy? How? Is it a crime that I want to show you that I love you?"

"No. I like it. I love you, too." An awkwardness hung in the air. "I'm just not used to being spoiled."

"Well, I enjoy spoiling, so hold onto your hat, honey." Randy winked at me and took a drink of tea. "Have you had anymore visits?"

"Visits? What do you mean?"

"You know, has *she* been back?"

"Rebecca? Funny you should ask. I was just dreaming about her."

"And?"

"And it was nice. I didn't realize how much I missed her." My smile grew as I was pulled back into the memories.

"Did she tell you anything new? Like where she is?"

I shook my head. "Not this time. We were kids. Not a care in the world. I miss those days."

"You and me both." Randy held his teacup between his hands. "I miss when my parents loved and accepted me."

"Are they still alive?"

"Yeah, well, I don't know. They stopped talking to me after I came out."

"Oh, Randy, I'm so sorry."

"Yeah, if it wasn't for Mandy, I wouldn't have any family."

"Did they disown her, too?"

Randy laughed. "Oh, honey, we're not *real* siblings. Well, we're as real as it gets, but we're not blood."

"Seriously? I never would have known. You are so much alike."

"Why? Because we're queer and annoying."

"No, because you're both sweet and caring, and sarcastic and funny."

"Aw, thank you." Randy placed his hand on his heart.

"It's their loss, you know."

A tear fell from Randy's eye.

"I'm proud to call you my little brother. I love you." I reached out my hand and gave it a squeeze. "It's a privilege to know you. You don't need anyone who can't love you for who you are in your life."

"I know. It just hurts sometimes."

"I can imagine it does. I know I miss my parents all the time, especially this time of year."

"Yeah, this is when it stings the most."

"We've got our own island of misfit toys here. Screw the others who can't see our beauty."

"Oh, Christmas movies. You're in trouble now." Randy laughed. "Thanks for being so kind, Tessa. It means a lot to me."

"I'd be lost without you." I finished my waffles and thought about our conversation. We were all a little messed up, I guess. People were never what you thought. Most everyone had something they were hiding.

"What are your plans for today?" Randy took our plates to the sink.

"I think it's time I get my divorce filed."

"You haven't started that yet?" Randy turned to give me a look of disgust.

"No. I've had other stuff on my mind. I meant to, but something always comes up."

"Tessa, you literally do nothing most days. You've got

second thoughts, don't you?" Randy came back to the kitchen table and leaned against the back of a chair.

"No, it's not like that." I looked down at the woodgrain in the table. "Okay, I guess it started out like that, and then I just got overwhelmed with everything. Besides, Tommy doesn't think we're legally married anyway." I felt heat spread across my cheeks when I realized what I had said.

"Tessa." Randy slowly shook his head as he stared into my eyes. "Have you learned nothing?" He let out a heavy sigh. "Are you dating that fine piece of ass?" He placed his hand over his mouth to hide it from dropping open.

"No. I am not." I stood up and pushed the chair in to put some more space between us. "I knew you had the hots for him. You dirty dog."

"Sounds like somebody's jealous."

"Absolutely not." I held back the laughter.

"No worries, honey, I'm sure there's enough man for both of us, if you get what I mean." He winked and kept his lips tight.

"Oh my god. You've been thinking about this, haven't you?" Laughter erupted when I couldn't keep it in any longer. "I can probably get his number for you."

"Probably? Just dig out your phone. I know he's been calling you. These walls are thin." He wiggled his eyebrows as an evil grin spread across his face.

"You've been eavesdropping?" Embarrassment oozed off of me as I tried to replay all of the conversations we had.

"No. But I could if I wanted to. Just remember that if you ever have a sleepover." Randy walked back over to the sink and ran the water. "Good luck today at the courthouse." He kept his back to me as the plates clanked into the suds.

"Thanks." I didn't know what to say after that interaction. Randy was a great friend, and like I told him, he was family, but the years of pushing people out seemed to dominate his emotions. It was obvious that humor and vulgarity were his choice distractions.

I pulled out the box of important documents from my closet and rummaged through until I found our wedding certificate. I turned the flimsy piece of paper over trying to figure out if it was legitimate, or if the whole marriage was a lie. It looked official. There was a county seal and signatures. Could I have really been that naive that I participated in a bogus wedding? At this point I was hoping the answer was yes.

The parking lot at the courthouse was almost empty. I pulled my car into the spot closest to the door in case I needed to leave in a hurry. It was funny how fear followed you everywhere, even places that should be safe. I took the folded-up marriage certificate and my purse and got out of my car. Before I shut the door, I scanned the neighborhood. I hadn't been this close to Keith since I left. What were the chances he would be driving by at this exact moment? The only thing I knew for certain was I had no idea what to expect.

I pulled open the heavy oak door and stepped onto the stone floor. Out of sight from the road, the chances of being seen by Keith dropped significantly, but I knew it was still a possibility. Hypervigilance. It was a new word in my vocabulary, but one that I could not shake. After I made it through security, the guard pointed me in the direction of the clerk.

The tap of my shoes on the polished floor made me feel fancy, until I remembered why I was there. As a little girl, every time I heard ladies' shoes tapping on the floor, I wanted to be like them. I couldn't wait to grow up and be able to dress up and be important. If I had only known what the future had in store for me, I might have not made that wish.

The glass window slid open and a heavyset woman with tight brown curls offered up an ice-cold welcome. "What do you need ma'am?"

Taken aback by her lack of social skills, I was at a loss. "I, ah, I need to file for divorce."

"Have you filled out the paperwork?" She pushed her round glasses up her nose as she sighed.

"No. I, um, wasn't sure where to start."

"You got a computer? Internet?"

"Yes. But I had some questions I hoped you could help me with."

"It's not part of my job to give advice ma'am. I just file paperwork. I don't care if he's your baby daddy, or your sugar daddy. I just date stamp the forms."

"I, ah…" I closed my eyes to try to regain my focus. "He's neither. I just wanted to know if you would be able to check and see if this is a real marriage certificate." I pushed the folded piece of paper through the slot in the window.

The angry woman unfolded it and took a quick glance before she started to laugh. "Is this a joke? Even my pug could tell this is phony."

"How? How can you tell?"

"Look." She pointed to the seal with her stubby finger. "1-800-marriage.com is your first clue. This is a gag gift. You know the thing you prank someone with? Where's the real one?"

"That's the only one I have." Humility was becoming a shade I wore often. "Can you do me one other favor?"

"What's that? Do you want me to take a look at your death certificate?" Her beady eyes peered over her glasses at me.

"No, ma'am. You see, I'm here trying to get a divorce from a man who murdered his first wife. So, I don't have my death certificate, but if you want to keep screwing around, maybe my sister can bring it to you after he finishes the job. I hope you have a great day, ma'am." I turned to walk away, embarrassed at my crassness. Her lack of empathy fueled the dormant rage living inside of me.

"Miss, I'm sorry." She stood behind the glass window and tapped on it to get my attention. "If you come back, I'll help you with that question."

"I'd hate to bother you." I continued to the door.

"Miss, I'm sorry. I was having a bad day. I shouldn't have taken it out on you. Come back, please. I want to help."

Confidence filled me as I turned around and met her at the window. I'd never stood up for myself before. I liked how it felt to be heard. "Would you please look up Keith R. Stevens and tell me who he is married to?"

"Sure. Just a minute." Her fingers typed away at her keyboard as her eyes drifted away from mine. "Hmm. There is nothing here, let me check one other place." She got up and walked to the filing cabinet in the back of the room. She pulled open the drawer and pushed files around before it slammed shut from the weight. "Miss, there is no one on record with that name. I went into the statewide database, and nothing came up. There is no record of marriage for anyone by that name."

"One more favor?" I tilted my head and smiled.

"Okay."

"Can you look up Rebecca Stevens. Or Rebecca Hayes?"

"I can give it a try." She repeated the search she had just done for Keith and returned to her desk. "Miss, there is no record of marriage for either Rebecca Stevens or Hayes." Her eyes dropped. "I remember hearing about Rebecca Stevens on the news. She's the one you're talking about, isn't she?"

"She is. Thank you for your help."

I left the courthouse with more questions than answers. Keith and my marriage wasn't legal. I was relieved about that. I just didn't understand why his marriage with Rebecca wasn't. I had a feeling there was more to this mystery than I'd ever be able to wrap my mind around. Just another lie to add to the book.

After leaving the courthouse I decided to surprise Tommy. I had never been to the police station before. Come to think of it, Tommy was the only police officer I had interacted with since I married Keith, or whatever that time in my life was. I pulled my car in next to Tommy's truck and started to send him a text. What kind of surprise would that be? I knew I needed to go inside and catch him off guard.

The police station was located in the basement of a community center. Small town cost saving measure. I guess there wasn't enough crime in Drakesville to warrant a building all to itself. I pulled open the rickety door and was greeted by a cute, young girl sitting at a small desk. Jealousy shot through me as I imagined Tommy flirting with her, sharing a cup of coffee with her each morning. Knock it off, Tessa. I straightened my sweater and pushed the hair out of my face.

"Hi there." I gave the petite blonde my biggest smile and

spoke to her like she was a puppy. "Is Tommy... I, ah, mean, Thomas Peters in?"

The girl giggled. "It's okay, I call him Tommy, too." She turned her head to look behind her at a board with names and magnets on it. "Yup, looks like he's in. Hang on." She picked up the phone and pushed a button. She looked up at me with a smile as she waited. "Hey, Tommy, I have someone here to see you." The flirty tone in her voice made me want to run back to my car. "He'll be right out. You can have a seat, if you'd like." She pointed to the stained cloth chairs lining the bare wall behind me.

"Thanks." I walked over to the waiting area and held my sweater tight against my body as I waited for Tommy to appear.

The girl at the desk giggled some more when Tommy and another man walked into the room. "Hey guys." She twirled a lock of her hair around her finger as she batted her eyelashes at them.

"Tess, what are you doing here?" A smile spread across Tommy's face when he saw me. Any ounce of jealousy I had disappeared.

"I just wanted to surprise you. I didn't know if you had time to go to Swiftwater's."

"Sure, yeah, I'd love that." He looked over at the other guy. "Jeff, is that alright with you? It won't be long."

The tall, broad-shouldered man smiled and gave Tommy a wink. "Sure, it's fine, buddy." He shoved his hands in his front pockets. There was a familiarity to him. His toned arms held my attention. I couldn't pull myself away. I bit my bottom lip as I studied him.

Tommy tapped my arm. "Tess, this is Jeff, he's one of the guys. Jeff, this is Tessa, she's a friend from back home."

A friend from back home? What the hell was that about? I pulled my attention away from Jeff and focused on Tommy, who seemed oblivious to how his comment hit me, but equally oblivious to my fascination with Jeff.

Jeff walked over and held his hand out for me to take. "Hey, Tess, it's a pleasure to meet you." His cheeks indented with dimples accentuating his square jawline.

"Nice to meet you, too. It feels like I've met you before." I kept my hand in his as I stared up into his hazel eyes.

"I get that a lot." He gave my hand a light squeeze before releasing it. "Have fun guys." He turned and walked back over to the girl at the desk. It didn't look like I had anything to worry about with Tommy and her as long as Jeff was around.

"Well, that was awkward." Tommy turned to look at me as he opened my car door.

"What?"

"The ogling and goggling over Jeff."

"Ogling and goggling?" I snorted. "He seems so familiar. I just can't figure it out."

"I'm sure you've seen him around. He's been a cop here for a while."

"That must be it. Do you want to ride with me to the café?"

"Are you sure you don't want to bring Jeff?" Tommy held my door open as I got in.

"Knock it off and get in."

Tommy climbed into the passenger seat, sitting on top of my paperwork. I pulled it out from under him, ripping the paper in the process. "Oh, shit, I'm sorry." He lifted his butt off the seat.

"It's nothing important. Just my phony marriage certificate. You were right, I was never really married to Keith."

"That's great news." Tommy wiped the smile off his face. "I mean, it is, isn't it?"

"Yeah, it's just so confusing. I asked the clerk to look up his marriage with Rebecca, and it didn't exist. There was no record for either one of them."

"You don't think they were really married, either? Why would someone do something like that?" Tommy looked out the window. "You know, if I were lucky enough to marry a beautiful woman, I'd be damn sure it was legal. I wouldn't want to mess something like that up."

"You think about being married a lot?"

"I don't know. I guess. I'm not getting any younger. It'd be nice to have someone to come home to and wake up next to."

"That would be nice." Silence filled the rest of the drive as thoughts of the life I was meant to have weighed heavy on my heart. Love should be *this* simple.

At the café Tommy reached for my hand and led me inside. We shared a soft smile confirming we were thinking the same thing. The life we both wanted was in reach. I just had to find Rebecca and clean up the mess with Keith before I could start anything new. Tommy deserved at least that.

Tommy ordered our drinks while I went to the ladies' room. I splashed cold water on my face and returned to our table. Tommy was waiting for me there. Although he wasn't as handsome as Keith, or Jeff for that matter, there was something irresistible about him. He was wholesome, the kind of guy you knew would make the perfect dad. One who you could imagine playing with the kids on the floor, giving horsey-back rides. One who would protect me and keep me safe. All that wrapped into a cute, stout package. A little extra man to love. It was his personality that made me fall in love with him all those years ago.

"What are you looking at?" Tommy's voice pulled me out of the trance I was in. I hadn't realized I was just standing in front of him with a goofy smile plastered on my face.

"You." I slid into the booth. "I was just looking at you and how cute you are." I adverted my eyes after, not daring to see his reaction.

"I like that, keep going." His smile grew as he reached across the table for my hand. "I thought I might lose you to that hunk back at the station. Once the ladies see him, I know there's no chance for me."

"Are you serious?" I lifted my eyes unsure if I should be angry or sympathetic. "Why would I fall for a guy I don't even know? You do know how long you've had my heart, right?"

"Hey, simmer down. I was just saying..." He paused. "I'm flattered. I'm glad you think I'm cute."

I placed my hand in his and held his gaze. This was what it was supposed to feel like.

"So, have you doodled my name on any notebooks lately?"

"No, but now that you mention it, I think I'll start."

"You can start with Mrs. Thomas Peters. It has a nice ring to it, don't you think?"

"I'll let you know once I see it."

"See what?" Tommy tilted his head.

"The ring. You keep hinting at something."

"Oh, I'm just teasing." Tommy looked down at my hand in his. "I mean, unless you want something more?" He rubbed my ring finger with his thumb. "I think my grandmother's ring would look stunning right here."

"Is that a proposal?"

"No. I'm just thinking out loud. I think we should start with dating first, don't you?"

"I'd like that." Butterflies danced in my belly as the warmth of his skin next to mine made me long for more of his skin touching mine.

"So, it's official. We're an item. Sorry ladies, I'm off the market."

"That's right. They better keep their hands off my man."

"I like the way that sounds." Tommy smiled. "Does that mean you're going to put *your* hands on me?"

"I'd like that." I bit my bottom lip as desire filled me. "I've been waiting years to be able to get my hands on you."

"It's getting hot in here." Tommy pulled at his collar.

"What's that on your shirt?"

Tommy rested his chin on his chest to see what I was pointing at. "That son of a bitch." Tommy dug at the yellow stain with his fingernail. "This is from the stud, Jeff, the asshole shot mustard on me while he was making his sandwich."

"Gross."

"Yeah, tell me about it. I hate mustard, and now I have to smell it the rest of the day."

"At least you have something to look forward to tonight." I winked before awkwardness overcame me.

"I can't wait."

This was a secret I couldn't keep from Emily. I wasn't sure how she was going to react knowing what we were going to be up to, but I couldn't keep it inside, and I couldn't tell

Randy. Before I knew Emily was a lesbian, I would have bet money that her and Tommy would have been the ones to end up together. They were always together. It was hard on her when we had to move away and leave him behind. In the era before the internet, friendships fell by the wayside when distance was put into the equation.

I arrived at Emily's house with a garlic pizza and a six pack of pumpkin craft beer. It had been a while since we had a girls' day and today felt like as good as any to have one. Today was cause for celebration. Bringing Emily's favorites was also my attempt at a peace offering, in case it was needed when she heard the news.

I gave the door a tap with my foot and waited for Mandy to let me in. It seemed like she was the official greeter in their house. I was about to give the door another kick when it opened. "What are you doing here?" Emily squinted at me as she looked into the sunlight.

"Is this a bad time?" I studied her face to see if I could figure out what was going on. "I can just leave this and get out of here." I lifted the six pack and pizza box.

"No, don't be silly. I'm just nursing this migraine."

"Where's Mandy?"

"She's got a deadline, she's in her writing cave. Come in." She held the door open with her eyes almost closed. "Can we eat in my bedroom? It's dark in there. I can't deal with this light right now."

"Okay, that sounds fun. It'll be like a slumber party." I followed her into her room and set the pizza on her bed. "Do you have any paper plates?"

She waved her hand at me. "Nah, we don't need them. We can be animals, right?"

"Sure. It's never stopped us before." I set the beer on the floor and sat on the edge of her bed. "Are you sure you're up to this? I can take a raincheck."

"Yeah, I'll be fine. I took some meds. They should kick in soon." She joined me on the bed, covering her lap with a leopard print throw.

"What in God's name is that?" I lifted my eyebrow and poked at her blanket.

"This?" She snorted. "This is a gift from Mandy." She put her finger to her lips. "Shh. I love it."

"The things we do for love, huh?" I pulled out a slice of pizza, the aroma of garlic hitting my nose. "I haven't had this since the last time we did this."

"Really?" She took a big bite and closed her eyes. "I don't think I could last that long without this in my belly."

"It's just not the same without you." I twisted the cap off a beer and held it out. "Are you up for this?"

"Damn it, I can't say no." She took the cold bottle out of my hand and pressed it against her lips. "Mmm." She licked her lips clean before taking another drink. "Just what the doctor ordered."

I laughed. "Umm, I don't think so, but hey, whatever works."

"Why do you seem like you're in such a good mood?" Emily tilted her head and looked me up and down. "What's up. Something seems different."

"Well, that's actually why I'm here." I put my slice of pizza down and rolled my shoulders back. "I'm not married. I never was."

"Wow, Tess, that's great news."

"I know. I went to the courthouse this morning to file, and the clerk told me our marriage was never official. She also said Keith and Rebecca's wasn't, either."

"Really? That's strange." Her eyes shot up. "Unless." Her mouth fell open.

"Unless what?"

"Unless he's like a serial killer. Maybe Rebecca wasn't his first victim. Maybe there's been others."

I squinted my eyes to try to comprehend what she was saying. "Wait. You think he's killed others?"

She shrugged her shoulders. "I don't know. Are there any other missing women in the area?"

"I have no idea. I guess I could ask Tommy." My cheeks burned as I said his name. He was who I really wanted to talk about, not Keith. "Speaking of Tommy…"

"I know, congratulations." Emily took another bite of pizza.

"Know what?"

"That you two are an item."

"How in the hell do you know that?"

"Tess, how do you think?" Emily shook her head and smiled.

"I have no clue. I wasn't sure how I was going to spill the

beans, and you already know. It literally just happened this morning."

She twisted around and picked up her phone. "Tommy texted me."

"Oh my god. What a little bitch."

"What? He's my gbff. Or I guess I'm his."

"Gbff?"

"Gay best friend forever." She turned on her phone and scrolled through the screen. "Look, it's even Facebook official."

"Oh my god. What the hell? I didn't think I was dating a twelve-year-old."

Emily's hyena laugh exploded. "Good one." She tossed her head back. "I think it's cute. I'm happy for you two."

"I can't believe he told you before I could. And what's with Facebook? Like seriously? We just made it official two hours ago."

"Welcome to the twenty-first century." She held her hands up. "It's cute. He's excited." She nudged my knee with hers. "Especially for tonight."

I felt my eyes widen. "He didn't."

"He did. I'll be awaiting details."

"Um, no. That's sick. Why do you want details about my sex life?"

"I don't. I'm just glad you're going to have one with a guy who I don't have to worry about murdering you." She took a long swig of her beer before burping. "Relax, Tessa, enjoy your life, laugh at the funny shit. Don't be so uptight."

"I know. I do need to relax a little. It's just so bizarre that my boyfriend is my sister's best friend. I didn't think of how weird it could potentially be." I took a drink, letting the pumpkin ale wash away some of the garlic. "You'd be proud of me. I stood up for myself today."

"That's great, Tess."

"Yeah, the clerk at the courthouse was being a real bitch. I told her off, and she changed her tone. It made me feel powerful, like I was in control for once."

"Good. Remember that feeling and any time you doubt yourself pull it back up. You're a badass."

"I never thought of myself that way before. I guess it is time that I learn how to take care of myself and not be so nice all the time."

Emily held up her bottle. "Let's toast to that." Our bottles clanked together. "I love you, Tess, I'm so proud of you."

"That means a lot coming from my cool, big sister."

"We've been through a lot together. There was no way I was going to let some douche bag take you away from me forever. Speaking of the d-bag, have you heard from him?"

"No. Surprisingly it's been quiet. I half expected him to show up today."

"Maybe he's scared that you're going to talk to the police about what you know."

"I don't think so. I have a feeling whatever he has in store for me is still on the way. I know I'm not free from him yet, not until we find Aunt Becky."

"It sounds so much more heartbreaking when you call her that. I can't get the image of her as a gangly teenager out of my mind."

"Funny you should mention that. She came to me in a dream last night just like that. She pretty much confirmed for me it really is her."

"I just can't wrap my head around it all. What a small world. What are the chances? It's like a made for TV movie."

"I know. If I wasn't the one who found Keith, I would have thought he might have known the connection."

"Twilight zone level shit." Emily finished her beer. "I'm feeling better. It seems like it was just what the doctor ordered." She stretched her arms over her head and rolled her neck. "Hey, did I tell you I did one of those DNA things?"

"No. When did you do that?"

"About a month ago. I should be getting the results back soon."

"What does it tell you?"

"I'm not really sure. Mandy bought one for Randy and decided I should have one, too. I guess it will show me our heritage, like where our ancestors are from."

"Oh, that's cool. I want to do it."

"Tess, I'll share mine with you. We're sisters, I don't think you'll get different results."

I laughed. "I'm so dumb."

"No, you might get different results, if Mom did the nasty with the milkman or something."

"Eww. What's wrong with you?" I bent down and grabbed her another beer. "I still don't understand how it all went down the way it did. I'll never understand why Dad snapped like that."

"I know, I think about that a lot, too. I try to find clues, but I never come up with anything."

"Same." I twisted off the beer cap and took another long drink. "I might need to stick around and sleep this off."

"Yeah, you're going to need your energy tonight." She wiggled her eyebrows at me.

"Oh my god, no. I don't want to talk about this with you." I giggled and tossed a pillow at her. It felt like we were teenagers again. "I've missed this."

"What? Talking about sex?" Emily wiggled her eyebrows again. "Shit, I've got to stop that or my headache is going to come back."

"Serves you right." I stuck my tongue out at her. "No, just spending time with you, sharing my life with you. You know, like we used to."

"I've missed it, too. I'm glad you're back. I can't wait to see what the future holds for you. For us."

"I really need to find Rebecca. It's all I can think about. I don't feel like I can even think about my future until we find her, and Keith is held accountable for what he did to her. It's my driving force."

"I get it." Emily set the empty beer bottle down. "Do you have any idea where she could be? Has she given you any more hints?"

"No, not at all. I haven't seen her again, either. That seems to have been a one-time thing."

"Maybe it's because you were in danger at Keith's and now that you're safe she doesn't have to use as much energy to get your attention."

"I guess, but she must know that I'm not safe while Keith is still out there. I know he hasn't given up on me. I have this feeling that he's going to sneak up on me and hurt me."

"What kind of feeling?"

"You know, the kind that I'm supposed to pay attention to. I just can't shake it. Everywhere I go, I catch myself looking over my shoulder, waiting for him to be there."

"To be honest I'm surprised that he hasn't tried anything else since he had that woman pretend to be me."

"I know. It's like I'm waiting for the other shoe to drop. It's not a matter of if, but when."

"It really sucks that you have to live like that. We need to find Rebecca so you can have your life back and make me an auntie."

"Whoa, slow down. Tommy and I just made things official today, actually only a couple hours ago."

"A middle-aged girl can dream, can't she?" She stretched out on her bed. "Come on, let's watch a movie until you sober up a little."

"It was only two beers, but that doesn't sound like a bad idea." I joined her in bed while she flipped through the channels.

"Hey, look, we can pretend we skipped school and watch these soaps."

"I secretly used to love sleeping on the sofa while Mom had these on in the background while she cleaned."

"Me, too. One time I missed a whole week because I couldn't pull myself away."

"You do realize that the story never really changes? You could have skipped a day a month later and you wouldn't have missed anything." I pulled a blanket over me, tucking it under my chin as I rested against Emily.

"I know. I guess it was more that I liked having the extra time with Mom. Not that I didn't like having you around, it was just different when it was just the two of us."

"I know what you mean. I liked that, too. She was a pretty amazing mom."

"She was. I miss her so much, especially this time of year."

I put my arm around Emily as we fell asleep together. If only for a few minutes we could let the memories surround us. Our childhood was near perfect, until the tragic day in September, when everything fell apart. We had to learn how to live all over again. Luckily, we had our gram and each other.

2 8

"That was incredible." Tommy pulled me close, the heat from our naked bodies made me crave him even more.

"It was. You don't know how long I've wanted to do that." I buried my head in his chest.

"I could tell." He laughed and he rubbed the middle of my back. "This wasn't exactly how I imagined our first date. I'm sorry I couldn't control myself. I want more from you than *that*."

"Don't be sorry, I was a willing participant. I wanted it more than you did, maybe. Let's do it again so I can prove it to you." I lifted my head to kiss his lips. Goosebumps covered my skin as he ran his fingers over my side.

"Give this old boy a little time to recharge." He kissed the top of my head. "Do you want to spend the night? I'd love to wake up next to your beautiful face."

"I'd love to, but I can't. I don't want Randy to know that we're dating."

"Are you sure he's not into you? Why would he care if you stayed here with me?"

"It's a long story." I let out a sigh as I tried to push Randy out of my head so I could enjoy being with Tommy for as long as I could before I went home. "Do you want to fool around a little more?" I kissed his chest before climbing back on top of him, straddling him as my hair cascaded around his face. I licked his lips and felt his excitement build as I pressed my body into his. "Come on, one more time?" I sat up and put my hands behind me and stroked the inside of his thighs.

He sat up to kiss me. "Ah, Tessa, I'm exhausted. I've got an early morning tomorrow."

I took the hint and got off of him. I covered myself with the flannel sheet and found my clothes I had taken off as soon as Tommy gave me the tour of his studio apartment. I pulled my sweater over my head and dropped the sheet on the floor when I found my jeans. "Yeah, you're right. I'm tired, too." I sucked back the tears so he couldn't see how bad his rejection had stung.

"Tess, don't be upset. I had a great time. I'm just super tired. I'd love it if you stayed here with me tonight." He rubbed the side of the bed I had just vacated.

"I'm not upset. I'm tired. It's been a long day for me, too." I gathered my bra and socks and stuffed them into my jacket pocket before putting it on.

Tommy got out of bed and pulled his sweatpants on. "It feels like you're mad." He put his arms around me and rested his head on my shoulder. "The thing is, I'd love to do it again. Hell, I'd stay up all night, but I don't have any more condoms. I wasn't expecting to make love with you tonight. I'm just not prepared."

"That's the only reason?" Relieved to know it wasn't me he

was pushing away, but the prospect of an unplanned pregnancy put me at ease.

"I swear. It felt so good. It's all I'm going to be able to think about until we do it again." Tommy yawned. "And next time I'll be rested, and we can make it last even longer."

"Next time." I smiled. "I like the sound of that."

"And next time maybe you can get permission to spend the night."

"It's not like that. It's hard to explain. He just wants to protect me."

"In that case, I appreciate his efforts. I'd like to spend some more time with him. You know, get to know him, have a beer with him. Ask him permission to date his daughter."

I gave Tommy a smack on his chest. "You're pretty funny, aren't you?" I gave him a kiss, letting my lips linger a little longer before I pulled away. "Goodnight, Mr. Peters."

"Good night, Tessa. I can't wait to read what you write in your diary about me." Tommy held the door open as he watched me get in my car.

Rebecca's journal. I had forgotten that Emily had it. Knowing what I do now, I wanted to read what she had to say. Did she talk about us? About her brother? Before I pulled out of Tommy's driveway, I sent a text to Emily. "Just leaving lover boy's now. I'll let him be the one to kiss and tell. Just wanted to be the first one to text you." I hit send and sent a follow up text. "Hey, do you still have Rebecca's journal? I'd like to read it." I tossed my phone in my purse and put my car in drive. The drive home was over a half an hour.

I had time to think about my future with Tommy, who seemed just as eager to take things to the next level as I did. It felt good knowing I had a man in my life who wanted to protect me. I knew Randy had good intentions, but I knew I could trust Tommy.

The uneasy feeling of knowing Keith could strike at any moment took over my serenity. I'd been out of the house for a few weeks now and he only tried to assassinate me once. I giggled when I realized how ridiculous that statement was. It wasn't funny, though, I knew it was a distinct possibility.

The gravel crunched under my tires when I made the turn into Randy's long driveway. The deeper into the woods I went, the safer I felt. I liked how secluded we were. It might be the only thing that had kept me alive. That, and Randy's overprotectiveness.

Randy was sitting in the dark at the kitchen table when I opened the door. I jumped back and placed my hand to my heart. "Jesus Christ, you scared the shit out of me."

"Good." Randy sat with his legs crossed and arms folded. "Do you have any idea what time it is?"

"Yeah, sorry. I left you a message to let you know I was going to be home late."

"Yes, I'm aware." His lips puckered as his leg bounced. "I didn't expect you to be this late."

"Hey, I'm here now. I'm sorry if I worried you. How was your day?" I pulled a chair out to join him at the table.

"Awful." He looked away and I noticed a tear streaming down his cheek.

"Oh, Randy, what's wrong?" I hesitated before I scooted closer to him and placed my hand on his knee. "What happened?"

"My ex came by today to get the rest of his stuff."

"I'm sorry," I said softly.

"So am I. I didn't think he was really going to be gone for

good, you know? I figured we'd fight and make up like we always have done." Randy sniffled. "I was just so lonely today, and then you never showed up."

"You should have told me, I would have come home."

"I didn't want to bother you." He turned his head to look away.

"Randy, I told you, we're family. If you need me I'll be here."

"I'm sorry to be such a little bitch." Randy pushed the tears off his face with the sleeve from his bathrobe.

"Stop it. You're not a little bitch. This shit is hard. It's even harder to go through it alone. But Randy, you're not alone. If you need me all you have to do is ask." I squeezed his knee before wiping the tears out of my eyes.

Randy held out his arms. "Can I have a hug?"

I reached over from my chair and bumped heads with him when I put my arms around him. "Get up so I can really hug you."

He stood up and fell into my arms. "Will you sleep with me tonight? I really need someone to hold me." He started to sob. His body heaved against mine.

I ran my hand on his neck as he continued to cry. "Of course, I will." This would be hard to explain to Tommy, but I didn't see any other option. "Let me take a shower and I'll be in to join you."

Randy took a step back and gave me a once over. "Why? You just had one this morning. Why do you need another one? I need you."

"Tommy." Embarrassment heated my cheeks. "I mean Randy, I've had a long day, I'd just feel better after a shower, that's all."

Randy crossed his arms and sniffled. "Just as I thought." He turned and stormed away.

"What? What's just as you thought?" I took a few steps toward him and stopped. What was he even talking about? There's no way he could have known what I had done earlier. Besides, so what if he did? I was a grown woman. Tommy was right, I didn't need Randy's permission. Randy was like an unstable jealous teen lover, but we were neither.

In my bedroom I sat on my bed and looked around the room. Guilt flooded me as I thought about how much Randy had given me. He saved my life. Without him I may have become Keith's next victim. I owed him at least a night of cuddles. I shook off the cringe factor that thought left me with. But if he needed me, regardless of how creepy it was, I needed to be there for him.

I slipped on my coziest pajama pants and an oversized sweatshirt before I put my hair up in a messy bun. I slid my slippers on and grabbed my phone to keep me occupied while Randy snored himself to sleep. I noticed Emily had responded to the text I sent her when I left Tommy's place. With the commotion with Randy, I had forgotten all about my request.

"I'm going to need more details!" She ended the message with a winking emoji. "Shit, I completely forgot about Rebecca's journal. Give me a few more days with it and I'll get it back to you."

With the amount of excitement Emily had when she left with the thing, I would have expected her to have read it five times by now. It seemed like there was something she wasn't telling me. Doubt crept in as I thought back to what Randy said about not being able to trust anyone. I stared down at the messages and felt unsure of anything. That feeling Gram always told us to listen to was screaming at me to listen. But Emily?

I climbed in bed next to Randy and pulled the covers around me before settling in behind him. I reached up and kissed his cheek before nestling into the pillow next to him.

"What are you doing here? Don't you need to go wash Tommy off you?" Randy rolled over, taking the covers with him.

I inched closer to him and tugged at the covers. I draped my arm over his belly. "That's gross. I'm here because I love you. And I think I need this as much as you do."

Randy put his hand on top of mine and gave it a squeeze. "Fine." He made a few grunting noises and backed his body closer to mine. "I love you, too."

As we drifted off to sleep together, I wasn't sure which one of us needed this more. It felt good to be able to give back to him, but it was also nice to feel needed. Our friendship was not one I ever would have imagined, but some of the best things in life fall into our laps when we need them most.

I tried to shake off the doubts I was holding onto about Emily. I needed to know where they were coming from. It had to be a message from someone, and it was one I needed to listen to. If I couldn't trust Emily, I might as well not exist. I thought she felt the same way about me.

I took the last drink of coffee and stretched my arms up over my head. Sleeping with Randy left me with a stiff neck and sore shoulders. I wasn't sure of the last time I was the spooner instead of the spoonee, but it didn't agree with me. I rolled my shoulders to try to loosen the knot. A hot shower would be the cure.

I brought my phone in with me to play some music. I needed something to focus on so my thoughts didn't carry me away. The vibration of an incoming text pushed me out of the music app. I opened the message, it was Tommy. "Good morning beautiful. I had fun last night." My body throbbed as I thought about last night, the last night before I ended up in Randy's bed.

"Me, too. I can't wait for a replay."

"Not a replay. I know we can do it better… and longer."

I sent a wink and kissing emoji and picked Sheryl Crow to sing away my worries. I sang along to some of my favorite songs from the 90s and let the hot water cascade onto my back. There was nothing a few nostalgic songs couldn't fix.

When I got out of the shower, I noticed there was another text from Tommy. I wrapped myself in a fluffy towel and dried my hair before I read the message. "I want to show you something cool. Meet me at the cabin ASAP."

I stared at the screen, confused by what he meant. What cabin was he talking about? The doubt I had pushed aside about Emily was now replaced by doubt about Tommy. Just when things started to feel *right*. Another text came in as I held the phone in my hand. "254 Wildflower Lane, Drakestown."

My shoulders fell and my body relaxed. I hadn't missed anything; he just hadn't finished the text. Thoughts that he sent the message to the wrong girl faded away with the new information. "OK, getting dressed now. I'll be there in about forty minutes." Drakestown was on the other side of Drakesville. It was more rural and had many seasonal camps.

I took the clothes I had picked out for the day into my room and found something else. I was hoping Tommy was going to have a surprise for me, the one he couldn't offer me last night. I traded my bra and panties for my sexiest black lace lingerie and slid on a button up top, leaving the top two buttons undone. I finished it with my favorite jeans and returned to the bathroom to put some mascara on.

I typed in the address Tommy gave me into my phone and placed it in the cupholder so I could hear the directions. My body trembled at the thought of what was to come. I imagined how good it would feel to be in Tommy's arms again and was excited I wouldn't have to wait much longer.

A feeling of dread settled into me and apprehension replaced the giddy feelings I had just been filled with. I turned the radio up and sang along to Alanis Morissette. I was close enough to the camp that I didn't need to listen to the directions any longer. I needed to shake whatever was trying to take away my joy and make me doubt everything good in my life. I danced along to the lyrics and tapped my hands on the steering wheel.

I turned my music down as I pulled my car onto Wildflower Lane. The gravel spun under my tires as the road slowly disappeared. The further in it was obvious this was one of the roads that only ATVs and snow machines traveled on. I parked my car next to a mailbox with 186 painted on the side. I pulled out my phone and sent Tommy a text. "I'm almost there. Left my car where the road ended. I'm going to walk the rest of the way. See you soon." After I hit send, I put my phone into my purse and took a last look in the mirror. I put on lip-gloss before getting out of the car and continued my journey on foot.

The crunch of dead leaves under my shoes sent chills up my spine. With just the sound of my thoughts the feeling of doom circled back, encasing me in a cloud of self-doubt. I pulled my phone out of my purse to play some music and check if Tommy had responded. There was no cell service. When I opened my music app none of my music would play. The songs I had just listened to said they were not downloaded. I tossed my phone back into my purse and continued on the path.

There hadn't been any more houses yet. I looked ahead of

me and saw the path continued straight up. There were no other cabins in sight. The hair on the back of my neck stood up when I heard the rustling in the woods beside me. I started singing the songs from my morning to try to channel the excitement I had been feeling.

The wind began to blow as I made my way closer to the top of the hill. My hair blew out of place, landing in my face making it harder to see. *Come on Tommy, come find me.* I tried to telepathically communicate with him because I didn't want to be alone anymore. Everything inside of me told me to turn around, but my feet kept pulling me forward. *Just a few more steps.* I knew it was going to be worth it once I reached Tommy's cabin. I tried to replace my fear with the pleasure that awaited me.

When I climbed to the top of the tiny mountain, I saw a mailbox on the left side of the road. I squinted my eyes and saw 254 in reflective numbers stuck to the side. The breath I had been holding released from my lungs. I increased my pace and jogged the rest of the way. I couldn't wait to feel Tommy's arms around me.

I walked down the path to the door and looked around the yard. An ATV was parked by the front door. Frustration sent a jolt through me when I thought about how easy Tommy's trip up to the cabin was. He was going to have to pay for this. I smiled as I thought about what it was going to be worth.

My knuckles tapped the door lightly before I turned the knob. "Hey Tommy, you better make this worth my wild." Paralyzed by fear I couldn't take my hand off the doorknob.

"Oh, don't you worry, I haven't had any complaints yet." Jeff stood in front of me. He had a gun pointed at my chest.

My eyes darted across the room trying to make sense of

what was happening. Keith sat at the kitchen table, a gun laid in front of him. I took a deep breath and closed my eyes. This was going to be how I lost my life. A gunshot. Just like my mom. And my dad. And my Aunt Becky. *Poor Emily.*

No. This was not how my life was going to end. I stepped into the cabin and walked over to Keith. "Hey, baby. I've missed you so much. I love you."

Keith held his hand out and I shimmied my way onto his lap. "Why'd you leave me then?"

I turned to the side and kissed him holding his face in my hands. I moved my hands down his body and hovered over his lap. I felt the erection forming in his pants, and I knew it was working. "Baby, let me make it up to you." With one hand I unbuttoned his jeans and the other I held his face close to mine while I kissed him.

"What the fuck do you think you're doing Keith? This isn't part of the fucking plan." Jeff slammed the door shut.

"Come on baby." I whispered in Keith's ear and nibbled it before I slid off his lap on to my knees and unzipped his pants. "I want to taste you."

"I've missed you so much Tessa." Keith leaned back in the chair and spread his legs.

"Are you fucking kidding me?" I felt Jeff behind me as I took Keith's penis into my mouth. "I don't want to watch this shit."

"Just give me a minute." Keith leaned back in the chair, his body shuddering under my touch.

"This is fucked up." I heard the door shut when Jeff left the cabin.

I picked my head up and made eye contact with Keith. "I want you to make love to me." I unbuttoned my blouse and let my cleavage spill out. I brought his hand to my breast while I kicked off my shoes and undid my jeans. I bent down to pull them off the rest of the way and straddled Keith in the chair.

I hovered above Keith's erection and pressed my breasts into his face. "I've missed this. I want you back, baby."

"I've missed you, too." Keith pushed me onto him, and I held his gaze as I slowly rode him.

"I want to come home with you." I kissed him and bit his lip as he pulled away.

"You can't," Keith moaned.

"Come on, baby. I *need* you."

"I need you, too."

"Then what's the problem?" I looked into his eyes and slid back down onto him. "I'll do whatever you want."

"Jeff won't let me keep you."

"If he's the only thing stopping you, I have an idea." I kissed his neck, keeping him inside me. "Why don't you kill him?"

Keith's body tensed under me. "I can't."

"Why not? Does he do this to you?" I reached under me and ran my fingernails down his thighs.

Keith's body trembled under me. I knew he couldn't resist my touch. "Baby, it's not like that."

"It seems pretty simple to me." I placed his hands on my breasts and slowly glided up and down on his shaft. "He can't make you feel like this, can he?"

Keith closed his eyes and put his head back as he gripped onto my sides. "Oh fuck. Oh fuck." I felt him come and kissed his neck.

"Come on, baby. Do it for me?"

I stepped off of him and pulled on my panties and jeans,

not taking my eyes off of him. The gun was in his hand and his eyes met mine. He set the gun back down and stood up to pull his pants back on. He came over and wrapped me in a hug. "I'll do it for you, baby. You promise you won't leave me?"

"I promise."

The door opened and Jeff walked in. "Are you done?" He shook his head and lifted his gun and aimed it at me. "You are a dirty little whore." He snickered and a sinister smile spread across his face. "Just like Tommy said."

My heart dropped. *Tommy was in on this, too?* He had to have been. Defeat crashed over me. Fucking Tommy. Randy was right all along.

"Tommy? Who's Tommy?" The anger in Keith's voice took away every ounce of hope I had. It was over. My life was over.

"Do you want to tell him? Or should I?" Jeff tossed his head back and laughed.

My eyes went from Jeff's gun to Keith's. There was no fixing this. No magic word or trick that could buy me any time. "Tommy's a friend of Em's. They went to school together."

"Really? That's all?" Jeff's laughter returned. "You believe this shit?"

"Who is he really?" The vein in Keith's forehead throbbed, his face turning redder by the second.

"He's just a friend. You know I love you. I always have." My attempt to calm Keith failed. He fired a shot into the ceiling.

"You're fucking him, aren't you?" Keith squinted his eyes as he raised his hand to point the gun at me.

"No. I'm not. He's just a friend, I swear." I held my hands up.

"Then why are you dressed like that?" Keith used his gun to point at my outfit.

"Because she was coming here to fuck his brains out. Isn't that right, Tessa?"

"No. That's not true." A tear slid down my face.

"Aw, isn't that cute. She cried just like her mama. I thought you were going to be different, but it looks like all you Blake bitches are the same." Jeff raised his gun back up, pointing it in my face.

"How do you know my mom?" I turned my head to look past the gun.

"You don't know?" Jeff slowly shook his head. "Oh, that's right. Everyone thinks Kenny did it. That fucker always took all the credit."

Anger pushed out every bit of fear I had left. "What did you just say?" I pushed my heated breath through my nostrils as my head turned to look at Jeff and then back at Keith.

"Should I tell her? Or do you want the honors little brother?" Jeff put his arm down as he waited for Keith to answer.

"Jeff, shut the fuck up. Not now." Keith dropped his head when he lowered his gun.

"What in the actual fuck is going on? What are you saying?" The words Jeff just said hadn't yet penetrated my brain. It was too much to comprehend. Too much to digest.

"Since Keith is too much of a pussy, I guess it's on me, just like everything else fucking is." Jeff pushed his gun into the back of his waistband and cleared his throat. "Where should I begin?" He cracked his knuckles and leaned against the kitchen counter. "So, you see, a long, long time ago your whore of a grandmother fucked our father." He pointed to himself and then Keith. "She got pregnant with a little bitch,

Rebecca." He pointed to a rolled-up garbage bag wrapped with duct tape in the corner of the living room. "This is what you were looking for, isn't it? You were so close. But what's that saying? Almost doesn't count?" Jeff threw his head back and laughed.

"How do you know my dad?" I demanded.

"Kenny? Well, he was our baby sister's favorite brother." Jeff crossed his arms against his chest. "How do you think it made her other brothers feel knowing we could never compete?"

"I don't understand." I looked at Keith and back to Jeff. "You married your sister?" I squinted my eyes as I looked at Keith.

"Oh, don't be such a prude. Do you want to hear the rest of the story or not?"

I tried to wipe the disgust off my face and nodded unable to connect any of the dots that Jeff was giving me.

"Rebecca was always talking about Kenny this, Kenny that. The last time she called Dad she was bragging about all the money her perfect big brother had saved up to put a down payment on a new house. Dad had to rub it in and make sure we knew what kind of fuck ups he thought we were. What was it he said?" Jeff looked over at Keith. "The little bitch told him it was about twenty thousand. Keith and I needed some money, so." He held his hands up at his side. "What were we supposed to do?"

"You killed my parents for twenty fucking thousand dollars?" My lungs burned from the rage boiling inside me.

"No. I killed them for three hundred dollars. It seems that little Rebecca was also a storyteller. She made it up to make

Kenny sound better than us, but he was more of a loser than we ever could be."

"How? How'd you do it?"

"Keith and I called Kenny and told him about a piece of land for sale. When he showed up, your mother was with him, even after we specifically told him to come alone." Jeff shook his head. "Your mom begged for her life when she saw my gun. She cried like a little bitch, just like you."

"You killed my mom?"

"Are you even listening?" Jeff's hand went to his waistband and rested on his gun. "Do you want to hear the rest of the story or should I just get this over with?"

"I'm listening."

Jeff took his hand off his gun and stepped away from the counter to join Keith at the table. He clapped his hands together. "Pop. That was the last thing your mom heard."

The emotion spilled out of my eyes as I imagined how afraid my mom must have been. I squeezed my eyes tight to try to push them back inside so Jeff couldn't see how upset I was.

"Kenny tried to come after me but turns out I was no match for him. He wasn't as great as little Becky made him out to be. He wasn't even man enough to save his wife."

"It wasn't good enough that you killed him, you had to make the whole world think he was some kind of monster?"

"A monster?" Jeff's mouth hung open and his hand went to his chest. "Does that make me the real monster?"

"Yeah, it does." With nothing left to lose I couldn't hold back. "You're a piece of shit. Who does that kind of thing? And for a few dollars?"

Jeff pointed at Keith. "That piece of shit right there. Why don't you tell her how you killed her precious Aunt Becky?"

"Fuck you, Jeff." Keith dropped his head and rested it in his hand.

"I think I'm a little late for that, isn't that right Tessie?" Jeff smirked at me.

"There's really not a lot to say. I mean, Rebecca is dead, I did it. That's all really." Keith lifted his shoulders.

"Oh, there's more to the story. Don't hold out on her. Tell Tessie how she got to enjoy her Auntie's sloppy seconds."

"Would you shut the fuck up?" Keith rubbed his forehead. "Enough, okay?"

"No. You're not getting out of this that easy." Jeff got up and kicked at the bag in the living room. "Should we open it?"

"Jesus fucking Christ. Just fucking stop. What's the point to all of this?" Keith picked up his gun and rubbed his fingers over the barrel.

The sound of plastic ripping made my stomach drop. "Do you think she wants to come out and play? How about that incest baby? Do you want to bounce him on your knee, Daddy?" Jeff bent down over the bag and pulled more of it open.

"Stop it. You know I loved her." Keith's hand trembled as he pointed his gun at his brother. "I said fucking stop it." As Jeff's hand went to his back, Keith fired. Jeff fell to the floor. Keith stood over him and emptied the gun into him. Keith started to sob as he stood over his dead brother. "I said fucking stop."

I took a few steps forward deciding what my next move should be. To comfort Keith or to get Jeff's gun before Keith did. I closed my eyes and pulled up the image of Rebecca, the same one from all of my dreams. Her beautiful white gown blowing in the breeze and smile on her face. *"Go to him."* I heard her say.

I took her instruction and stood behind Keith. I put my hand on his back and rubbed it. "It's okay." Keith turned and pulled me into him and broke down in my arms. I rubbed the back of his neck and he cried. "Don't worry. I still love you, Keith." A calm came over me and I felt like the worst had passed.

Keith pulled out of my arms and looked down at me. "I don't believe you." His face was stained with panic. The same panic I had felt moments before.

"Baby, I love you."

Keith looked down at Jeff's body that was sprawled over Rebecca's remains and then back to me. "I know you're lying."

The calm I had channeled remained. Something told me it was going to be alright. I smiled and held out my hand for Keith. "No, I do love you. I always have. I don't care what you've done." The words that left my mouth didn't sound like me, but they kept coming. "You're everything I ever wanted in a man. You're strong and handsome. You're great in bed." I bit my bottom lip and took a step toward him.

"You really think so?" A smile returned to Keith's face.

The door of the cabin opened slowly. Tommy stood in the entrance holding his gun. He held his finger to his lips and stepped inside. Keith's back was to the door, he hadn't heard Tommy enter. Tommy motioned for me to step to the side. I took Keith's hands and rubbed my thumbs over them before I gave them one last squeeze and stepped out of the way.

Keith fell to the floor. Tommy shot him in the back of the head. My nightmare was over.

Tommy rushed toward me and I backed away, still unsure who to trust. "Tessa are you okay?"

"How did you know I was here?"

"When you sent the text telling me you were almost here I couldn't figure it out. I texted you back and when you didn't answer I knew something was up. One of the guys helped me retrieve the deleted texts. As soon as I saw the address, I knew Jeff had gotten into my phone."

"How'd you know that?" I crossed my arms, tightly hugging myself.

"Because I've been here with him before with some of the other guys." Tommy took another step closer to me.

"So, you weren't in on this?"

"Tessa. You know me better than that." He held his hand out for me to take. "I love you."

I took his hand and my emotions spilled out. Tommy pulled my body close to his and held me. "I thought you were part of this." I buried my head into his chest. "I'm sorry."

"You have nothing to be sorry about. I can understand why you'd think that."

"I didn't know what to think. I'm so happy you're here." I squeezed him tight, not ever wanting to let go of him.

"I'd like to know how you were able to send me that text when you got here. There is absolutely no cell service on this road at all. It's like a miracle."

"Rebecca. She saved my life. She must have made sure I was able to send it to you." I dropped my head and pressed my eyes closed. "She's over there."

"You found her?"

"I guess I did." I wiped the tears off my face. "Fucking Jeff. He must have seen the map I sent you."

"You never sent me the map. You gave it to me when I got to Webster trail."

I shook my head. "Remember that picture I sent that you said you never received?"

Tommy nodded. "It was of the map?"

"Yup. How did Jeff get access to your phone all the time?"

"I didn't know he did. I guess I just left it on my desk or in the cruiser."

"And you don't have a password on it?"

He shrugged his shoulders. "I didn't think I needed one. I don't have anything to hide."

"It all makes sense now." I thought back to everything Rebecca had shown me and tried to tell me. Every piece added up. "The fucking mustard."

Tommy tilted his head. "Mustard?"

"Rebecca brought me to this place in one of my dreams. There was a plate with just the crust from a sandwich." I walked over to the table and saw the plate. "And a napkin covered in mustard." I held up the crumpled-up piece of paper stained yellow. "She did show me where they took her, I just didn't know what she was trying to tell me."

"Wow, Tess, that's unbelievable." He wrapped his arms around me and kissed the top of my head. "I'm so glad your aunt was looking out for you."

"It's all so surreal. I wish I could have saved her." I closed my eyes and saw Rebecca smiling back at me.

"You saved her now. That's something. Now she can have the funeral and burial she deserves."

I looked up at Tommy and smiled. "You're right. She's free now, and thanks to you, so am I."

"No, that's all you. You're the hero here."

"No." I looked at Keith's dead body on the floor. "If you hadn't have come when you did, I know he would have killed me. I was going to get Jeff's gun, but I wasn't sure if Keith had fired all of his rounds into him. If there was even one bullet left, I would have been the dead one. Rebecca told me to go to Keith. I had no idea how I was going to get out of that mess. I was out of ideas."

"Well, it doesn't matter who killed him, all that matters is that you're safe."

"Thank you, Tommy." I took his face in my hands and gave him a kiss. "Me, too." The smile on his face told me he knew what I was talking about.

Emily, Mandy, and Randy were waiting for us when Tommy brought me home from the police station. I hadn't spoken to any of them since everything happened at the cabin. "Don't you ever scare me like that again Tess." Randy pushed past Emily and Mandy and raced to me. He squeezed me so hard I thought my eyes were going to pop out of my head.

"Yeah, what he said." Emily joined us in the driveway. "I'm just so glad you're okay." Emily pushed Randy off of me and threw her arms around me neck. "You don't know how scared I was."

"I'm sorry. I know." I closed my eyes to try to see Rebecca, but she wouldn't come.

"Actually, you don't know." Emily took a step back and looked into my eyes. "That journal." She closed her eyes and inhaled deeply. "If I had read the whole thing when you gave it to me, none of this would have ever happened."

"What do you mean?" I saw the look of betrayal in Emily's eyes.

"Let's go inside and I'll tell you." Emily took my hand and led me into the kitchen where everyone took a seat around the table. Fresh baked chocolate chip cookies and banana bread were ready to be served.

"You've been busy." I gave Randy a smile.

"Yeah, well I bake when I'm stressed." Randy sat with his elbows on the table and his face in his hands.

"I don't understand why you were stressed when you all knew I was okay?" I looked around the table and studied everyone's face.

"That's what I'm about to tell you." Emily pushed her chair closer to mine and took my hand. "I just want to apologize for being a shitty sister. I could have prevented this if I would have read that fucking journal like I said I was going to." She hung her head.

"It's okay, Em. I'm fine, and Rebecca has been found." I pushed a tear off her cheek. "I've got something I need to tell you, too."

"Let me go first? I want to get this off my chest." Emily held up Rebecca's journal. "All of the answers were in here the whole time." She flipped through the pages. "She went through hell." She opened to a bookmarked page and began to read. "Ever since Keith found out I was pregnant he's been acting funny. Even though we talked about having a family, he's insisting I have an abortion. There's no way in hell I'd ever do that."

I knew what she was going to say, but I stayed quiet and let her continue.

"There's more." Her hands trembled as she turned the page. "Keith introduced me to his friend Jeff today. He seems like a nice guy. There's something about him that feels familiar. I can't place it, though. It felt like Keith wanted me to start dating him or something. It was weird." Emily turned the page. "I was right. Keith gave Jeff my email and we've been talking. He's been flirting with me, and the truth is, I kind of like the attention. He listens to me talk about the baby. He thinks I should leave Keith. I told him about all the times Keith has hurt me. He told me he knows how to make him stop." Emily paused to wipe her eyes dry.

"Do you want to take a break?" Mandy pulled her chair closer to Emily and rubbed her back.

"No, I need to keep going." Emily pushed out her breath and continued reading. "I told Keith that Jeff thinks he should be a man. That didn't go well, he threw me into the wall. Again. This time I didn't need to go to the hospital, though. It's over between us. Jeff can give me what I need. He told me he would help raise the baby." Emily closed her eyes before she turned the page.

"Take your time." Mandy pushed the hair out of Emily's face.

Emily's voice trembled. "I told Keith I was leaving him for Jeff. He got so angry. He told me Jeff was my brother. At first, I thought he was lying to try to make me not leave him, but he knew things he shouldn't have. Keith pushed me into the wall and tried to choke me. When I fell to the ground, he kicked me in the stomach. He told me he was my brother, too."

I bowed my head and squeezed my eyes closed. I knew what was coming.

Emily turned the page. "I called my mom and asked her why she didn't tell me. Why did she let me marry my brother? She said she didn't know. She told me my dad was promiscuous and there may be others out there. She warned me if Keith was anything like my dad, I should be careful. She doesn't know about all the times he's already almost killed me. I feel so sick. I don't know what to do. I confronted Keith about the whole incest situation. I needed to know if he knew we were related, or if it was a surprise for him, too. He told me he knew. He knew who I was, and he found me so him and Jeff could kill me. He said he fell in love with me and couldn't help himself. He didn't mean for it to go this far. I'm furious."

Emily looked over at me and reached for my hand. "The next part is going to be hard to hear."

"I have a feeling I know what she's going to say." I squeezed her hand before she pulled it away to turn the page.

"Keith told me the reason he wanted to find me was because him and Jeff thought I knew about Kenny. I had no idea what he was talking about. He thought I was playing dumb, but I didn't have any idea what he was about to tell me. Jeff killed Kenny and Rosie. All this time we thought Kenny did it, but he was set up. Who does that? I'm going to pack my stuff and move back home with mom tomorrow while Keith is at work." Emily set the journal on the table and turned her head to look at me. "That was her last entry. They must have killed her before she had a chance to get away."

"That's what I was going to tell you. Jeff told me right before Keith killed him."

"I don't understand why he would have killed them. And all this time we were made to believe Dad was a monster. All these years I felt like I didn't even know my own father."

"I know." I closed my eyes to stop the emotions from spilling out. "Jeff said Rebecca had told him that Dad had money –twenty thousand dollars saved up to buy a house. He said he and Keith needed the money, so they lured Dad out to look at the land and shot Mom and then Dad. Then they made it look like a murder-suicide."

"All these years." Emily shook her head.

"I know. It makes more sense now, though. Dad was who we thought he was. He was never someone who snapped. He really did love us; all of us."

"It's all so twisted. Who in their right mind marries their sister? And then gets her pregnant?"

"Right? I can't even imagine what Rebecca went through." The image of Rebecca's remains at the cabin sent a chill up my spine.

"That's why she led you to Keith. She wanted us to know the truth about Dad."

I turned to look at Emily and thought back to it all. "You're right. She was the reason that I found the ad for the perfect used car in a town I had never been to. And then met Keith and we fell in love in record time. The dreams. All of the dreams where she gave me messages, even when I didn't understand, she knew I would when I was ready. Then all of the activity in the house, knocking over boxes, spilling out pictures. The map that she put in my box of books because she knew he was going to take the tote of evidence. The late-night visit also makes sense now, too. She was desperate for me to not tell him about the baby. And the baby—I bet she was the one who messed with the test."

"Maybe she thought you were related, too." Randy added as he bit at his fingernail.

"No, I think she didn't want him to get his hands on an innocent life. He was evil and so was Jeff."

"I had no idea what a piece of shit Jeff was. I'm so sorry I introduced you to him the other day." Tommy cracked his knuckles. "If the prick wasn't dead, I'd kill him."

"That's what I'm talking about." Randy held his hand up for a high-five. Tommy obliged. "I was wrong about him, Tess. You've got a good one here."

"I sure do. I don't know what I would do without him, without any of you." Joy replaced the sorrow I had been drowning in. "You're my family now. I never want to lose any of you."

"While we were waiting for you to get back from the police station, I logged onto Ancestry.com and did some digging." Emily took out a piece of paper from her pocket and unfolded it. "Rebecca's dad, Howie, was a man whore." She handed me the piece of paper. "That's a list of all of his kids that were listed. Most likely there's more."

"Holy shit. There's at least twenty-five names here." I scanned the list. "I bet it was one of their sisters that was waiting for me at the café that day."

"Oh wow, you're probably right. That would explain why that woman looked so much like Rebecca." Emily shook her head. "I can't believe so many of those siblings are that evil. That's probably the reason Grammy Blake didn't try to stay with Howie. He was probably just as bad."

I handed Tommy the list. "Do you recognize any of these names?"

He scanned the list. "No, but if they're anything like Jeff and Keith they probably have different last names, too."

"Do you think any of them will come after me?" The thought took my breath away. Just when I thought I was free.

"I doubt it. They're probably glad their dick brothers are dead. And chances are they don't know each other. It looks like most of them are half siblings. Rebecca didn't know Keith or Jeff were her brothers, so that tells me they probably don't hang out at family reunions together." Mandy picked the list off the table where Tommy had put it and started counting the names. "Thirty-three kids. You've got to give that dirty bastard credit."

"Gross. Who sleeps with that many women?" I stuck my tongue out at the thought.

Emily looked over at Mandy and they shared a smile. "This is the perfect time to change the subject. We weren't going to say anything, not after the day you've had but I don't want to keep secrets from any of you." Emily held up her left hand, a diamond ring sparkled under the kitchen light. "I said yes."

"Oh my god, Em, I'm so happy for you two." My eyes filled with tears; the kind that get pushed out from a full heart. "This is the best news to end a lousy day with."

"I know a good one when I see one, too." Emily's smile made everything better for me. I hadn't seen her this happy since we lost our parents all those years ago.

"Does this mean you're moving to California?" I asked hoping for the answer I needed to hear.

"No, not unless all of you come with us. There are too many important people here, we can't leave any of you behind. Maybe we'll go there for our honeymoon."

Randy was the only one at the table not wearing a smile. His lips in a tight, straight line. I knew he was hurting. I got out of my chair and sat on his lap. "What are you doing?" A smile spread across his face.

I reached up and kissed his cheek. "I'm letting you know how much I love you. How much we all love you. You know

Mr. Right is out there. When you stop trying, he'll come to you."

"Doubtful." Randy tried to push me off his lap. "Come on, Tessa, you're hurting me with your boney ass. If you'd eat the cookies I bake you, we wouldn't have this problem."

"You're a goofball. But I'm serious. Stop trying so hard. You're one of the best guys I know. Someone is going to snatch you up." I jumped off his lap and returned to my chair.

"This might sound crazy." Tommy leaned back in his chair. "But one of my good friends, Ben, just went through a breakup. He's the nicest guy." He winked and looked at Randy. "I think you'd be cute together."

"Well, what are you waiting for? Give that bitch my number." Randy's mood changed at the prospect.

"I'm exhausted. It's been a hell of a day." I covered a yawn. "I really hate to leave you all, but I'm going to fall asleep out here. I love you all. Every one of you." I gave Emily a tight hug. "I'm so happy for you. I can't wait to help you plan your wedding." I whispered in her hear and kissed her cheek.

"I love you. Thank you for being my sister and sharing this journey with me."

Tommy stood up and gave me a hug. "Sweet dreams, Tessa. I'll call you in the morning." He kissed my cheek quickly and pulled away.

"What in the world was that?" Randy raised his eyebrows. My heart sank as I tried to think of a way to explain away the relationship. "A real man doesn't kiss a woman he loves like that." He smirked and shook his head. "Why don't you stay here tonight with her? I'm sure she could use someone to cuddle with." Randy winked at me before standing up and stretching. "I'm beat. I think I'm going to go listen to a book on tape or something. You know, so I won't be able to hear anything."

I fell asleep in Tommy's arms. For the first time since my parents died, I felt safe. There were no uncertainties or unknowns hanging over my head. I had people I loved and trusted. I had a family.

Rebecca stood in the same field of wildflowers we played in together the other night. She held a baby boy on her hip and bounced him. His giggles surrounded us, and I could feel my heart smile. "Thank you, Tessa, for saving us."

"But I didn't save you. I was too late."

"Nonsense. There was nothing you could do to stop them, but you helped free us. Because of you, we get to go home." A bright yellow light began to form around them.

"Will you tell my dad I know the truth?"

"No, but you can." Her cheeks lifted into a gorgeous smile. "I love you, kid. I always knew you were special." She turned to walk away. She turned around before she entered the light. "You're going to make a great mother someday." She kissed the baby on the top of his head. "Just don't forget who you are. You've got a real gift you need to use. You're one of the lucky ones." She turned and faded out of sight.

I sat on the ground, the grass tickling the sides of my legs. I picked a daisy and started to pull off the petals. What gift was she talking about?

"Tessa Rose." The sweetness of her voice made me jump to my feet.

"Mom? Mommy?" I ran toward her and threw my arms around her.

She pushed the hair out of my face, just like she always used to do. "I'm so proud of you. You've grown into such a beautiful woman." Her smile was angelic, and I was reminded that she was gone.

"I miss you so much. I just wish you didn't have to go." Tears began to fall. "Please tell Daddy that I know the truth. I never thought he was capable of that"

"Oh, honey, I know." His deep voice came from behind my mother.

"Daddy? Oh, Daddy, I've missed you so much. I knew you loved us too much to take Mom from us that way."

"I'm so sorry you had to grow up so fast. You and Em are incredibly strong girls. You have so much left to do, and I know you will succeed at anything you put your mind to."

"I don't want you to go. I need you." I pulled at his hand to try to make him stay.

"You have all the strength you need inside yourself. Don't you ever forget it." He leaned in and kissed the top of my head.

I held the hand of my mom and dad as we stood in a circle. "We have to go baby girl. Give our love to Emily. We've never stopped watching over you two." My mom picked up my hand and kissed it, letting go as she waited for my dad.

My dad did the same and went over to my mom. He took her hand and they walked into the same light Rebecca did. My head hung as my heart stung from loss, as fresh as it had been so many years ago.

"Lift that beautiful chin up, Tessa girl."

The pain that filled my heart evaporated when I saw my gram standing in front of me. "Grammy? Oh, Grammy, I've been wanting to talk to you."

"I know, dear, but there was too much at stake for me to interfere before. You passed the test with flying colors." Her round cheeks rose in a smile. "I'm ready to work with you, and help you learn how to use your gift."

Warmth from her love wrapped around me. "I wasn't sure I was like you."

"You always have been. I knew the minute your momma brought you home from the hospital."

"How could you tell?"

"There was that little spark in your eyes. I knew you could see and hear all that I could. I didn't want to scare you when you were a little girl and then when you lost your parents it was too much for you to handle." She took my hand and placed it to my heart. "But you're ready now."

"What if I mess it up? What if I'm not good at it."

"Oh, Tessa, the first step is believing in yourself. You have what it takes. You found your Aunt Becky, didn't you?"

I nodded as I tried to absorb everything she was saying to me.

"I've got to go, honey." She kissed my cheek. "If you need me just close your eyes and I'll be there. You've never been alone. We're all here watching out for you and Emily. Don't be so easy to give up on your dreams."

"I love you, Gram."

"I love you, too." She blew me a kiss.

I opened my eyes, still able to feel the love from the visitors in my dream. Tommy was on the other side of the bed, still asleep. I laid next to him as I pulled up the messages I had received. I was never alone. That was always something I felt but I was never quite sure. It was what I always hoped for, but it seemed too far-fetched to be real.

Now there was no doubt it was real. I would never be lonely for the rest of my life. I snuggled next to Tommy and thought about the first steps I would take to learn how to use my gift. Excitement filled me as I thought about all of the people I could help. If I was able to help Rebecca, maybe I could help others like her, too.

The fear I had felt about these gifts vanished when the good outweighed the bad. It was time to get serious and stop wasting the time I had left. I knew better than anyone how quickly life could be whisked away from you. There wasn't always a tomorrow promised. I had to make the most of the rest of my days.

3 2

SIX MONTHS LATER

It felt like we'd been waiting for this day forever. Today was the day we get to lay our beautiful, spunky Aunt Becky to rest. The police confirmed the remains in the beat-up garbage bag were hers. Emily and I planned a small funeral so we could give Rebecca and her unborn son a proper resting place.

The dandelions were the only flowers filling the lush green fields. The sea of yellow helped bring some cheer to what should be a somber day. However, today wasn't as sad as you'd expect a goodbye to be. Rebecca's death brought us closure. Celebrating her life was the least we could do.

Emily, Mandy, Randy, Tommy and I stood around the white box. I rubbed the top, resting my hand where I thought her heart would be. "I picked this beautiful casket for you, Aunt Becky, because it reminded me of the gorgeous white gown you visited me in. It's elegant, just like you."

Emily joined me by Rebecca's side. "Tess did a great job. With this, and with everything else." Emily dabbed the side of her eyes with a balled-up tissue. "I don't know how I'll ever repay you for giving us the truth about our dad."

"She said you already did." I couldn't help but smile as I heard her voice in my head. "She's here with us, she can hear you."

"I'm sorry, Aunt Becky, that we lost touch over the years. I always thought about you. I just didn't know where to start." Emily hung her head as she gazed at the wooden box.

"She said you have nothing to be sorry for. She could have just as easily looked for us, but she was embarrassed." I blinked my eyes to try to hold off the tears so I could finish the message. "She said it hurt too much to be reminded of Kenny after he died. She loved him more than anything and when she heard what people thought he did she couldn't face us. She was ashamed. She's sorry for abandoning us."

"It's okay." Emily sniffled. "I love you."

"She loves you, too. She said she'll look after us." I placed my hand to my mouth when I heard what she said next. I took a step closer to Emily and whispered in her ear, "She's going to look after my baby, too."

Emily's eyes went wide, and her hand went to her mouth. "Are you?" She moved her lips but no sound came out.

I lifted my eyes. "I don't think so."

"Wait, what's going on?" Randy took a step forward to join us.

"Oh, nothing." Emily and I started laughing.

"Come on, you can't leave us out." Randy crossed his arms and gave his best pouty face.

"Randy, knock it off, let them have their time together." Mandy pulled on Randy's arm.

"No, he's fine." I held my hand out to Tommy. "Why don't you all come join us?"

Tommy and Mandy added their hands to the top of the casket. Randy followed suit. "Rebecca, you have some pretty special nieces. They're in good hands now." Mandy gave the box a tap.

"I second that." Tommy added as he put his hand on mine.

"She said she's so glad you all came to celebrate her today. She wants us all to know how important it is to enjoy every day. Don't let the little stuff take over. Tomorrow is a gift, don't waste it."

"She's a wise woman." Mandy put her arm around Emily. "I bet that's where you two get your awesomeness from."

Emily and I looked at each other and laughed. "We come from a long line of awesome." Emily put her hand to her heart. "And thanks to Aunt Becky we never have to doubt that again."

Rebecca and her baby were laid to rest next to our parents and our gram. Emily and I couldn't find her mother's grave and thought she would like to be near her favorite big brother. We bought her a headstone with an angel etched into the pink granite. After the small service we all went back to Randy's place where he had a big spread of food waiting for us.

"Holy shit, Randy, how long did this take you?" Tommy stuffed a jalapeño popper into his mouth.

"Oh, it's nothing really." Randy blushed as he loaded the table with the rest of the dishes.

"Do you want some help?" I joined him in the kitchen.

He swatted at my hand. "No, get out of here and go join the others. I've got this."

"You've out done yourself." I kissed his cheek before I left the kitchen.

A knock on the door surprised us all, except for Randy by the smile on his face. "Oh, I forgot to mention I invited someone to join us. I hope it's okay." Randy took off his apron and wiped his hands off before he made his way to the door. "Hey, everyone, I'd like you to meet Ben." He pulled him into the house by his hand. A tall handsome man dressed in khakis and a cream sweater gave us an awkward wave. "Hi everyone." His nervousness melted away when he noticed Tommy. "Oh, hey man."

"It's so nice to see you, Ben. Seems like it's been forever." Tommy walked over and slapped him on the back. "Happiness looks good on you my friend."

"Right back at you." Ben's perfectly trimmed beard lifted with his smile.

"Oh, so you're the hunk I've heard so much about." Mandy wiggled her eyebrows. "You're right, Randy, he's a hunk. Rawr."

"Mandy." Randy gritted his teeth and shook his head. "Oh my god, shut up."

"What?" Mandy snapped a carrot between her teeth. "That's what big sisters do. It's my job to humiliate you."

"She's not wrong, Ben is a hunk." Tommy smirked. "You know if I didn't find Tess, I was considering him myself."

"Wow man, I don't know what to say. You're not really my type." Ben scratched his beard. "Can I get a drink? I'm feeling a little naked right now."

Randy took Ben's hand and dragged him into the kitchen with him. "Keep your paws off my man."

Laughter spread around the table. "We're sorry, we didn't

mean to make you uncomfortable." I smacked Tommy on the chest. "We're all just so delighted to see Randy happy."

"Now we're all one big, happy family. No man or woman left behind." Tommy lifted his beer.

I lifted my glass of apple juice to his bottle for a toast. "We will never leave anyone behind again."

"What's with the juice?" Tommy tilted his head and looked at me.

A smile spread across my face. "Can't a girl just enjoy some nice cold apple juice?"

He arched his eyebrow. "Yeah, I guess. It's just weird that you decided today of all days to trade in your beer for apple juice." He lifted his shoulders and pressed the bottle to his lips.

Emily poured herself a glass. "Nothing wrong with a nice cold glass of apple juice." Emily winked before she took a drink.

If there was any truth to what Rebecca had said at the funeral, I didn't want to take any chances. Tommy and I weren't married but we were living together. I was the happiest I had ever been in my life. It might not be perfect timing, but when is it ever?

"Your gift really seems to be blossoming." Mandy turned to look at me. "You really heard all that stuff from your aunt today?"

"Yeah, I've been working with Sara and reading a lot of books. I really want to use it to help other people like Rebecca. I know she's not the only one out there that needs my help. Like she said, I need to make every day count. If I was blessed with this gift, I feel like I need to make the most of it."

"I think that's very admirable of you. Personally, I'd be

scared shitless to talk to ghosts." Mandy leaned back in her chair.

"I don't look at them as ghosts. They're people just like you and me."

"Except they're dead," Mandy added.

"Right, and they deserve to enjoy every second of what awaits them in death. If I can help them cross off their to-do lists, I want to."

"Shit, those things never go away? A fucking to-do list in the afterlife." Mandy shook her head. "Death sounds even less appealing."

"That's where you're wrong." I smiled as I thought about all that awaited me. "All the people you've lost are there waiting for you. Mom, Dad, Gram, and now Rebecca. It's like a big family reunion."

"Okay, it's growing on me. I'm just not ready to kick the bucket yet." Mandy tipped back her glass of wine.

"I love how sentimental you are, honey." Emily rolled her eyes and laughed. "I'm glad you want to stick around here with me and all these crazies."

"What was that you said Tess? About us being from the island of misfit toys?" Randy laughed.

"Nah, I was wrong." I looked up at Randy and smiled. "We're not the misfits, everyone else is. People would give anything to have this many special people in their corner. What we've got is real. That doesn't make us misfits, it makes us limited editions."

"She's right." Emily nodded. "What we have is rare. The world is an ugly place, but what we've got here is beautiful. When we lost our parents, I never thought I'd have a family again. I couldn't trust anyone. I didn't let anyone in."

"She's right, she had the highest wall I'd ever seen. When I found out about Mandy, I was so happy to see she had let someone in. And then when I got to know you, I knew she waited for a reason. You were just what she needed." I wiped a tear out of the corner of my eye. "I can't believe your wedding is in a few weeks."

"Oh, don't remind me." Emily sighed. "Don't get me wrong, I'm excited. There's just so much to do."

"Fuck it, let's just elope." Mandy hit her fist on the table making the dishes bounce and fall with a symphony effect.

I dropped my head. "We know how that ends." Emily and I laughed.

"Yeah, our little wedding will be perfect. It'll be worth the stress."

"The hardest things have the biggest rewards." I took Tommy's hand and gave it a squeeze. Surrounded with love from this side and the other, my heart was full. As terrifying as the world can be, I knew we'd always be alright. As long as we were together.

"Hurry up, Tommy, we're going to be late." I tightened the back of my earring and slipped my foot into my shoe.

"I'm coming, I'm coming." He stood in front of me and straightened his tie. "How does it look?"

"You look amazing." I kissed him on the cheek. "Now, let's go."

When we arrived at Randy's house, you could see the big white tent in the back yard. We were the first guests to arrive, just as I had hoped. Tommy opened the car door for me. "I've got to go find Em. Why don't you go see if Randy needs any help?" I reached up and kissed him before rushing into the house.

Emily was in her bathrobe when I opened the door to my old room. "Thank God you're here. I'm a mess, Tess."

"You're going to look beautiful." I set my purse on the bed and took her wedding dress off the back of the closet door. "Come on, let's get this thing on you."

"I don't know if I can do this." Emily's voice trembled. "This isn't how I imagined it."

"Oh, Em. Today is going to be perfect." I pushed the bouncy curl out of her face.

She shook her head. "Mom and Dad should be here. Dad should be the one to walk me down the aisle."

"They *are* here. I know it's not the same, but they wouldn't miss this day for the world." I sat next to her on the bed, her gown draped across my lap. "And your niece or nephew's daddy is going to give your hand to the best woman on this planet."

Emily lifted her head. "What did you just say?"

"I took a test this morning. Tommy doesn't know yet. I didn't want to make today about us, but I couldn't keep this from you."

"Oh my god, Tess. Rebecca was right." A smile spread across her face. "We're going to have a little baby to spoil."

"I know. I can't wait. But today is about you. Let's get you ready." I gave Emily a hug before I stood up and shook the dress in front of her like a red cloth to a bull.

"So, they *really* are here? You're not just trying to make me feel better?"

"I wouldn't lie to you about that." I closed my eyes. "Mom wants you to know how proud she is of you. She said she knows Mandy is going to make you very happy."

"Really?"

"And Dad said that he can't believe how beautiful you are. He'll be right by your side as you walk down the aisle today. If you pay really close attention you might be able to feel him."

Emily wrapped her arms around herself. "Thanks Tess. That really helped."

"Good, now let's get you dressed." I unzipped the garment bag and pulled out the long flowing white dress.

Emily took off her robe and stepped into the gown. When it was on, I pulled the zipper up her back. Her hair fell around her shoulders and I pulled back a lock with one of our Mom's barrettes. I took a step back and put my hands on my hip. "Wow, Em, you're gorgeous."

She stood in front of the full-length mirror and looked at her reflection. "You know, I think I can see them around me."

"Close your eyes."

"I see them. They are here." Tears spilled out of her eyes.

"See, I told you."

"Gram's here, too." I saw goosebumps sprout on her arms, the tiny hairs standing on end.

"They are wrapping you in a hug, Em. They're always around, all you have to do is close your eyes and they'll come." I brought her white Birkenstocks over and placed them on the floor by her feet. "Come on, Em, there's a bunch of people waiting on you."

Emily slipped her feet into her sandals and took a deep breath. She shook her hands at her side. "I can do this."

"It's time to go." Tommy knocked at the door. "Can I come in?"

I opened the door for him and gave him a kiss before I hurried to my position.

"Oh my god, Em, you're beautiful." I heard Tommy gasp as I waited by the back door for the music to start.

Emily had her arm wrapped around Tommy's as she made her way down the pathway of red rose petals. I couldn't hold my tears back when Tommy gave her a kiss on the cheek.

Emily joined Mandy down by the water, squeezing my hand on the way to her spot.

The ceremony was breathtaking. It was everything I had hoped for my big sister and her new wife. She deserved happiness more than anyone I knew. Mandy and Emily had their first kiss as wife and wife before walking back down the path together.

Before the party started, Emily yelled for Randy, Ben, Tommy and me to join them for the family photos. "Tell her I'll be right there." I gave Tommy a kiss before I ran to the house to grab my purse.

I joined the group and pulled a stack of frames from my bag. I printed off and framed a picture of Mom, Dad, Gram, and Rebecca. I handed a picture to Mandy, Emily, and Tommy. "I wanted to make sure they would be here for the pictures."

"Oh, Tess, this is perfect." Emily sniffled. "How did you ever think of doing this?"

"I had a little help from some friends." I smiled as I remembered Gram giving me the idea.

We posed for pictures by the water as a family, then just Emily and I before the photographer whisked the newlyweds away. The rest of us watched as their happiness was immortalized. "That was such a sweet thing of you to do." Randy kissed my cheek. "I've got to get up there and get the food out. You two stay here." Randy winked at Tommy and took Ben by the hand.

"What was that about?" I asked Tommy.

Tommy cleared his throat. "I don't know. He's a weird guy."

I turned my attention to the water as the sun beat down on

it. The trees were popping with their new leaves. Everything looked so alive. The secret I was keeping from Tommy was biting the tip of my tongue. I turned around to take Tommy's hand and saw him bent down on one knee. My hand went to my mouth and my knees started to shake.

"Tessa Rose Blake, I love you with every beat of my heart. You are the peanut butter to my jelly. The pepperoni to my pizza. You are my best friend. My partner in crime. You are everything to me. I can't imagine spending my life without you. Will you marry me?" He held open a ring box.

"Yes, yes, a thousand times yes." I held my hand out and heard people clapping. The photographer had captured our special moment.

"This is my grandmother's ring. I know she would have loved you." Tommy slid the solitaire diamond on my finger and pulled me into a hug.

"I know, we've been talking." I held my hand out to take a look. "But she didn't mention this."

"You've already met?" Tommy tilted his head.

"Yes, and I have a secret of my own."

"What do you mean? Are you okay?"

I put my arms around his neck and whispered in his ear. "You're going to be a dad. I took the test this morning."

"Holy shit Tessa, we're going to be parents. Oh, my god, that's awesome." Tommy gave me a kiss.

"Yeah, it's even more awesome you asked me before you knew. That means you really want this."

"Of course, I do. I meant all that stuff I said."

"How long have you had this planned?"

"For a little while. Emily and Randy helped me pull it off." He turned around to look at them.

"I can't believe you all kept this a secret from me."

"I wasn't worried about them." Tommy laughed. "I was more worried about your friends I can't talk to."

"And today of all days." I looked up at Emily. "Mom's birthday."

"I know, June fifth already gave us so much when we got Mom, but now a wedding, an engagement and a baby."

"A what?" Randy looked at me and then at Tommy. "Did I just hear what I thought I did?"

"Yes. I didn't want to steal the show today. I promise I was going to tell everyone tomorrow." I put my hands on my hips. "You can keep his secrets for God knows how long but you can't keep mine for an hour."

"Sorry, it was too exciting to hold onto." Emily took Mandy's hand and raised her eyebrows.

"Go ahead." Mandy rolled her eyes. "Little miss big mouth has another secret to share."

"Mandy and I were approved for adoption. We've been waiting for the right moment to share this with you all. I didn't want to jinx anything, so we kept it to ourselves, but we got the call the other day. We're going to be mommies." She squealed.

"Wow, Em, that's amazing. Our babies will be able to grow up together. You two are going to be the best mommies."

"That's right, I'm going to teach her everything I know." Mandy laughed.

"You better not." Randy's laughter harmonized with his sister's. "Since everyone is sharing, Ben and I have something to share, too." Randy pulled Ben closer. "Ben's moving in."

"Wow, man, I'm so happy for you." Tommy put his hand up for a high five.

Ben and Randy went for it at the same time. We enjoyed another laugh together. Everything was falling into place for each of us. "Looks like you're going to get that big family you always wanted." Emily moved the hair out of her face.

"I can't wait to see what else is in store for us."

The good almost always outweighs the bad. When you really listen, you can hear the answer to most every question. When you're unsure, I've learned it's best to just trust your gut.

ACKNOWLEDGMENTS

Writing a novel is a beautiful, but messy process. The words flow (most of the time) and the world keeps on spinning around me. The characters come to me with a story to tell and it's just my job to share it with you. Together we unleash secrets.

Thank you to my husband who listens to me talk through characters and scenes, and even listens to me read an entire, random chapter in order for me to get it right! Thank you to my kids who help me work through the plot and listen as I uncover the next layer of the story and pick up the slack around the house when I am deep in the writing process and can see nothing else except the computer screen. And a special thanks to my daughter, Alana, who helps with naming characters.

I cannot forget to thank my rescue dog, Charlie, who sits by my side as the story unfolds and demands we go for walks when we've been sitting for too long. I owe many story developments to those walks! He even listens when I can't wait to share the next great idea with someone.

And many thanks to the people who helped bring Rebecca Remains to life:

Indigo Hearts Design for the beautifully, haunting cover.

Proofreading by the Page: Samantha Wiley and Rachel Pugh for editing and proofreading.

Sara Moore, Debbie Russell, Michele Avery, and Caitlyn Page for beta reading.

Itsy Bitsy Book Bits Team for going above and beyond with everything that you do!

To the Coffee Queens: Thank you for your support, encouragement and push to keep writing. You have all helped me so much with your friendship and kindness. Who knows, maybe I've got a romance novel in there some place!

Thank you to the readers. Without you, my characters would never have any fun! Your honest feedback is always appreciated and helps improve my craft. Reviews help other readers as much as they help me. Please consider leaving one.

ABOUT THE AUTHOR

Jessica Aiken-Hall, author of her award-winning memoir, *The Monster That Ate My Mommy* and the *Scope of Practice Trilogy*, lives in New Hampshire with her husband, three children, and three dogs. She is a survivor of child abuse and domestic violence and is a fierce advocate. Her mission is to help others share their story.

She has a master's degree in Mental Health Counseling, with over a decade of experience as a social worker. She is also a Reiki Master and focuses her attention on healing.

When she is not writing, she enjoys listening to Tom Petty, walking along the beach, looking at the moon, and watching murder shows.

To follow what she's doing next check out http://www.jessicaaikenhall.com.

Boundaries: Scope of Practice Book 1

Confidentiality: Scope of Practice Book 2

Accountability: Scope of Practice Book 3

The Monster That Ate My Mommy: A Memoir